Long Black Veil

Jeanette Battista

DEDICATION

To readers everywhere and lovers of great music.

CONTENTS

Jeanette Battista

Long Black Veil

ACKNOWLEDGMENTS

To my family, both the one I inherited and the one I created: thank you for your everlasting support.

To my readers, who are the best part of this job: thank you so much for giving me the opportunity to entertain you.

To all of the people who made this book happen either through editing or art: Tracey, Nan, Bev, Char, Claudia, and Ashley. Thanks to my awesome agent, Pam van Hylckama Vlieg, for being, well, awesome.

Thanks to Mike Ness for his version of Long Black Veil which began this endeavor. And finally, to the one and only Johnny Cash, whose version of Long Black Veil kept me company on many a long night of writing. Sir, you are greatly missed.

.

i

She walks these hills, in a long black veil
She visits my grave, when the night winds wail.
Nobody knows, nobody sees,
Nobody knows, but me.

-Long Black Veil
Marijohn Wilkin and Danny Dill

PROLOGUE

Devon stood at the base of the steps of the Town Hall, her shadow thrown out behind her like a cape from the street light above. It was early-March cold, and her breath frosted the air around her. She wished Brock could have picked a warmer place to meet, oh like say, *anywhere* else, but knew why he hadn't. There still weren't many places they could go and not attract attention. There was no way they could go to his house since he was grounded and his parents were actively pretending she didn't exist, and Gammy's trailer was out of the question. So Devon was stuck waiting around after her shift at the drugstore, jumping up and down and hoping she didn't turn into a Devsicle before he got there. She could only hope he'd be on time—it was nearly eleven o'clock already—because she couldn't stave off frostbite forever.

It was sort of creepy, with the lights glinting off of the snow and the rest of the street so dark and quiet. Knowing about the two murders that had taken place here didn't dial down the eerie vibe either. Granted, she and Brock were probably the only ones who did know about them, as much research as they'd been doing in the past months, but that didn't help her insides, which were busy tying themselves in knots. She knew it was just the lateness and the cold making her jumpy. But knowing it and *knowing* it were two entirely different things.

She heard a sound and turned toward Main Street. There was Brock cutting across the parking lot on his way to her with a smile on his face. She waved, relieved, and began to cross the road to meet him.

A car engine roared to life. She stopped, turning to see the silver flash of a car's grille bearing down on her. Devon tried to get her legs to move, even as Brock yelled at her to get out of the way, but they didn't seem to be working.

Something slammed into her and she was flying through the air, and then falling in a cloud of her own breath and white mist.

CHAPTER ONE

Devon liked winter in the mountains the best. She knew it was weird, as everyone else—including the tourists, the ones who bothered to stop in town anyway—loved autumn. It was because of the riot of color from the leaves turning that transformed the mountainside into a visual brushfire. It was a feast for the senses: the bright blast of color like a Crayola bomb going off, the smell of wood smoke and leaf rot, the sound of small animals crashing through piles of dead leaves, and the feel of bite on the wind, as if the very air had developed teeth. Taste was covered by the hand-pressed apple cider sold at the general store and along the roadside near a particularly beautiful vista of nature that had a convenient turnoff.

To Devon, that was just a prelude to the real show: winter. That was when the bones of the trees were visible against a pale grey sky, when the clouds lowered their fluffy white heads and shook the snow from them. Winter was when twilight seemed to last forever, and the wind had not just teeth, but the jaws to go with them. It was air so cold it burned your nose, causing pain to shoot up into your sinuses until your head pounded. She loved it.

But winter was still months away as Devon stepped off the bus, minding the rainwater that gathered at the side of the road. She waited until the bus drove away, then turned and began the long trudge to her grandmother's place. As she tried to avoid the puddles made by the light rain—she hated getting her boots all wet since they took forever to dry and smelled like boiled cat poop until they did—she thought about how she still didn't think of her grandmother's house as home, not even in her head. Devon had been living with her Gammy for ten years now, and it still wasn't home. Granted, she wasn't big on cross-stitch samplers or ceramic dogs that seemed to follow her with their eyes to the point she thought she might need to stock a baseball bat for the inevitable time they came alive to murder them, but Devon had expected to feel some kind of connection to the place by now.

She'd been eight years old when her mother had been arrested for drugs, theft, prostitution, and heaven alone knew what else, and Gammy had been called to come and get her. Gammy couldn't come right away, so Devon had been sent to a group home for the several days it took her grandmother to arrive. When she laid eyes on her, Devon had almost cried with relief to be gone from that place and the kids in it. The fact that she'd no longer be dragged pillar to post around the Shenandoah Valley was a bonus.

She hadn't cried though, and Devon knew her grandmother had appreciated it. Gammy was imminently practical. There was no point in crying over something that couldn't be helped, over something that was as immoveable as the mountains her people came from. Gammy had gathered her up in a tight hug and collected her things and then took her back to the mountain town her family had left nearly eight years before. They passed the hours in silence, with Devon slipping in and out of an exhausted sleep.

The gravel road became a dirt track that led up to the foothills at the base of the mountains. Devon followed it, her backpack full of books heavy on her shoulders. The day was grey and misty, the tops of the mountains wreathed in clouds like smoke from a pipe. It was still warm during the day in late

September, but the humidity and the rain made everything feel clammy and sick. It was almost like the world had a fever.

She passed by the old stone church, no longer used and worn out in a tumble-down sort of way. There was a small cemetery adjacent to it, the stones still sticking up out of the overgrown grasses and choking weeds. Devon kept walking. She let her gaze wander as the path opened up on her left to give her a glimpse of the dense green hills seeming to roll on until they broke like a tide against the mountain's base.

Devon stopped as her eyes caught movement. Someone was walking on the hillside. The rain had mostly stopped, so it wasn't that strange, but they didn't get many visitors up this way. Devon looked closer and saw black fabric spooling out behind the figure in the gentle wind. It was a woman; Devon could tell by the way she moved through the grass and by the ripple of movement in the long clothing she wore. She was dressed all in black, including a veil of some kind that covered her head and face.

She was too far away for Devon to call to her. The woman probably lived high up on the mountain and was off to visit a friend, although she couldn't recall any neighbors of her Gammy's that dressed like this. The cut of the clothing seemed odd, almost like it belonged to an earlier time, and most of what Gammy's friends wore came from the nearest WalMart.

The corner of a book began to dig into her back and she jostled her pack to readjust it, taking her eyes off the woman for a moment. When she looked back up, there was no one walking the hills. Devon looked around slowly. The woman was just…gone. Devon stared at the place where the woman had been, wondering if she had just had a hallucination brought on by too much studying.

A gust of colder wind blew droplets of rain down on her. Devon gathered her rain slicker closer, ducked her head and continued trucking up the path that led to her Gammy's trailer. Better to think about the there one minute, gone the next hill walker where it was dry and warm.

A chorus of meows greeted her as the trailer came into view. It was an old single-wide on a poured foundation. The beige siding was showing its age, although how old that would be Devon didn't know; Gammy had lived here for as long as she could remember. The steps that led to the front door had seen better days, but the window boxes were full of flowers and greenery and Gammy still kept the yard neat as a pin.

Devon looked down as two cats took turns winding around her ankles. She petted each of them, making sure to keep the affection equal. "Hey Eden. Lambert." Eden was a petite black shorthair with a splash of white across her chest and nose. Lambert was their tom, a huge grey monstrosity that was the scourge of small rodents this side of the mountain. A purr like a backhoe rumbled deep in his chest. She was surprised that they had come to greet her even though the rain was passing. They both hated getting their fur wet. She knew that the rest of the afternoon and evening would see them sitting on the front steps grooming themselves to within an inch of their lives.

The cats followed her as she climbed the sagging steps and let herself in the front door. A strong odor declared war on her nostrils as soon as she stepped inside. Eden and Lambert fled back to the yard. "Gammy?"

Her grandmother came from the small but neatly appointed kitchen, wiping her hands on the dishtowel she had tucked in her apron. Devon moved further into the house, toeing off her boots and stacking them in the rack by the door before going any farther. She hung up her rain slicker on one of the coat hooks. The trailer was small, but was pleasant and tidy. Gammy didn't allow clutter inside; she said it made the house look ratty.

"How was school, hon?" Gammy looked Devon up and down with sharp brown eyes, as if she could tell just by looking at her granddaughter everything she'd been up to that day.

6

"It was good." She swung her backpack down onto a chair at their kitchen table. "I've got a ton of homework." Devon looked at the giant black pot steaming away on the stove—it was the source of the noxious smell. "What's in there?"

Gammy walked back and gave it a stir with a huge wooden paddle. "Evan Greaves has got himself a sick horse. I'm fixing up a batch of liniment."

Devon raised an inquiring eyebrow. "Don't you usually brew that stuff up outside?" She knew the answer to that question already because she often helped Gammy get the logs going in the fire pit they had out back.

"In case you hadn't noticed, it's been raining off and on all day." Gammy made a scoffing sound. "You sure you're the brightest in the class?"

"I was until a horrible medical procedure rendered me stupid. Now I'm in remedial classes and struggling mightily." She smiled when her grandmother clucked at her.

Devon was a senior this year and she had the highest GPA in her class at the end of last year. She knew that the only way she was getting out of this podunk mountain town was on a scholarship, so she worked hard to keep up her grades and her extracurriculars. She volunteered at the small branch of the local library, she ran cross-country, and she loaded her plate with as many AP classes as the school offered. But a scholarship was not guaranteed and Devon wasn't going to risk getting sloppy.

Gammy opened a window in the kitchen, gesturing for Devon to do the same in the living room. She did so, hoping that would help some of the smell to dissipate. "That stuff is strong."

"It'll either cure it or kill it," Gammy said, popping the lid back on the pot.

Devon shivered. She still felt wet and cold, even in the warmth of the trailer. She thought she'd have enough time to shower before Gil arrived. The woman in black came back to her and she remembered how weird her sudden appearance—and disappearance—was.

7

"I'm going to take a quick shower," she told her Gammy, making her way back to her bedroom. It was the last room in the house, all the way at the back past the family room with the wood-burning stove for heat, Gammy's room, and the bathroom. The hallway was decorated with samplers that Gammy had sewn long ago, and family portraits from before Devon was born.

She closed her bedroom door with a faint sigh. It was tiny with barely enough room for her bed, a dresser and a nightstand. A small television sat atop the dresser and a plastic framed long mirror hung on the back of the door. Several shelves were hung on the wall and these contained her favorite books, the ones she couldn't bear to part with at the used bookstore two towns over. Her twin bed had one of Gammy's old quilts on it, with a grey and green hand-knit blanket folded up at the end of it. It wasn't much, but it was way better than she'd ever gotten from her mother after her father had died.

Devon pulled off her clothes, dropping them in the clothes basket at the bottom of her closet. She closed the accordion door and wrapped herself in her robe, then proceeded on to the bathroom she shared with her grandmother. She was about to turn on the water when there was a knock at the door.

"Gil's here."

Devon slipped her robe on with a sigh. Her best friend had the most unfortunate sense of timing. "I'll be right out." She waited until her Gammy had gone back down the hall, then trotted back to her bedroom and threw on sweats. She twisted her red-brown hair into a knot at the top of her head and went out to meet him.

"Don't get all gussied up on my account," Gil said as he looked at her critically.

"I thought you'd take longer. Jackalope." Gammy didn't like cursing so Devon had to be inventive.

Gammy tutted at her, "Language." Apparently, she hadn't been inventive enough.

"Outside," Devon said, pointing to the door. She pulled the rifle she used for hunting—it was her grandfather's—out from its spot under Gammy's bed, snagged a box of bullets, and went to join him.

"Hunting practice?" Gammy asked.

Devon nodded. Gil's father despaired of his heterosexually challenged son ever doing what the rest of the boys his age did. Gil had no interest in hunting, but he figured it would make his father happy if he learned to shoot a gun. For the past couple of years, he'd been joining Devon in her hunts for game so she could teach him the basics. Today though, the shooting practice was not all he was here for. Devon needed to talk to him.

She joined Gil out front and they took off, walking northwest higher up the mountain. They moved through the woods cautiously. You never knew when someone might be up here hunting something, although it was too early for deer season. Still, not everyone followed the Wildlife Commissions rules and it paid to be careful on the mountain. Devon held the rifle with the barrel down across her body. Gil shuffled alongside her, as surefooted as a goat.

Devon found a likely area and sat on the ground. She propped the rifle along a fallen log, using it as a brace. Then she gestured to Gil. "Go ahead."

He lay down with a sigh and sighted. "I'm not that interested in hunting squirrels today." He raised his eyebrows at her, inviting her to tell him what was really going on.

"I know, but Gammy expects me to bring something home." She sat next to him. Devon had been supplementing their meager food budget for as long as she'd lived with her. Gammy's Social Security didn't offer them a whole lot beyond the basics, so they had to be frugal. They bartered extra vegetables from their garden with their neighbors, Devon had a job, and Gammy sold her remedies and such, but there were times that if they wanted meat, they had to get it for themselves. "Hold it tight against your shoulder."

"I have shot a rifle before," he sniffed, not at all offended.

"Yes, but you're a crap shot," she teased. That was the difference between them. Gil didn't need to hunt for food. He could afford all the bullets he wanted. He wasn't as concerned with waste.

"True enough, much to my father's dismay." He sighted, then said, "Why are we out here instead of sitting on an actual couch? Aside from the smell, that is."

"I can't talk about college in front of my grandmother." She took the rifle from him and positioned herself to shoot if something that looked like dinner popped its head up.

"I still don't get why not. It's not like your grandmother is stupid or blind. She has to know you're looking at leaving," Gil whispered. Devon held up a hand to silence him.

They were quiet for a few minutes. Devon saw faint movement and waited, barely breathing. She sighted, breathing out once to steady herself, and squeezed the trigger. The crack of the rifle split the woodland silence. Before the sound of the shot died out, Devon had already placed the rifle on the ground, moving away from Gil so she could retrieve the rabbit she'd hit.

She brought the dead rabbit over to a nearby flat rock, her knife already in her hand. As Gil ambled over, she began to skin and dress the rabbit. She and Gammy would be having stew tonight. It was a lean week for them, so this meat would be a treat.

"Nice shot," Gil said, coming up next to her. He stayed far enough back to avoid the discarded viscera. "So what's the deal? Why'd we have to have a pretend shooting lesson?"

"Gammy changes the subject whenever I bring it up. I think she's afraid of what will happen to me if I leave." She never took her eyes off of the rabbit she was skinning. "Reach into my jacket pocket."

Gil stuck his hand in her right side pocket and extracted a folded sheet of paper. He raised his eyebrows at her, then unfolded it and began to read. It didn't take him long. When he was finished, he folded it back up and returned it to her pocket.

"So what do you think?" Devon asked anxiously.

"Where did you find out about that?" Gil tucked his cold hands into the pockets of his jeans.

"The guidance counselor dropped it off during last period. Do you think it's legit?"

Gil shrugged. "If the counselor gave it to you, I don't see why it wouldn't be. I wonder why more people haven't heard of it before?"

Devon finished up. "Can you reach in my other pocket and get me the rag?"

"Sure. Just don't touch me with those rabbit hands."

"Oh, you mean like this?" She wiggled her bloody fingers at him. He took a step away from her and then another. She followed him slowly, chanting, "Bunny fingers, bunny fingers..."

He laughed. "Stop being so disgusting." He reached into her pocket again and handed her the rag. "Are you going to apply for it?"

Now it was Devon's turn to shrug. She cleaned off her knife and then her hands as best she could. She put the rabbit in her game bag, wiped her hands one last time and picked up her rifle. "I guess."

"That's going to be a hell of a lot of work," Gil answered. Devon snorted. Gil did everything in his power to get out of doing as much work as possible. Applying for a scholarship that would require as much research as this one would was something he'd never even consider.

Then again, he didn't have to. His parents had enough money to send him to any college that would accept him. If there was anything that was going to keep him out, it would be his grades, not his parents' bank accounts.

But this scholarship promised a free ride. "I'm just surprised I haven't heard of it before. I've been doing nothing but research on scholarships for the last year."

"This one sounds pretty out there. I don't know of anyone who'd be willing to do the work for this one." Gil rubbed his chin.

"How's the beard coming?" she teased. He gave her the finger.

"Come on, we'd better get back." Devon hoisted the rifle, barrel down and across her body once again, and set off with her game bag. She knew better than to ask Gil the Squeamish to carry it.

"Five generations," Gil shook his head. "That's a lot to prove." He was referring to the scholarship she'd just shown him; it required proof that at least five generations of your family had lived in at least one of three specified counties. Devon's family qualified; her kin had been in these mountains for as long as there had been mountains, or at least it felt that way.

"I think I can swing it." It was going to mean a lot of afternoons in town and a lot of late nights.

Gil raised an eyebrow but said nothing. She was glad he kept quiet. Getting her college paperwork finished was already enough of a hassle. And she was trying to do as much as she could outside of the trailer. She didn't want to tell Gammy she was planning on leaving, on going as far away as college could take her. She wasn't ready for that conversation just yet. Gammy didn't seem to be ready either.

They tromped back through the woods, not being as careful with their noise this time. When they reached Gammy's yard, Devon walked Gil to his car. "Sure you don't want to stay for Bugs?"

Gil made a face. "I'll pass. I prefer my rabbits marshmallowed, thanks anyway." He paused before getting in his car. "Seriously though, if you need any help, just ask."

"Got it." She leaned in and gave him a quick peck on the cheek. Then she waggled her fingers at him one more time. "Bunny hands!"

He slammed the door in her face.

Gammy was happy to get the little bit of extra meat that the rabbit provided. This was the end of the month and the money from Gammy's Social Security check had run out. They had another few days before the new one came, and her grandmother made a living being frugal, so they weren't in desperate straits, but the meat was a welcome addition. Otherwise the stew would have been vegetables only.

Devon wasn't above hunting to supplement, but sometimes she really wished she didn't have to. Gil had been her friend since she'd moved back, but he was a town boy. He didn't need to worry about extra meat during lean times. It embarrassed her to have to hunt in front of him, but it was the only excuse she had to talk to him alone without making Gammy suspicious.

While Gammy handled dinner, Devon opened more windows to help clear out the heavy medicinal smell from the liniment. As fresh, damp air flooded the trailer, she went and took a shower, like she'd originally planned to do. Gil's early arrival had been unexpected but not surprising, as he often dropped by when his home life got a little too stressful. His parents were barely civil to each other on good days, so when the house was unbearably tense, he sometimes fled here. Whatever the reason, Gil was one of the few town folk that Gammy welcomed into her house with open arms. Not that many townsfolk were keen on visiting them.

The hot water sluiced down over her. Devon scrubbed her feet and hands, glad to feel the warmth seep back into them. She hated days where she couldn't get warm, and this was one of them. Only a hot shower took the edge of the chill off and brought her back up to normal temperature. She wrapped herself in her robe and turbaned her hair in her towel and went to join her grandmother in the kitchen.

"How was Gil?" Gammy asked, mixing dough up for biscuits.

Devon pulled her math book from her bag, along with a notebook and pencil before sitting down at the small kitchen table. She had a problem set in Calculus to get through. "He's good."

"Family doing well?" Gammy always asked after everyone's families. It must be a mountain thing. Or maybe it was an old person thing.

"Suppose so." Gil didn't really talk about his family, so neither did Devon.

There was a heavy pause in the conversation. Then Gammy said, "I talked to your mama today."

Devon stilled. Gammy didn't often mention her mother; it was best for all concerned if the woman wasn't brought up. Devon looked at the calendar, suspicion beginning to gnaw at her. "Mom's birthday is today." She took up her pencil carefully, afraid she might break it in half if she didn't keep a tight rein on herself.

Gammy nodded. "It is."

Devon didn't ask anything else and her grandmother didn't offer. It was a painful subject that they danced around, neither of them mentioning the past or how Devon had come to live here. Thinking about her mother always tied Devon in knots and it always made Gammy terribly sad for a few days after, so they just let it lie. It made things easier that way.

Devon tried not to think about life with her mother after her father's death. She didn't want to think of the men her mother brought home, of the smell of liquor on her mother's breath. She didn't want to remember the glazed empty look in her mother's eyes from the meth, or to conjure up the memory of hunger tearing at her insides when her mother forgot to buy food.

And she knew Gammy didn't like being reminded of what her only child had become.

The silence that filled the room was uncomfortable, but Devon did her best to ignore it. She focused on her math problems, trying to work through them as a way to keep her mind busy. Gammy kneaded dough and cut out biscuits. Eventually the tension eased and the quiet became companionable.

They did not mention her mother for the rest of the night.

CHAPTER TWO

Devon slept poorly that night and awoke with a pounding headache. She managed to drag herself to school and make it through her classes, but she was glad when lunchtime rolled around so she could go see the school counselor about the scholarship information the woman had passed along. She traded out books at her locker for the latter half of the day, then went to the front office to sit in the hard-backed chairs in front of the counselor's closed door.

After a few minutes, which Devon spent reading the next chapters in her English assignment, the door opened. Ms. Kilgore stepped out, smiling at the underclassman whose face was splotchy and red. Devon didn't recognize the boy, but she gave him an encouraging smile. Sometimes high school could really suck; she understood how that kid felt.

Ms. Kilgore motioned her to come inside. Devon gathered up her things and took a seat in front of the guidance counselor's ancient looking desk. Ms. Kilgore came around and sat down behind it, a smile on her face. "What can I do for you today, Devon?"

Devon took out the folded sheet of paper with the scholarship information on it. "I wanted to talk to you about this."

Ms. Kilgore nodded. "Sure thing. What do you want to know?"

"What kind of proof are they looking for? I mean, I know it says proof of five generations born in the county, but do I have to prove that they stayed? That they owned land?"

Ms. Kilgore smiled. "I don't think additional information could hurt your chances. I would start with birth records and move on from there. If you can find land deeds or anything that shows your family has been active in the county, I can only think that would help your submission." She folded her hands atop her desk. "How are you doing with the applications?"

Devon rifled through her notebook and pulled out a small pad. Flipping it open, she found her list of colleges. She and Ms. Kilgore had sat down together and made a list of all of her choices, including sure things and longshots. "I've got apps ready to go for three schools. I'll finish up the last two this weekend."

"Running into any problems?"

Except for money, no. Devon worked a part time job at the drugstore and lately all of her meager paychecks seemed to go directly to college application fees. "Nope, I'm good."

Ms. Kilgore nodded. "I thought of you immediately for that scholarship," she said, pointing to the paper Devon still held. "You're going to be valedictorian, you have great extracurriculars and community service, and I know your family goes back generations. If you're having trouble finding proof, check the town records."

Devon looked down. Ms. Kilgore knew how hard she had worked to get where she was, and Devon figured the counselor knew how much she wanted out of this town. She was glad that Ms. Kilgore was on her side in this. It made her feel a little less alone since she didn't want to talk to Gammy about her college choices.

"You're doing a great job, Devon. You should be proud of everything you've accomplished."

Devon thanked Ms. Kilgore and got up. She still had some time left in her lunch period, so she headed outside. Gil had lunch the period after her, leaving her few choices of people to sit with. So long as it wasn't raining or freezing cold, she preferred the quiet outside, and she tried to avoid the cafeteria as much as she possibly could. She found an empty spot in the small courtyard outside the back doors of the school and got out her sandwich.

She'd maybe taken two bites when the doors flew open with a force that surprised her. Then the senior cheerleaders walked through them, as though making an entrance into a gala event rather than onto the blacktop that led to the student parking lot. Leading them was Skylar Preston, a petite blonde who had been spray tanned to within an inch of her life. Nothing in nature matched that burnt sienna color she'd seemingly chosen out of a crayon box.

As they swept by her on the way to their cars for a quick smoke, Devon saw Skylar look her way. The cheer captain said something Devon didn't catch, but it caused the rest of the girls to erupt in laughter. Devon thought about calling after them to ask Skylar how Brock was, knowing that the power couple had broken up over the summer, but decided against it. The girl wasn't worth the aggravation, and she had learned long ago that it was best to stay out of Skylar's way.

The cheerleader and the basketball star. Skylar and Brock had been a couple since freshman year. Everyone had just assumed they'd be together forever, going to the same college and then getting married before settling down back in town. It had come as a shock when they'd broken up, with the current rumor being that she had called it quits with him.

Devon thought it was clearly another sign—besides the rampant obsession with tanning—that Skylar was deranged. Brock Cutler was...*Brock Cutler*. He was the total package: good student, an athlete, gorgeous, from a solid family, and rich. If Skylar had wanted to trade up, Devon hated to tell her that there wasn't any more up beyond Brock. Devon knew that Brock had no idea she was alive, but even if she didn't have the buying power, there was nothing that said she couldn't window shop.

She watched the retreating backs of the gaggle of girls absently, trying not to think about much of anything. Skylar flipped her long blonde ponytail, making Devon grimace. The ponytail flip. She remembered how Skylar had treated her in middle school; she'd made a point of trying to embarrass Devon whenever she could. Most of the time, she hadn't cared, but Devon had always wondered why Skylar had singled her out from all of the other mountain girls that went to their school.

Devon folded up the aluminum foil her sandwich had been wrapped in and tucked it into her messenger bag's front pocket. No point in dredging all of that stuff up again now. She just had to make it through the rest of this year and then she could put Skylar, her mother, and everything else well behind her.

CHAPTER THREE

The Hall of Records was really just a room buried in the back of the Town Hall offices adjacent to the courthouse. The building was fronted with Doric pillars, which the architects probably thought made it look stately and imposing. Devon thought it looked like someone with a fetish for ancient Greece just plonked a temple down in the middle of brick and clapboard store fronts and went about their merry way.

She climbed the wide steps leading up to the front doors, her messenger bag holding her financial aid and scholarship applications bouncing at her hip. She was most concerned with gathering the information she'd need for the scholarship Ms. Kilgore had given her. It was offered specifically to Appalachian families, but there was a catch: applicants had to prove they'd been living in the area for at least five generations. It meant a lot of sifting through files to find what she'd need in order to apply.

So Devon was headed to the records room. She needed to pull old birth certificates, death certificates, land deeds, and anything else that might prove her family had been in the area for all of this time. Her Gammy had already given her a helpful list of names of her forebears, so she at least had a place to start looking. But Devon didn't kid herself; it was going to take some time.

She still had a few months before the applications were due, but that didn't mean she could just sit around and wait until the last minute. Not with her future away from this town on the line.

Devon waited at the front desk, watching as Mrs. Welbourne—a pillar of the community and inexhaustible local volunteer—gave instructions to someone on the other end of the phone. She tried not to fidget. Mrs. Welbourne returned the receiver to its cradle and smiled at Devon. "What can I help you with, dear?"

Devon pulled a manila folder from her bag and opened it to reveal a stack of papers. "I need to do some research for some scholarship applications. I'm going to need to copy some records, like birth certificates and stuff like that."

"How far back do you need to go?" Mrs. Welbourne put her reading glasses on her nose and looked at the pages in the folder.

"Five generations."

"Lordy." Mrs. Welbourne smiled. "You're going to need the archives for some of it." She took another glance at the papers Devon had arrayed before her. "Seems like an awful lot of work for a scholarship." She shrugged. "We've got an intern with us—I'll give him a call and have him meet you at the Records room. He can get what you need from the archives."

"Thank you very much." Devon scooped her pages back up and into the folder in one smooth motion. "This probably won't be the only time I'll need to come here—I've got a lot of research for all of these."

"Well, I'm glad someone is finally taking an interest in their history, even if it is just for a scholarship." Mrs. Welbourne leaned over the desk. "All we usually get in here are title searches and land grants. Just follow the signs down the hall. They'll lead you right to it."

Devon nodded and took off down the main hallway, turning left down a side hall where the sign indicated. She passed a couple of doors, finally coming to a stop in front of an open one. The Records room was a large square, bisected by a long counter. Behind it were filing cabinets; they lined the walls of the entire room. A computer sat on the counter. Two wooden chairs sat sentinel on either side of the door.

She laid her bag down on the counter, then leaned over it, trying to see if there was anyone working. The computer monitor's screen saver was on. "Hello?"

"Hang on!" a male voice called from the back of the stacks, followed by a collection of thumps.

"Everything okay back there?" She craned her neck to get a look.

A tall young man walked between filing cabinets to join her at the front. He wore jeans and a polo shirt. Devon recognized him; he was Brock Cutler, the captain of the varsity basketball team, popular, good looking, former boyfriend of Skylar Preston, and son to one of the richest families in town. The town golden boy. Devon had had a couple of classes with him when they were underclassmen, but when she started taking mostly AP classes, their schedules diverged. But she knew him on sight—heck, everybody did.

"Hey, sorry it took so long." He looked at her bag on the counter. "What do you need?"

Devon slid her bag back over her shoulder, suddenly unsure. Why on earth was Brock even back there? "Mrs. Welbourne said she was calling an intern."

"Uh huh. That's me."

"Seriously?" Devon thought an intern would have been someone, well, more like her. Someone who needed the credit on their transcripts or the paycheck, if there was one.

He crossed his arms over his chest, frowning a little. "I can't be an intern?"

"Oh, no. That's not what I meant. I mean, I just wouldn't have thought…" she trailed off, watching as his mouth set into the beginnings of a scowl. "You know what? Let me try that again." She shook her body like a dog shaking off water. "Hi, I need some help with the archives, please."

He laughed suddenly, a bright and shocking sound. "Sure thing. Whatcha got?"

Devon pulled out her file folder and thumbed through the contents. "I need proof of residence for the last five generations of my family. Birth certificates, death certificates, land records—that kind of stuff."

He whistled. "That's gonna take a while. Like more than one day, awhile."

Devon nodded. "I figured. I thought I would start with the most recent— my parents—and move backwards."

Brock walked to the end of the counter and flipped it up so Devon could pass through. "Come on back." He gestured her through. "You know the years you're looking for?"

"Some of them, yeah." She slid through, feeling like she was breaking the rules. "Should I even be back here?"

He nodded and pointed to the computer. "Oh yeah, no problem. I have some shelving and requests to find so as long as you put everything back where you found it, we're good."

"Um, okay." She looked around. "Is there a copier around here I can use?"

"Yeah, it's in the back. Just keep a list of the copies you've made and you can pay at the front desk." He turned and showed her how to search the database to find the filing cabinet or archive shelf where the records she needed were. When he was sure she understood what to do, he began to walk away. "I'll be down in the basement archives if you get stuck."

"Okay. Sure. Thanks." Devon pulled out her notebook and a pen and sat in the high swivel chair in front of the monitor.

Brock cocked his head and looked at her. "You look familiar."

Devon turned halfway around in the chair. "I'm Devon Mackson. We go to the same high school. We were in the same Civics class sophomore year."

She waited for his reaction to her last name. Everyone in town knew the name and the scandal associated with her mother and father. Even Gammy's fearsome reputation as an upstanding Christian woman—and folk healer—couldn't stand against the town's opinion of Devon's mother. Her stint in prison only proved how trashy she was in their eyes. And so was Devon—guilt by association, by birth.

She thought she saw a flicker in the back of his eyes, but she couldn't be sure. He ran a hand through his dark brown hair. "Oh yeah. I remember now."

Devon highly doubted it. She turned back to face the monitor, uncomfortable with his eyes on her. In the class they had shared, she'd sat behind him in the second row to the left. She had spent a lot of time staring at his arms as they rested at the edges of his desk. He had very nice arms. But she knew he would never have noticed her, even if she had painted herself chartreuse and stood on her head on top of his desk.

"You had all the answers," he continued while she swanned about in memories of sophomore year. "You always blew the curve for the rest of us."

"Sorry." She began typing search criteria into the screen. She made a *what the hell* face where he couldn't see. Why should she be sorry? She was smart and she studied. If other students didn't do as well as she did, it wasn't her fault. She felt like she was trying to hide something.

"Anyway, let me know if you need something down in the archives; just shout." He tromped off back down the stairs.

Devon jotted down her first set of results, then entered in more dates. She knew her mother and father's birth dates, and she knew her father's date of death. She'd need records for her grandparents, at least one set anyway. She'd already picked Gammy's brain for family names and dates and had only come up with the vaguest of ranges. She knew her grandmother had boxes of old family papers; she planned on going through those after she'd gotten as far as she could here.

She grabbed her notebook and hopped down from the chair, heading to the rows of filing cabinets that lined the walls. Devon started pulling files, leaving a marker in the spot so she knew where to return each folder. Birth records were the simplest to pull so she started photocopying those she could find. It was boring, monotonous work, but Devon slogged through, knowing it would be worth it if she got the money.

Returning the first round of files, Devon started on her second pass. These were questionable relatives—they may or may not be part of her immediate family—but she wanted to have their information just in case. She believed in being thorough. She took the next set of papers over to the copier, keeping track of her copies in her small notepad where she kept everything about her college apps. She put in the first certificate and hit the Start button. The copier started up with a clonk and began to run the job with the noise of a commuter jet taking off.

"Hey," came a voice from behind her.

She yelped, jumping straight up in surprise. Devon hadn't heard anyone coming up behind her. Then again, the French Foreign Legion in full regalia could have been behind her and she wouldn't have heard them over the whine and wheezes of the copier.

She whirled around, coming face to face with Brock. "Take it easy," he said, holding his hands up in what she assumed was supposed to be a comforting gesture. "I didn't mean to sneak up on you like that."

Despite her heart lolloping through her chest like a psychotic thoroughbred, Devon managed a smile. "You startled me. The copier's so loud, I didn't hear you."

Brock picked up the notepad that had fallen when he'd scared her. He returned it to her. "My shift here's almost over and the place closes in about ten minutes. Just wanted to let you know."

"Thanks." Devon gathered up her copies and the originals once the machine finally stopped with the noise like an elephant dying. She turned and saw his hazel eyes surveying her.

"Did you find what you were looking for?" Brock leaned against one of the cabinets. He looked relaxed, completely at ease with himself and his surroundings. Devon envied him that quality. She wished she had something like that.

"Some of it, yeah." She began to put the originals back where she found them. "You were right. It's going to definitely take more than one day."

He took some of the stack of folders from her and began to reshelve them. "Sounds pretty important though." He closed a file drawer with a push. "I work here Tuesdays and Thursdays," he began, his hands busy with sifting through upright stacks of files. "I can help you out, if you want."

Devon gave him a sharp look. Why would he volunteer to help her? Maybe he was bored—it couldn't be that exciting down in the archives below. A little company and some different work might just be a change of pace for him. She shrugged. "I work most Wednesdays and Fridays at the drugstore," she said, not wanting him to think that if she showed up here it was because of his schedule. She may have had a crush on him in sophomore year, but she wasn't the type of person who usually stalked the object of her affections. "I'll be back to finish up though. Thanks for the offer."

He shrugged, eyes still on his filing. "No problem." He shut the last drawer he'd been working on, his hands empty. "Catch you at school."

"Sure," she said, watching him grab his backpack and make his way through the door. When she couldn't see him any longer, she finished up what she was doing, reeling a little from his words. He'd see her at school?

He'd never seen her at school before, and she somehow doubted he'd start now.

Still, it gave her a very warm sensation down in the pit of her stomach to think that he might.

CHAPTER FOUR

The halls were crowded as they always were in the rush to get to first period. Devon slipped through blocky bodies that took up more than their fair share of the hallways as she tried to get to her locker. Getting impatient, she stopped being so polite and just began to shove her way through. It earned her a few dark looks and a couple of muttered curses, but at least she was able to grab her books for the next two periods.

She slammed her locker shut and turned to go back the way she'd come. Her first period class, AP Physics, was at the end of the hall, which was in the process of emptying out as the warning bell rang. There were still plenty of people lingering outside of classrooms, but Devon found she didn't have to push her way through a wall of jocks to make any progress. It was like being a salmon trying to swim upstream, except instead of the current, she was swimming against student athletes. She grinned; that sounded dirtier than she thought it would

Devon rushed past the swirl of people where two hallways met in a T. She knew she had time, but she hated being late to class. She skirted a few stragglers, intent on getting to Mr. Ryan's physics class, when a hand caught her arm.

"Hey Devon."

Her head swung around, her eyes first lighting on the hand on her arm, then on Brock Cutler's very handsome face. The skin at the corner of his hazel eyes crinkled as he smiled at her. She liked his smile quite a lot. He had nice, white, even teeth.

She reminded herself to breathe because suffocation didn't suit her, and managed a weak, "Hi." *Pathetic.* She tried again. "I didn't see you," she explained.

"Late for class?" he asked, though he was just as likely to be late as she was.

"YO, Cutler!" One of the other basketball players was waving Brock over.

"You're being paged," she remarked with a grin. "Better go."

"See you later," Brock said, then yelled to his teammate, "I'm coming, dude!"

Devon continued on to physics, but she found her mind wasn't on the homework they were going over. Brock Cutler had stopped her in the hall to say hi to her. He'd meant it when he'd said he see her around. She wanted to find Gil and tell him everything right away, but they wouldn't see each other until English. If anyone would understand this minor social coup, it would be him.

*****

After she'd finished lunch, Devon went to the restroom. She avoided the one directly across from the cafeteria; the girls with reputations for sleeping around hung out there, reapplying their metric ton of makeup and gossiping about boys. She didn't feel like navigating that minefield, so she headed for the bathrooms at the other end of the school, closer to the back entrance and the student parking lot.

She was just pulling up her jeans when she heard the restroom door open. One girl was in mid-sentence, "…do you think you're going to do?"

Devon didn't recognize the voice, but she did recognize the one who answered her. "I'm going to get him back. Brock and I were meant for each other." It was Skylar.

Crap. Devon didn't know what to do. Should she wait until they left to come out of the stall? That felt too much like eavesdropping, and besides, she had just as much right to use a restroom as anybody else. But to walk out there with all of them standing in front of the sinks just felt weird.

Skylar continued. "He was devastated when I said we needed time apart. He'll be so glad that I decided we should get back together."

Oh for God's sake, man up, she thought, mentally kicking herself for being a gigantic wuss. The cheerleaders did not have sole possession of a freaking bathroom! Devon flushed the toilet and stepped out of the stall. Four sets of eyes swiveled in her direction. She ignored them, making her way to an unoccupied sink to wash her hands. The silence was nerve-wracking. She took her time, trying to appear completely unconcerned that she'd crashed a cheerleader gossip session. She couldn't wait to get out of there, but she wasn't going to let them know that.

"What are you doing in here?" Skylar snarled.

Devon raised an eyebrow at her. She grabbed a few paper towels from the dispenser and dried her hands. "If I have to tell you that, maybe you shouldn't be graduating this year." She smiled sweetly at the blonde.

One of the girls snickered. Skylar shot her a glare that, if weaponized, would have annihilated the giggler on the spot. Then the cheerleader gave Devon her full attention. Devon had to fight the urge to fidget as she was speared by the other girl's blue gaze. "Nice shirt," she commented.

Devon looked down. She was wearing her usual button down with one of her grandfather's old woolen vests over it. She'd been going for a kind of nerdy chic aesthetic today. Usually she didn't bother with clothes, but today she'd felt like trying something different. She looked at Skylar dubiously, not believing for a second that the girl meant her compliment. She waited for the rest of it, trying to look bored.

"No really," Skylar said, her voice bright. "Poor white trash and dumpster chic are totally in this season."

Devon eyed Skylar's skintight ensemble. Her shirt had sequins and her jeans looked like they'd been painted on. "As opposed to trashy pop singer, which apparently never goes out of fashion." She couldn't believe she was trading insults with Skylar. Senior year must be messing with her head. Still, it felt good to give as good as she got. She threw the paper towels in the trash can and walked at her regular pace to the door. But she stopped before she opened it and said in her most insincere voice, "Good luck with Brock. I hope everything works out for you crazy kids." Then she pulled the door open and was through it before Skylar could come up with a response.

*****

She wasn't able to get back to the Records room that week. Friday night found her at her shift at the drugstore. It was slow, like Friday nights always were. It gave her time to restock shelves and do any chores that the shop owner, Mr. McCalhan, came up with for her. When she was through, he usually let her work on her homework until closing time.

Devon was at the front of the store, restocking the candy and gum section, when the bell above the door rang. She finished stacking Twix bars in their cardboard boxes and took herself to the front of the store. She passed the aisle that held the aspirin and other medicines on her way back up to the register, when she saw a tall guy peering at the bottles and jars.

"Can I help you find something?" Devon asked, stopping at the mouth of the aisle.

The customer turned and Devon felt her stomach flip over. Brock stood there, holding two different boxes of medicine in his hands. "Hi."

"Hi," she returned, then mentally rolled her eyes. *Sparkling conversationalist, Devon.* She tucked a stray strand of hair behind her ear. "Do you need some Tylenol?" *Oh that was so much better.*

"Not me. My mom." He showed her the boxes in his hand. "She's got a migraine. I was sent on a mission of mercy."

"Well, you don't want those," Devon answered, taking the medicines from him and putting them back on the shelf. She looked at the various boxes of pills, then pulled one off the shelf specifically for migraines. "This one should work much better." She handed it to him.

"Cool," he said, taking a look at it. He seemed to be studying the ingredients rather more intently than she thought they warranted. "So how late do you usually work?"

"Friday nights I work 'til closing." She checked her watch. "In about a half hour." Devon began to walk to the register. Brock followed behind her.

"Do you work every Friday?" he asked as he put the box on the counter.

"Pretty much," Devon answered, ringing up his purchase and bagging it.

"That's kind of…"

"Pathetic," she finished for him. He handed her a ten dollar bill. She handed him his change. "I know." She tucked a stray strand of red-brown hair behind her ear.

"I wasn't going to say that," he said, smiling at her. "I was going to say that's kind of impressive." He paused, considering. "In a pathetic sort of way."

Devon laughed. "So what are you doing here if it's so pathetic? Why aren't you out with your friends?" She passed him his bag.

Brock shrugged, shifting his weight as though he was uncomfortable. "Eh, didn't feel like it."

Devon didn't say anything, just stared at him, waiting for him to say more. When he didn't expand on his explanation, she said, "That was a good thing then." She gestured at the bag. "You were available for a mission of mercy." She gave him a small smile. Her eyes met his and time seemed to slow down.

"You have pretty eyes," Brock said softly. Devon didn't say anything—couldn't say anything. Her eyes were a watery green, more like jade than the vibrant green of emeralds that most redheads sported. No one had ever said anything about her eyes before. "I never realized it before."

"Thanks," she managed to whisper, unable to look away from him. What was going on? Things like this didn't happen to girls like her. They just didn't. He should be busy living out his fairytale with Skylar.

At the thought of Brock's ex-girlfriend, Devon snapped back to full awareness. She ripped the receipt tape off the roll and handed it to him. "Almost forgot to give you your receipt." She cringed at the dorkiness of that statement. *And here's why things like Brock Cutler don't happen to you*, she thought. *You are an epic dork.*

Brock seemed to snap back to himself as well. "Yeah, thanks." He cleared his throat. "Speaking of missions of mercy, I'd better get this to my mom before her head falls off. See you at school Monday."

"Sure. Thanks for coming in." She watched him walk away, her stomach still doing that fluttery thing that made her think she'd swallowed a bunch of butterflies.

It didn't take her long to close up the drugstore; they hadn't done a lot of business so it took her no time at all to count down the register. Mr. McCalhan always drove her to bottom of the mountain road that led to Gammy's trailer every night she had to work a close. When he pulled to a stop on the verge, she thanked him, shouldered her messenger bag and began her trek up the path.

Being out in the woods at night never bothered her, not on the mountain anyway. She knew its paths and byways like she knew the lines on Gammy's face. Devon had walked this path so many times, she could do it blindfolded.

It was certainly more pleasant in the spring and summer when the sun took longer to set, but she wasn't bothered by the deep black night. The stars provided enough light on clear nights for her to find her way.

She was coming up on the old church and she slowed down without realizing it. She felt drawn to the church, even more than she usually did. Devon stopped and looked around. Everything was still under the light of the half moon. She began to walk again, but froze when she though she saw something moving off to the side. After a few still moments, she moved closer to the church feeling a chill crawl along her skin.

She caught another flash of movement out of the corner of her eye. Moving at an angle to the main building, Devon tried to keep whatever it was in her line of sight. Her breath misted around her in a white plume. The cold was shocking; the temperature must be dropping quickly on the mountain.

A flutter of black disappeared around the corner. Devon could have sworn it looked like fabric of some kind. She sprinted to the back of the church, desperate to get a better look. Who would be all the way out here? She turned the corner and caught the briefest glimpse of a female shape wearing a dark dress.

"Hello?" Devon called, but the woman was moving around the church, going back to the front of it. Devon saw a dark train streaming out behind the figure as if a light wind blew past her, but Devon didn't feel any air stirring.

She followed the woman, but she always seemed to be just a moment behind. Devon saw the end of the veil disappear behind the church door that was suddenly open. She didn't remember the door to the church being left open. But when Devon stepped inside, there was no one there. The church was frigid; clouds of Devon's breath obscured the air around her.

She could have sworn she saw a woman go in here, but the church was empty. Devon took a walk around the aisles, looking over the room, but there was no one there. A shiver eeled down her back and she wanted nothing more than to be safe behind her bedroom door. With one last look around, Devon quickly left the church and hustled the rest of the way to Gammy's.

She couldn't stop from looking behind her at odd intervals, unsure of what she wanted to find there. At times she could swear she could see a shape watching her from a distance. The third time she turned back to check, she thought she saw a dark veil blowing in a nonexistent wind. Devon ran the rest of the way to the trailer.

CHAPTER FIVE

Saturday meant chores. Devon woke early, determined to have everything done well before it was time for Gil to pick her up. Saturday night was diner night, the one night she allowed herself to actually feel like a regular high school student. Most of the juniors and seniors gathered there at some point in the evening to eat and hang out with their friends. Couples would usually stop by before their dates to grab some food and be seen by everyone else. If you wanted people to know you were together, you went by the diner on a Saturday night.

A couple of the kids from the cross country team were going to be there, as well as a few of her friends from class, so Devon knew there would be plenty of people that she knew there tonight. She'd worked hard this week and she figured she owed herself a little socializing.

She blew through her chores and even got a jump on some of her homework. Then she took a shower, put on her nicest pair of jeans and a sweater, and even gave in and applied a bit of makeup. Then she brushed out her hair so that it shone under the fluorescent bulbs of the bathroom, deciding to leave it down for once. Then she went out to the living room to wait for Gil.

Gammy gave her the once over as soon as she set foot in the front room. Devon saw a strange expression flit across her grandmother's face; it had almost looked like fear. But Gammy wasn't afraid of anything or anybody. Devon was going to ask her about it, but the older woman spoke first.

"Don't you look pretty tonight," Gammy said, putting down her knitting. The television was on, but so low you couldn't hear what the actors were saying. She was waiting for her shows. "Is this all for someone special?"

Devon felt her face heat, but she shrugged and answered, "Nope. There's no prince on the horizon to steal me away. Looks like you're stuck with me." She didn't want to admit to herself that she sort of hoped Brock might show up at the diner with the rest of his crowd.

Gammy patted the cushion next to her. When Devon sat, her grandmother brushed her hand down Devon's head, stroking her hair softly. "I want you to be careful, my girl, you understand?"

She looked at Gammy, completely at a loss for what she might mean. She didn't understand, not at all. "I'm always careful, Gammy." She cocked her head, trying to see her grandmother's face.

Gammy frowned. "You're getting older, Devon. And you're a lovely girl." She squeezed Devon's shoulder. "Just watch yourself."

A honk sounded in the front yard. Gil. Devon snapped her mouth shut around what she was going to ask. What did she have to be careful of besides the usual? Gammy smiled sadly. "Get going. That boy won't wait forever."

Devon planted a kiss on her grandmother's cheek, then went out to meet Gil.

*****

The diner was packed when she and Gil walked in. They were lucky that Roxanne, Jamie, and Shelton had already scored a table. Devon spotted the waving arms flailing over the top of a booth towards the back of the restaurant. She pointed Gil in the right direction and followed him back.

They slid into the booth, making sure to save space for Zach and Haley. Greetings were exchanged all around, news traded, and good-natured insults bandied about. Devon took a look around the diner, trying to catch a glimpse of who else was there.

She heard a familiar, overly loud laugh, and turned toward the sound. Skylar was holding court; she and her crowd had pushed several tables together and were cutting up and making life difficult for their waitress. Devon sighed, just happy that she hadn't been noticed thus far. She really didn't want Skylar to ruin her one evening out.

Gil nudged her, bringing her attention back to the table. "What's everyone ordering?" he asked.

"Shouldn't we wait for Zach and Haley?" she reminded him, though she really didn't want to. Haley was perpetually late, so late that they usually told her to be anywhere a half an hour ahead of time. They dubbed it Haley lag time. Zach was the one stuck driving her, so he was always late by default.

Roxanne showed her phone. "Just got a text. They're running late. Said not to wait for them."

"Don't have to tell me twice," Jamie said, rubbing his hands together. Devon knew he had a ridiculous metabolism—the sheer amount of calories he ate each day would probably bloat an elephant.

They flagged down their waiter and placed an order for fries, onion rings, cheese sticks and milkshakes all around. Devon was handing over her menu when a booming voice yelled out, "Cutler!"

She fumbled the menu, nearly slapping Gil in the face with it. Once the waiter had taken it and left to put in their orders, Devon was able to see who had shouted. It was Micah Landsdown, a behemoth of a varsity football player, who was currently sitting next to Skylar. Everyone at their table was looking at the door where Brock was standing.

Devon felt alternately hot and cold, as if her body's ability to regulate her temperature had gone haywire. She swore she was flushing, but her hands felt ice cold. She glanced away from the door, looking at anything that wasn't Brock.

"What is wrong with you?" Gil hissed in her ear, then looked around the end of the booth. His smile was only slightly mocking. "OH."

She kicked him under the table. Gil was the only person she had ever told about her crush on Brock—she'd told him once, and swore that she would slaughter him if he ever mentioned it again. "Nothing," she answered him firmly, giving him a hard look.

"Sure it is," he said archly, but then let the matter drop.

Devon glanced back to the door. She saw Brock acknowledge Micah and the people at his table, but he made no move to head over there. Instead he seemed to be looking for someone else. She dared a look at Skylar; the cheerleader definitely didn't look happy that Brock was taking so long to come over. Devon hid a grin.

"Dude," Micah said, his voice still far too loud for the venue. "We've got room."

Brock shook his head. He began to walk to another table. "I'm good, bro." Devon noticed that he was choosing to sit with a couple of members of the basketball team, and she wondered what that was all about. None of them were in his league, most of them being non-starters. They were second tier popular, nowhere near his level.

Devon chewed her lip. Maybe he was avoiding Skylar. She couldn't blame him. The girl was so toxic that flowers probably withered and died when she walked past them. Gammy's words suddenly came back to her, and she realized that it was good advice. This was a situation that she was better off out of. She pushed thoughts of Brock and the reasons for his odd behavior out of her mind and focused on having a good time with her friends.

The food came after a wait significant enough to enable Zach and Haley to join them. They shared their food with the latecomers so they wouldn't have to order separately and everyone set about demolishing the cavalcade of fried foods in front of them. Devon downed her vanilla milkshake in a hurry, immediately regretting it when she got cold.

"I'm going to get my jacket," she told Gil. "Give me your keys."

He handed them to her and Devon slid out of their booth. She hustled past the front tables, glad that Skylar was too busy shrieking with laughter at something Micah had said to be bothered to notice her passing close to her table.

The night was cool, but not unreasonably so, as Devon walked to Gil's car. She opened the passenger door and pulled out her jacket. She shrugged it on and closed the door, but didn't go back inside. It was quiet in the parking lot and after the raucousness of inside, it was a welcome change. Devon leaned against the car, elbows propped on the trunk, and stared up at the night sky.

After a few minutes she heard footsteps crunching on the gravel of the parking lot. Devon lifted her head to see who it was.

"Brock?" The tall frame looked like his, although his face was backlit from the lights of the diner.

"Devon?" He came closer so she could see him better. His hands were jammed deep into the pockets of his jacket.

"What're you doing out here?" She looked around to see if anyone else was with him, but he seemed to be alone. Stranger and stranger.

"Mind if I join you?" he asked.

Devon didn't answer; she just scooted over on the back bumper of Gil's car to give him room to sit. She made a point not to look at him, keeping her gaze on the cars in the parking lot. She felt the car dip as he settled his weight beside her.

"Just wanted to get some air," Brock said, answering her earlier question. "You here with anyone?"

Devon cocked her head to check his face, unsure of what he meant by that question. Of course she was here with people—what was the point in coming to the diner on a Saturday if she wasn't? Or did he mean something else by it? His face was alternate swathes of shadow and light, so she wasn't able to get a good look at his expression.

"Yeah, a couple of friends," she volunteered, still trying to get a good look at his face. "You?"

He shook his head, surprising her. "I'm not sure why I came," he said with a shrug of his shoulders.

Devon crossed her arms across her chest, feeling the temperature drop a little as the wind breezed across the lot. "Can I ask you a question? Besides that one, I mean."

Again the shrug. "Sure."

She took a deep breath. "Okay." Devon paused, unsure of how to put what she wanted to say out there in a way that wasn't completely offensive. Finally she gave up. "I don't get you."

He smiled; she saw his teeth flash in the light coming from the diner. "That's not actually a question, you know that, right?"

Devon elbowed him lightly, feeling an ease with him that she never expected. What the heck was going on here? "What's changed?"

Brock turned his head so he was facing her, all of his attention on her suddenly. Devon found it both frightening and exciting. He was looking at her—seeing her. She clamped down on the giddy feelings that were bubbling up her throat, ready to explode into giggles at the first opportunity. She stared back at him.

He smiled again, this time a little ruefully. "You're the only one who's asked me that." He stopped, as if trying to figure out what he wanted to say next. "Everyone just asks what's my problem or am I mad."

"Would you rather I ask that? Because I totally can," she teased, trying to lighten the mood.

He pushed his shoulder into hers. "Please don't. I can't take it."

Devon wanted to touch the place where his shoulder had bumped hers. It *tingled.* How was that even possible? Their legs were almost touching as they sat on the bumper. She could move her knee over just the slightest bit...

Brock continued, unaware of the nearness of their legs or anything else, for that matter. "I'm just tired of it all. Don't you get tired of it?" His voice sounded dry and dusty, like a drought-parched streambed.

She thought a moment before answering. "Depends on what the 'it' is, I guess."

"Going to school, getting good grades, having to be the perfect...everything. I'm just so sick of it." His voice dropped to nearly a whisper.

"I guess I don't, considering I'm too busy enjoying the experience of everyone in school thinking they're better than me just because of where they happened to be born." She scowled. "But that's nothing in comparison to you." She couldn't keep the sarcasm out of her voice. *Really? Mr. Perfect Life was having an existential crisis with her?* "I feel your pain." She nodded. "Totally."

Brock sat there for a few seconds, looking a little flabbergasted. Suddenly he burst out laughing, causing Devon to jump in her seat beside him. He looked over at her, still laughing, and managed to get out, "I guess that puts me in my place."

Devon was glad the parking lot was so dark so Brock couldn't see her flush. She didn't know what had gotten into her to say something like that to him. Still, she was glad she had. "No, really," she began, making patterns in the gravel with the toe of her shoe. "What's changed?"

"Nothing," he replied, sighing. He stood up. "That's the problem." He looked toward the diner. "We'd better get back inside before your friends send a search party out for you."

"And before yours think you were eaten by wolves."

"Sometimes, the wolves might be preferable," he muttered, leading the way back to the front door.

He held the door open for Devon, following her back inside. They went their separate ways, but all the way back to her table, she could feel eyes on her. Some were friendly. Some weren't. And some were Brock's.

CHAPTER SIX

"Did you find the box with my mom's birth certificate?"

"There's a box under my bed. It has all of the land deeds and birth and death certificates I could find." Gammy took up her needles again. "They sure got you working hard on this senior project." She speared Devon with a look that made her swallow nervously.

Devon hadn't been exactly honest when she originally asked Gammy for the family records. Gammy was particular about who she shared family history with, and Devon had been afraid that Gammy wouldn't let her have a look at the papers. So she'd fudged the truth a bit; now it was a senior project that was worth half her grade rather than a scholarship that meant all of her future. She and her grandmother had never really discussed what would happen after she graduated; Devon got the distinct impression her grandmother didn't want to really think about her leaving.

"Thanks," Devon said, disappearing down the hall.

Her grandmother's room was like Devon's own: small but tidy. She had a ridiculous number of handmade afghans stacked atop the twin bed, and an old blanket rack that housed several quilts. On the nightstand stood a picture of her husband, dead some twenty years, and a small lamp. Devon turned it on, then knelt next to the bed and flipped up the bedskirt to reveal the stacked plastic bins under Gammy's bed.

Devon found the bin she was looking for after a few moments of searching. She lugged it out from under the bed, disturbing a small cardboard box as she pulled it free. She reached for that one and noticed that it had her mother's name scrawled in black marker across the top of it. With a glance at the door, Devon pulled open the top, revealing stacks of letters, photos, and tons of other memorabilia that must have meant something to her mother at one point.

She didn't hesitate. Opening up the bin, Devon upended the contents of the Lorelei box into it and slid the now empty cardboard box under the bed. Part of her felt bad about stealing her mother's things, but a larger part needed to see what the woman had been like before. She'd asked Gammy to tell her about her mother, but Gammy always begged off, like the subject was just too painful. But here were things of hers that Devon could see and touch and read. She couldn't pass that up, not even if it hurt Gammy.

She was probably going to hell for it. But she could live with that right now. She gathered up the box and returned to her room.

Devon dumped everything from her mother's box onto her bed and began to sift through the things her mother had thought important enough to keep. Being orderly, she began to sort everything into piles. There were some movie ticket stubs, a few buttons with stupid slogans on them, a journal or diary of some kind, a couple of keychains, a few small stuffed animals, and a bunch of pictures. She put the book aside and began to flip through the pictures.

They were from high school. The first one had her mom and dad smiling at the camera, squinting in the bright sunshine. They were sitting on some bleachers so Devon assumed they were at a football game or something like that. The next picture had her father with another guy she didn't recognize.

They looked dirty, like they'd been rolling in mud, and the teen she didn't recognize held a football. She flipped through the rest, but it was all of the same three people: her father, her mother, and this young man she didn't recognize.

All that remained to go through was the book. Devon laid her fingertips on the book's cover. A sense of dread suddenly filled her. She wasn't sure she wanted to know what was in here. Did Gammy know? Had she read this? Why hadn't she showed Devon these things before?

Devon swallowed. She felt like if she opened this journal there was no going back. Her eyes flicked to the door, then back to the book. She didn't know how much time she had. No matter what the journal said, she had to know.

She opened the book to the first page. It was a diary. The first entry wasn't dated, but the girlish scrawl was not that of an adult. Devon skimmed the first entry; her mother wrote about her classes and some girls who were bothering her and hanging out with Deacon and Jackson. Nothing earth shattering there. Devon had known her parents were friends for years before they ended up married. But Jackson she'd never heard of before.

Devon paged through entries, reading randomly. A lot of what was written was more of the same, high school details, nothing really important. A few references to Grandmother Mackson that detailed the woman's chilly behavior, but that didn't exactly surprise Devon. As she flipped through more pages, a photograph fell on her bed. She turned the photo over in her hands. Her mother and the young man she didn't know stared adoringly at each other. He'd obviously taken the picture; his arm was stretched out, holding the camera so he could capture the shot. Devon looked closely at their faces. She'd never seen her mother look so happy. Devon flipped the photograph over. 'Lorelei and Jackson' was written in the same girlish script from the diary on the back. A heart was drawn next to Jackson's name.

Devon grabbed the journal and held it upside down by the front and back covers and shook the book. Nothing else fell out. No pictures of her father. Nothing. Just this one picture of her mother and a young man Devon didn't even know. Lorelei obviously loved him, even Devon could see it. It made her stomach hurt.

She gathered everything back in the bin except for the journal. Tucking the photograph back into the diary to keep her place, Devon put it in the drawer of her nightstand. She'd return Lorelei's things back to the box to Gammy's room tomorrow. But she wasn't done with her mother's diary.

CHAPTER SEVEN

Devon brought her mother's diary to school with her the next day. She had to wait until lunch to devote any serious time to it. Zipping up her jacket, she headed out to the stone table at the back of the school where she could eat her bagged lunch and read in privacy.

The sun was a buttery yellow, limning the half-bare branches of the trees with gold. It was cool and dry this October day, one of those perfect fall afternoons where the sky looks unreal in its clarity of blue. The weather was turning colder, but it was still warm enough to sit outside if the sun was on you. It wouldn't stay that way for long though.

Devon sat on the table to better bask in the sunshine, her feet on the stone bench, knees drawn up close to her body. She set the diary on her knees and opened it to the page she'd left off with last night. This entry, like the others before it, detailed the minutia of Lorelei's high school days. But there was a pattern Devon was noticing. Lorelei never mentioned Devon's father, Deacon, in any of these entries. But she spent a good amount of time talking about Jackson. She glanced at the photograph of her mother and Jackson once again.

She flipped to the next entry. This one was a departure from previous ones. Her mother mentioned Deacon's mother—Devon's grandmother—in this one:

Went over to Deacon's house after school today. We were all working on a project. Mrs. Mackson was there. Pretty sure she doesn't like us all hanging out at her house. The look she gave me when I walked in with Jackson and Deacon could've curdled cream. I haven't done anything to her, but I know she's not really happy with Deacon being friends with a mountain girl. Glad Jackson's family doesn't have that problem.

That wasn't surprising. Charlotte Mackson made no secret that her son had married beneath himself when he'd wed Lorelei. She was a cold, proud woman. Devon had always been a little bit afraid of her. She hadn't seen her grandmother at all since she'd come back to town to stay with Gammy. It was interesting that her mom felt it too, even when she was just friends with Deacon.

Devon went back to the diary, absently eating her peanut butter sandwich. It was more of the same, with no further mentions of Lorelei's future mother-in-law. An empty page demarcated the years, so Devon knew she must be into her mother's senior year entries now. She wished there were dates for the entries, but she managed to crib together a loose timeline based on events her mother wrote about.

She was only a couple of entries into Lorelei's senior year when the tone and content of her mother's writing changed:

He brought a girl to lunch! Her name's Saundra—a new student who moved from a town even smaller than this one. I don't like her, or the way she hangs all over him. She actually made him get up and leave lunch early. Deacon and I finished eating by ourselves. I know D was bothered by his behavior, but he tried to hide it. I'm so mad, I could kill him.

Devon raised her eyebrows. Yeah, that wasn't psycho jealous at all. Her mother didn't sound at all rational about Jackson getting a girlfriend. She took a sip of her generic soda and thought about her mother's words. Obviously

Lorelei had it bad for Jackson, but he didn't feel the same way about her. Where was her dad in all of this? Her mother gave him only the barest of mentions, and those only in conjunction with the three of them doing something together. How did they ever wind up getting married?

She read on, her eyes scanning the pages quickly. Jackson was absent more and more, leaving Lorelei and Deacon alone. There were a few more diatribes about Saundra and Jackson and their relationship, but now Lorelei seemed focused on Deacon. Devon chewed on her lip. So had her dad been the second choice, the man she picked because she couldn't have Jackson? Or had Lorelei come to love him once Jackson was out of the picture and no longer there to blind her?

Devon came to the last entry:

Deacon asked me to marry him today. Must tell Jackson.

There were several blank lines, followed by a two word sentence.

It's OVER.

Devon flipped through the rest of the book, but there was nothing else written. There was still about a quarter of the journal pages left, but Lorelei had stopped writing in it after that final entry. What was over? And why did Lorelei have to tell Jackson about the proposal?

She looked at the photograph that she had been using as a bookmark again. There was her mother and Jackson, their heads close together. But in the bright sunlight Devon caught something in the photo that she hadn't seen in the lamplight of her bedroom the night before. Far in the background was someone all in black—a woman. Devon felt her heart speed up. It couldn't be...

She was jolted out of her thoughts by a ball of something slimy and gross smacking into her chest. Grease spattered the blank pages of the journal, and Devon's face and clothes. She jumped up and a ball of aluminum foil containing what was someone's cafeteria lunch hit the ground. A giant grease stain decorated the middle of Devon's jacket.

Devon looked up to see Skylar and a few of her cheerleader minions staring at her with evil little grins on their faces. Devon shoved the journal back in her bag and grabbed what napkins she had, trying to wipe off the worst of it.

"Sorry," Skylar simpered, clearly not sorry at all. "I was aiming for the trash."

The girls all burst out laughing and walked away. Devon watched them go, going alternately hot and cold. She wanted to chase after them and pound some sense into Skylar, but that really wasn't going to help matters. Instead, she gathered up her things and went to the closest bathroom to try to clean herself up.

*****

"What happened to you?" Gil asked when she slid into her seat next to him in English class.

"Skylar Preston." Devon took off her jacket and bundled it up in a heap at her feet.

"What is that stuff?" He looked critically at her jacket, as if trying to psychically divine what the stain was.

"Taco grease. She threw an aluminum foil ball of it at me while I was reading at lunch." She pulled her notebook and pen out of her bag, settling in to take notes.

"Be-yotch!" he hissed, disbelieving. "Did she apologize?"

"That's making the assumption that she didn't do it on purpose." Devon cut her eyes at him. "I'd just really like to forget about it, okay?" She especially didn't want to remember the barbed insult that the cheerleader had hurled at her.

"Fine." Gil's eyes bored into hers. "Let's talk about Brock and your diner rendezvous."

Devon groaned, dropping her head on her arms. "You do not QUIT, do you know that?"

"It's one of my finer qualities. And you're avoiding." He wagged a finger at her.

"I am not avoiding because there is nothing to avoid. We just both happened to be in the parking lot at the same time. No big deal." The last thing she needed was rumors flying about her and Brock Cutler. That might send Skylar right over the edge. Although the look on her face might be worth it...

"Are you trying to tell me that if Mr. Cutler was interested in going on a date with you, that you would turn him down? You must have ovaries of steel." He leaned forward. "Come on, Dev. You've liked him since sophomore year!"

She put her head next to his. "Liked, Gil. As in past tense. He's just being friendly because we've had to work together when I'm in the records room."

"Looks more than friendly to me," he said, his voice knowing.

"You're impossible." She pulled back as Mr. Harris walked into the room. "And don't you go starting any rumors," she warned Gil as she opened her notebook to a clean page.

"You are just no fun," Gil pouted before turning around to face front. "None. At. All."

CHAPTER EIGHT

Devon wasn't in the mood to do more research in the records room. The last person she wanted to see was Brock, especially since she smelled of taco stink and depression. All she really wanted to do was go to Gammy's, shower about fifteen times, and then pull the covers over her head and forget that diaries, scholarships, and high school ever existed. Unfortunately, there was still too much for her to do, so unless she wanted to stay on the mountain forever hiding from one Skylar Preston, she was going to have to drag her butt to the archives.

But she didn't have to be happy about it.

She signed in at the front desk and walked down the hallway until she came to the records room. Dumping her stuff off at the computer, Devon stood at the top of the stairs leading down into the archive basement.

"Brock?" she called. It was a Tuesday. He should have been working. She waited a few moments, then shrugged. Maybe he wasn't feeling well and had called in sick. Or maybe he had the day off. Either way, it wasn't any of her business.

She settled herself behind the computer, pulling file folders out of her bag. She also got out her small notepad; it had all of the possible names she still had to check. She entered the names into the search screen, notating where the record was likely located on her notepad. Only one name was still in the filing cabinets in this room. The rest were in the archives below.

Devon first pulled the files from the cabinets. Once she had those, she took her list and climbed down the stairs. The lights weren't on in the basement room, but the illumination coming from the top of the stairs helped her find the light switch. She flipped it up and the old fluorescent lights flickered to life with a low buzzing sound.

She stopped at the first rack. There didn't appear to be a layout or map anywhere in the room that she could see, so she had no idea how the boxes holding the old files were laid out. Each box seemed to be labeled, but to her eyes, there looked to be no rhyme or reason to how they were shelved. She began a methodical search, aisle by aisle to try and locate the ones she needed.

Heavy steps pounded down the stairs. Devon stuck her head out into the main aisle and looked at the doorway. "Brock?"

He came in, sweaty, disheveled, and out of breath. "Yeah, hey. Just give me a minute and I'll help you." He began to shuck off his jacket and backpack.

Devon left the stacks, wondering what had caused him to run. It surely wouldn't have been a big deal if he were a few minutes late; Mrs. Welbourne seemed to adore him, so she doubted he'd be in any trouble. "Don't worry about it. Catch your breath."

He threw her a welcome smile. She felt her breath catch in her throat and reminded herself of what she had told Gil in English class. Just because his smile made her stomach do funny backflips didn't mean she still harbored any feelings for him. She watched as he put his stuff away neatly.

Then he turned, his nose twitching. "Does it smell like Taco Bell in here to you?"

Devon blushed and looked away. "Um, yeah. That would be me. I had a little altercation with some taco grease today." She gestured at the splotch that had soaked into her shirt through her jacket.

"It looks like the taco won." He grinned.

She found herself grinning too. "Not so much the taco as Skylar and her friends," she answered, smirking at him. She found Skylar's comment didn't bother her if she saw the funny side of things.

Brock, however, lost his smile. He abruptly changed the subject, holding out his hand for her notepad. "What are you looking for?"

Well, that certainly killed the mood. Who would have thought Skylar's name could be used as a prophylactic? She'd have to remember to pass that along to her the next time the cheerleader lobbed a big greasy ball of taco meat at Devon's head.

"I'm kind of lost down here," she said as she followed him into the stacks. "There's not a map or anything that I could find so I was just going up and down the aisles."

"There's a layout, but I don't think it makes sense to anyone but the person who set it up. And I think he died like ten years ago." He led her unerringly down an aisle off to the right of the main stacks. He walked two shelving units in and then plucked a box from the shelf second from the top.

"That's helpful," she said, taking the box he passed her. When he didn't answer, Devon put the box on the floor and asked," Is everything okay? You seem a little...distracted."

Devon was expecting him to tell her to mind her own business, but he just dropped down to the ground. He leaned his back against the boxes stacked up on the shelves and rested his forearms on his raised knees. "Can I talk to you?"

I thought that was what we were doing? But she didn't say it aloud. "Sure. I won't tell anybody."

He ran a hand through his brown hair. The blonde highlights glinted briefly in the fluorescent lights. Finally Brock said, "It's my parents."

Devon took a seat on the floor across from him, mimicking his slumped stance against the boxes. "Go ahead," she waved him on.

"I don't even know where to begin..." he said, then stopped. He took a breath and started over. "Okay. My parents both have these ideas of what's best for me, you know? But they've never actually asked me if I want any of it. It wasn't so bad in middle school or even a year or two ago. But now..."

"We're going to college," Devon finished, having an idea of where this was going.

He rubbed his neck. "Yeah. We're going to college. And now all they do is talk at me about it. Mom wants me to go one place, Dad wants me to go to his old school. Mom wants me in pre-med, Dad wants me in pre-law. But they never ask what I want."

Devon twined her fingers together to keep her hands still. "What is it that you want?"

His laugh held bitterness. "That's the thing! I have no idea. Ever since I was a little kid, they've always told me what to do, how to behave, who to be friends with." He paused, his voice soft. "I've never had to make up my own mind."

"Why start now?" It came out harsher than she meant it to. *Oh, to have this boy's problems.*

Brock looked at her strangely, then nodded as if determining that is was indeed a fair question. "Because I should?" He sounded unsure. "I don't know. I mean, I'm going to college in the fall. This is the rest of my life we're talking about. Shouldn't I do something I want to do?"

"Are you asking for permission?" Devon prodded.

Brock just looked at her. His eyes were a combination of green and brown and grey, and they were very unhappy. "I have a lot of expectations on me," he said, as if she wouldn't understand.

Devon bit back a sharp reply. "And I would know nothing of expectations, is that what you're telling me?" Oh she knew the expectations everyone in town had for her. But she was determined to show them she wasn't going to wind up like her mother. She stood up, gathering up the box as she went. "Look, Brock, the way I see it, your problems are pretty simple. Do you want to be trapped in a life you don't want because of somebody else's expectations? Or do you want to find the person you're supposed to be?"

She took herself upstairs and back to her research without saying another word. Devon made her copies and headed home, without returning the box to the archives and without saying goodbye.

CHAPTER NINE

The next morning, she found a note in her locker. It read:

D-

Thanks. You gave me just the kick in the head I needed. See you Thursday.

-B

With a small, secret smile on her face, Devon folded the note and put it in one of the hidden pouches in her messenger bag.

CHAPTER TEN

Devon walked to her locker after the last bell rang, mentally going over the list of things she had to do this weekend. There was the paper in AP English that was due Monday, a test in AP History to study for, calculus homework, some physics problems, not to mention more forms to fill out for college scholarships. She expected she'd be spending all of her time at the library this weekend. But first there was her shift at the drugstore, stocking the shelves and working the register.

The combination lock stuck, so she had to try the combination three times to get the stupid thing to open. Devon rummaged in her locker, stuffing the books and notes she'd need into her messenger bag. If the year kept up with the teachers giving this much homework, Devon was pretty certain that her bag would not make it to graduation.

"Hey Devon."

She jumped when she heard the voice behind her. She hadn't realized anyone was there with the sound of the kids pouring out of classes and on their way to the parking lot. She closed her locker and turned to talk to Brock.

"Didn't mean to sneak up on you. Sorry about that." He had his hands stuffed in his coat pockets, his own backpack slung over one shoulder. It looked considerably lighter than hers.

"No problem. Mind's on other things, I guess." Devon tried not to stare at him, but then she realized she was looking everywhere but him which had to look even weirder. She settled for looking at the tip of his nose. She tried to stay calm.

"That's cool." He looked around, eyeing the students passing by them for a few moments. "So, you're coming to my Halloween party, right?" He still wasn't looking at her when he asked.

Devon blinked. And blinked again. Brock Cutler had just invited her to his huge Halloween bash. It wasn't something that she'd been expecting. She'd never been invited, and she'd always turned down Gil's attempts to get her to go with him to it. She knew she didn't belong there. The popular kids, the ones with money, the pretty girls and the hot guys, those were the ones that got the invites. Devon knew she was pretty, but she also knew that she came from the wrong family. Everyone knew her mother was in prison for drugs and prostitution, and nobody wanted a girl with a mother like that within fifty feet of their social gatherings. Devon knew she'd probably have more success if she had leprosy and stuff just fell off of her at random intervals.

But here was Brock, actually asking her himself! She wiped suddenly sweaty palms on her jeans. "I'll have to check my work schedule."

He nodded. "Cool. Hope you can make it."

"Make what?" a deep voice asked.

Devon saw Micah and Skylar walking up to Brock and she suddenly wanted to be anywhere but where she currently was. Skylar was frowning at her, as if Devon was something she stepped in and had to scrape off the bottom of her shoe.

Devon hitched her bag up higher on her shoulder. "I'll catch you at the Records room," she said, and didn't wait any longer to make her escape.

She heard Skylar asking Brock what Devon had meant by that, and then she was too far away to hear what he said. Devon was glad to hit the fresh air and began her walk to the drugstore. As she walked she thought about Brock's invitation and Skylar's frown. If she went to the party, then she'd most definitely be rubbing elbows with the high and mighty Miss Preston and all of the other girls just like her. Devon would rather gnaw her foot off than socialize with them ordinarily, but she might make an exception for one night. It wasn't as if she was going to suddenly start campaigning to be prom queen or anything with them.

She began to think while she walked. She certainly wasn't an *it* girl, and Devon knew her background better than anyone. If she went to the party, Skylar and her harpies weren't going to like it, and while it was Devon's last year—hopefully—in this town, she still had to make it to graduation. And she had no doubt that Skylar could make Devon's life a living hell until then.

Still. Brock *had* asked her to go. And it was his party—he could invite whoever he wanted to. Devon shook her head. She was being ridiculous. Whether or not he invited her, it wasn't like she was required to attend. She could say no. But he'd been so nice to her at the Records room over the past couple of weeks. He was funny. And pretty cute. Maybe he was trying to feel her out, to see if she might be interested...

No. Devon stopped dead in the middle of the sidewalk. She was being beyond ridiculous now and well into unicorns and rainbows and fairies fantasy territory now. There was no way Brock was going to ask her out, no way that the captain of the basketball team and local heartthrob was interested in her. This wasn't a Disney fairytale; things like this did NOT happen in real life, and to pretend otherwise was just stupid. And Devon Mackson was not stupid.

*****

Devon walked up the wide brick steps that led to the large wraparound porch and the Cutler's front door. She could already hear the raucous sounds of music and talking, and suddenly she felt like she should be anywhere but where she was right now. She froze, knowing deep in her bones that she didn't belong here.

Gil's hand in the middle of her back propelled her forward. "You can't be chickening out now," he taunted.

Devon glanced back at him. He was dressed as the anti-Bieber, presumably to annoy his little sister who had a massive thing for the singer. Every time Devon looked at him, she had to resist the almost unstoppable urge to roll her eyes right out of her head. Gil *committed* to his costumes.

She shook her head. "Not really, it's just…." she trailed off, searching for the right word. Finally she shrugged. "I feel weird."

"Come on," he assured her, taking her hand and leading her up the rest of the steps. "It's a party. You'll have fun." He eyed her critically for a moment. "Although you could have come up with a more creative costume."

Devon looked down at what she was wearing. She didn't have money for a proper costume, so she'd just grabbed her Gammy's dowsing rod and threw on a flannel shirt. Water witch wasn't the most exciting costume, but it was cheap. And at least it wasn't slutty, like all of the store-bought costumes for teen girls seemed to be. Really, Little Red Riding Hood with a skirt that barely covered her ass? She highly doubted Red dressed like a truck stop stripper, even with all of the sexual overtones in the fairytale.

Gil knocked on the door, then let himself in. Devon followed behind, unable to get away even if she'd wanted to due to the tight grip he had on her hand. Maybe he suspected she was likely to bolt at the first opportunity. He was right to be suspicious; she wanted to break for the hills right now.

The living room was packed with people from school. Gil greeted them loudly as he shoved his way through the press of people. Devon noticed the curious looks she got as they passed. This wasn't her crowd, not that she had one. These kids were popular, good-looking, and had money, along with the entitlement to go with all of it. She wondered for the fifteenth time why she'd agreed to come in the first place.

Brock stopped Gil at the doorway between the cavernous dining room and the kitchen that looked like something out of the future. Devon swallowed nervously. There was the reason she'd agreed to come, standing there, all six feet of him. Brock Cutler: even his name sounded chiseled and refined, like the name of someone on a soap opera. For a second, Devon wondered if that's where his mother had picked it out from.

He looked up from greeting Gil, who had finally let go of her hand so he could head into the kitchen to get a drink. Devon shook the feeling back into it and tried not to stare at Brock. His invitation was the only reason she was here; she could admit that to herself, even if she wouldn't dare do so to anyone else.

They stared at each other. Brock broke the silence first. "I'm glad you came." He smiled a little, and it felt like it was just for the two of them. "I don't think I've ever seen you at any parties."

That's because I'm never invited to them. Aloud she said, "I have to work a lot." *Yes, that's the reason; it has nothing to do with the fact that I'm the equivalent of social napalm.*

"No work tonight though." Brock gestured to the kitchen. "Help yourself."

"Your parents don't mind you having a party like this?" Devon would not have pictured the upstanding Cutlers being at all okay with their middle son holding a rager at their finely appointed family manse. But before a few weeks ago, she wouldn't have pictured Brock talking to her either.

He frowned the slightest bit, but Devon caught it. Brock cracked his neck and then answered, "They're out of town and it's Halloween. And it's sort of expected since my brother threw them all the time. It's like a tradition." He shared a look with her, acknowledging their conversation about expectations. He took a closer look at her. "What are you supposed to be anyway?"

Devon held up her split stick. "A water witch?" She hated the way she answered him like a question. "Because it's Halloween?" Gah, she had to stop doing that!

Brock gave her a half-hearted chuckle. He probably couldn't wait to get away from her and her lameness in case it was catching. He opened his mouth to say something, but a loud "Bro!" swallowed whatever it was he was going to say.

Devon slid away into the safety of the kitchen as more pinstripe suit clad guys crowded around him. They were all guys from the basketball team, although Bro—Micah Landsdown—was the quarterback of their high school's football team. He thought he was a huge playa with the ladies, but all that meant was that he had no idea what the cheerleaders said about him in the girl's bathroom. He was Brock's best friend.

He was also a giant douche.

Devon saw him point at her and nudge Brock. She turned away, not wanting to see what he might do next. She found Gil talking to Tara, a tall girl from the volleyball team, and sipping a beer. She joined them.

"You're drinking beer?!" Devon mocked as she leaned against the countertop.

"I'm in costume, remember?" He took a swig and made a face.

"You're in costume yes, but you're not an alien. What have you done with the real Gil?"

Tara laughed. "Hey, Devon."

They were in National Honor Society together, so Devon knew her from meetings. They'd had a few classes together their junior year, but this year they barely had any of their AP classes together so their paths hadn't really intersected much.

"Hi Tara. Nice costume." Tara was wearing short shorts and a white t-shirt that read *Merlotte's* and her blonde hair was pulled back in a ponytail.

"Thanks." She cocked her head, appraising Devon. "Um, are you in costume?"

"Yeah," Devon said, again holding up the dowsing rod, "I'm—"

"Sad is what she is," Gil interrupted, throwing an arm around her. He handed her a can of PBR. "Come on, let's see who else is here."

Devon waved goodbye to Tara, following Gil once again, like some kind of puppy. He knew everybody, which wasn't surprising since his family was one of the richest in town. Money bought a lot of friendship, but it didn't bother Gil, especially since it had saved him from any number of beatings from the hilljacks at school once his sexual orientation became widely known. Between his parents and his own social clout at school, he was pretty much accepted anywhere, and if kids didn't like it, well, they kept it to themselves.

Devon cracked open her beer and took a sip just to be doing something. It tasted like all beer did to her—like her Gammy's liniment mixed with gutter water—but it gave her hands something to do and if she looked like she was drinking she'd probably fit in better. Gil dragged her into a conversation with a few of his newspaper friends and they all talked about school papers and the horrible teachers for a while. Devon found her gaze straying to Brock.

He was surrounded by his teammates in the living room. A few of them were playing a game on the X-Box, but most of them just hung around drinking. Devon noticed Brock didn't have a drink in his hand. She set her nearly full can on a console table and tried to pay attention to what Anthony was saying, but her eyes kept sliding to the other room.

This Brock felt so different from the one she had glimpsed during their afternoons in the Records room at City Hall. That Brock felt real, this one felt like a put on. She remembered what he'd said earlier, about the Halloween party being a tradition from his brother's time, and she wondered if he'd really wanted to throw it at all. The two Brocks didn't add up—it all just felt so disjointed. She got that he had a certain status to uphold, but which Brock was the real one?

He caught her looking at him. He smiled and lifted his chin in greeting. Devon waved, giving him a smile in return, then returned her attention back to the argument over who was tougher: Mr. Sweeney for Calculus or Ms. Denton for AP Chemistry. Gil was arguing heatedly for Ms. Denton, even though Devon knew he hadn't ever had either teacher for anything. He just liked arguing.

Gil left to get another beer—his fourth maybe? Devon hadn't been keeping track, but it looked like she'd be designated driver tonight. She stayed, finally feeling a little closer to belonging. A few of her classmates from yearbook had joined the little group hanging out in the hallway between the bathroom and the kitchen, and Devon was beginning to relax. Maybe Gil had been right in making her come. Maybe she wasn't the social leper she thought she was.

Brock edged his way through the crowd of people, coming to a stop next to her. Devon was amazed how many of her schoolmates were here—at least half of the senior class, as well as some of the more popular juniors from the basketball and football teams had crushed their way into Brock's house.

"How's it going back here?" he leaned down to ask. "You having a good time?"

"Yeah," Devon answered, glancing around nervously to make sure he was talking to her. It seemed like he was. "Although any more people and I think you'll have a fire hazard on your hands." As soon as the words left her mouth, she wanted to smack herself. *Could she sound like any more of a buzzkill?* Maybe if she concentrated hard enough she could will a black hole into being directly underneath her to swallow her and her ineptitude whole.

Instead of making fun of her, Brock laughed like he appreciated her joke. "True that." He pulled her away from the press of people. "I wanted to ask you something."

Devon tried to make her heart slow down; it had started doing double-time at the touch of his hand on her arm. She hoped that Gil would stay gone just a little bit longer. "Sure, go ahead." She hoped it came out more casual than she felt.

"I know you're really good in English—well, really good in everything, actually," he began. Devon nodded. "Anyway, I was wondering if you could help me with my college application essay. It's kicking my ass."

Devon tried not to let the disappointment show on her face. Of course he wanted her help with a paper. That's why he'd been so nice to her at the Records room and why he'd invited her to his party—a party that she never normally would have received an invite to. He was trying to be nice to her so she'd say yes when he asked for her help. *Stupid, Devon.* They weren't friends. They weren't *anything*. She was just a way to help him get into college. To meet his *expectations*.

Before she could formulate any kind of coherent response involving actual words, the buzz of conversation picked up around her. Kids began jostling for position, as if something was happening, or was going to very soon. Devon looked up, unsure of what to expect. Loud hoots and catcalls began to filter in from the front of the house, followed by shouts of laughter. Brock had his head up too, his eyes trying to see beyond the heads of everyone in front of him.

The crowd in the hallway began to move to the sides and Devon had a sudden sinking feeling in her chest. She caught a flash of orange as people began to push and shove to get a better look at what all the commotion was about. All she wanted to do was get away.

"De-VON!" A very loud, twangy, put-on Southern drawl cut through the murmurs. "Devon!"

Skylar shoved her way to where Devon stood next to Brock. She had a herd of the senior class mean girls with her; all popular, all gorgeous. They were wearing their Halloween costumes and Devon was not surprised to see a large number of slutty Red Riding Hoods, Alice in Wonderlands, and Bo Peeps among them.

But Skylar's costume was different. She was dressed in an orange jumpsuit, like the kind people in prison wore. Devon's prayers to be swallowed up by a black hole increased by a million. She wanted to die.

"Hey Devon, do you like my costume?" Skylar's smile was rotten at its heart, the sweetness in it a complete lie.

"What the hell, Sky?" Brock asked, sounding angry.

"Oh hush, you," she said, throwing him a pout. Devon could see that her eyes were a little glassy. She was probably lit. "I was just asking Devon a simple question." Skylar turned back to Devon, taking a step closer. "Do. You. Like. My. Costume?"

Devon had no idea what she looked like, but knew she had to pull herself together. This was clearly not the place to lose it. As it was, she was likely never going to live this night down. Still, she would be damned if Skylar Preston would know how much her costume had hurt her. She mustered every ounce of calm she had and managed to get out, in a normal voice, "Orange is a good color on you."

A few kids close enough to hear what she'd said laughed. Devon's mouth twitched from nerves. She saw Skylar's eyes narrow and knew that her torture wasn't finished yet.

"I know," the girl said, brushing imaginary dirt of the orange jumpsuit. "But it doesn't suit me nearly as well as it does your mom." She turned a megawatt smile on Devon. "Wouldn't you agree?"

"Burn!" Micah shouted, already halfway drunk. "She's got you there!"

Devon felt her hands grow cold. The sounds of the party began to dim, almost like she was hearing them underwater. She tried to rally. "I wouldn't know, since I haven't seen my mother in a decade." Weaksauce was what that was. And everyone knew it.

"Poor Devon. *Poor* little orphan girl." Skylar's sincerity was cloyingly false.

Devon gritted her teeth. This was why she was so desperate to get out of this town, this right here. She would go as far away as scholarship money and student loans would take her and she wouldn't come back until she could rub everyone's face in her success. And maybe not even then.

Brock grabbed Skylar by the arm and pulled her back down the hallway. "That's enough."

A few boos rang out from those disappointed at being deprived of a fight as the two disappeared into a room at the front of the house. Devon caught looks of pity, but when she tried to meet anyone's eyes, they turned away, suddenly deeply interested in something else. She didn't know which one was worse.

She was done. So very, very done here. But she wasn't going to run crying out into the night like some pathetic little bitch. She wouldn't give any of them the satisfaction of seeing her run. Instead Devon went to find Gil. She was amazed he hadn't immediately appeared in the thick of it, like some kind of conflict genie, as drawn as he was to drama.

He found her first. "Are you okay?" His voice was trembling, as if he was holding back anger.

"I'm good." It was a lie, but it was all she had right now. "But I have to get out of here."

"I'll drive you."

"NO!" She said it too loud, and immediately quieted. "No. You've been drinking. Just stay here and sober up. I can make it home on my own." She had to get out while she still had some dignity left.

"But it's like miles…" he trailed off when he saw the look on her face. "Be careful. I'll call you in the morning."

"Sure, fine, whatever." Devon was already moving towards the back of the house. She planned to use the back door and cut across the side lawn. It would put her closer to the road and would have the added bonus of having fewer people to run into. It would be a long, cold walk, but cold was exactly what she needed right now.

*****

It was way beyond late when she finally hit the gravel road to Gammy's house. She was wrung out and tired and just sick of it all. She'd walked fast at first, rage and embarrassment fueling her footsteps. It had been a huge mistake going with Gil to that Halloween party; she should have known better. She wasn't their kind and everyone knew it, including her. She would have been better off just passing the night with Gammy, watching her knot charms and all her other mountain superstitious stuff. Gammy didn't believe in going out on Halloween, but she didn't stop Devon. Now she kind of wished her grandmother had.

Her legs hurt and her feet ached and she was full on tired. All she wanted to do was get to the trailer and crawl under the covers and never come out. Devon forced herself to plod on, shocked when she felt wetness on her cheeks. Angrily she wiped away the tears. Tears were stupid. They didn't do any good. At least she had held off the waterworks until she was alone and almost to Gammy's.

She passed the old church. The moon was out, almost full, so it cast good light on the ramshackle stones. Devon slowed, the adrenaline from her furious pace slowly leaking out of her. She took a deep breath of cold air, feeling it crystallize inside her. It would be nice if she could feel this cold all the time; if ice could just take up residence in her body and she could just not *care*. Nothing could hurt her if she were made of ice, not Skylar or Brock or her mother.

A sharp wail cut through her reverie. At first, Devon thought it might have come from her accidentally—the sound had been that close by. But it went on, a wailing keen that she imagined a banshee must sound like. It froze Devon's feet to the cold-rimed earth. It was so public, and yet so private, all at the same time.

She waited for the sound to die, then moved in closer. It sounded like it came from the far side of the church. It was late for mourning, although when Devon thought about it, was there a preferred time for grief? Like 7 to 10 was okay, but anything between 1:30 and 5 was right out?

Devon stifled a hysterical giggle. She must be getting beyond tired, to laugh at the jokes in her head. She tried to move as quietly as she could. The keening wail started up again, not so long this time, and swallowed by a harsh sob. She felt badly for a moment, like she was eavesdropping.

This kind of grief wasn't supposed to be witnessed.

Still, whoever it was might need help. They might be out of their minds with sadness and need someone to call a loved one or whatever. Devon didn't remember anyone being buried out here recently, but maybe someone's grandmother had wandered away in their dementia. Wouldn't be the first time that an old person had wandered off thinking it was fifty years in the past. That was part of why she dreaded leaving Gammy alone.

Devon rounded the front of the church, hanging back in its shadow. She could see someone standing in front of a headstone. A woman, Devon amended silently, taking in the long black dress the motionless figure wore. A

71

biting late autumn wind blew the long thin veil she wore out behind her. It streamed like a banner, a black flag unfurling beneath the moonlight.

Devon couldn't look away. The woman reached down and placed her hand on an eroded grave marker. She bowed her head as though in prayer and the keen came again. Devon had to stop herself from jumping as she recognized the sound—it was the wind blistering down the mountain. It sounded so strange out here; nothing like the sound the wind usually made when she was safe inside her Gammy's trailer.

Devon stepped out of the sheltering shadow of the forgotten church. "Hello," she called to the woman, trying to be heard over the sighing grasses and the screaming air. "Do you need some help?"

The woman turned slowly, so slowly that Devon thought her eyes might be working strangely. Everything seemed washed in light, like a flash had gone off. She saw the woman's face, dark tears streaking down her hollow cheeks. One hand stayed on the grave marker, while the other was lifted towards Devon, reaching for her. Devon felt the spiky urge to back away surging up her spine.

The full moon disappeared behind a heavy cloud, blotting out the light for the briefest of moments. Devon looked up, and when she returned her gaze to the old cemetery, the woman was gone.

Devon shook her head, feeling thick and dumb. She checked her watch; it was just after midnight. She looked back at the gravestone, marking where it was in her mind, then turned back to the path to Gammy's. She tried to tell herself that the shivers coursing through her were because of the cold wind howling down the mountain.

But she'd never been very good at lying to herself.

CHAPTER ELEVEN

It was late when Devon crawled back to wakefulness. Sunlight was streaming in through the slats in the blinds that covered the one window high up in the wall. Devon covered her eyes with a groan. She was awake. Dammit.

The party last night came flooding back to her. So she hadn't dreamed it then. She'd hoped it was something her overactive imagination had cooked up just to torment her, but no such luck. School on Monday was going to be a nightmare.

She levered herself up on one elbow and checked her alarm clock. It was 10:30, well past the time she usually slept. Devon was surprised that Gammy had let her sleep so late, especially on a Sunday. Still, Gammy knew she'd been upset when she came home, so perhaps she'd decided Devon could use a break. Either way, Devon wasn't going to complain.

Yawning, Devon kicked her feet over the side of the bed. It took her a minute to push herself up and when she did, she immediately regretted it. Her whole body ached, but most especially her legs. She staggered into her robe and slippers and teetered her way down the hall and into the living room.

"Gammy?" There was no answer.

Devon continued on into the kitchen and found a note on the counter. It read:

Went to church with Stella. Left breakfast on the stove for you. We'll talk when I get home.

She took a look on the stove and, sure enough, there was the plate covered with aluminum foil. Devon pulled it off to reveal a plate of Gammy's buttermilk silver dollar pancakes and thick strips of bacon. She smiled; Gammy didn't often make her favorite breakfast anymore. The old woman must have known she needed a treat. Sometimes Devon wondered if Gammy wasn't a little bit psychic.

She heated up the plate in their small microwave and took it into the living room to eat. She plopped herself down on the sofa and began to dig into the pancakes. They weren't as good as straight from the griddle but they were certainly better than cold cereal or a PopTart. Devon chewed and thought about what she should do today.

She still had some research to do for her scholarship applications, especially the one that required proof of her family's history in the mountains. And she had her senior writing project to begin. She could go into town and try to knock some of it out at the library. She could, but the thought of going back into town before she had to made her feel queasy.

The encounter with the woman in black last night came back to her. Devon still found it so odd—how had the woman been there one minute and gone the next? Devon knew she hadn't been at her best last night, but she didn't think she'd lost time or anything else that could explain the woman's sudden disappearance. And what was she doing out there so late at night? Who was she visiting in that old graveyard? No one had been buried there in decades.

Devon swallowed the last of her pancakes, her mind still on the woman at the grave. That wasn't the first time she'd seen her. A woman dressed in black clothes had been walking the hills back in September. And she'd seen her on the night she'd seen Brock at the drugstore. And again, after she'd started going to the records room regularly. The logical part of Devon warned that it probably wasn't the same woman in every instance, but her instincts said that it was. She told logic to shut up.

It looked like Devon knew what she was doing today.

*****

The wind was whipping the misting rain almost horizontal as Devon made her very slow way back down the gravel path. She was wrapped in her waterproof coat and a knitted hat, her head pulled into her collar like a turtle in its shell. The damp seeped into her bones, making muscles already sore from last night's long walk home howl in protest. She thought about just forgetting all about the church and trudging back to Gammy's and installing herself on the couch, under a warm blanket, reading a book.

But there was something that pulled her on, despite the weather. Devon felt drawn to the mystery of this woman and her strange disappearances. So she put on her big girl panties, sucked up her whining, and didn't stop until she came to the church.

She oriented herself as best she could, trying to picture exactly where the woman had been standing. Devon walked over, looking for footprints or some sign of someone standing there, but saw nothing. That wasn't surprising—the ground was wet from the constant drizzle and any print that might have been there was long gone. Instead, she looked over the headstones. She positioned herself where she thought the woman had been in relation to the headstones. *There, that was the one.*

The headstone was covered in lichen and worn down by the elements. Devon knelt down for a closer look. It was hard to read the name on it. She ran her fingers over the stone, pulling at the vegetation and brushing away the grit and dirt. She felt the carvings of a name and dates beneath her fingers. She looked closer.

Daniel Holfsteder

August 21, 1894 - April 1, 1914

That was impossible. Devon pulled away and sat back on her heels. How could anyone still be alive that would mourn for this man? And especially one so young? Devon had seen the woman's face last night and she had looked to be barely in her twenties. It didn't make sense. Who was she? And what had this man been to her to have her crying that like?

She heard the sound of wheels on the gravel path. Devon pushed herself away from the ground and caught the taillights of a car heading toward the trailer. Gammy was back. Devon took one last look around the small cemetery, but found nothing else interesting. She jotted down the information on the grave marker for later. With a sigh, she headed back up the mountain.

When she opened the door to the trailer, Gammy was already in the kitchen, a clean apron on over her Sunday clothes. She was chopping vegetables and placing them into piles on the large cutting board. Devon came in, shucking off her damp coat and hat before joining her in the kitchen. Gammy handed her a carrot to munch on.

"How was church?"

Gammy didn't stop what she was doing, her hands working automatically. Devon wished she was that skilled in the kitchen. Gammy performed miracles on the little they had. "It was very edifying. That young preacher has quite a following."

Devon had heard of him. A lot of the girls at her school had suddenly developed a keen interest in religion and Sunday service was usually packed. His sermons—and how cute he was—were the topics of conversation every Monday. "The girls like his handsome face," she said around a bite of carrot.

"Faces don't matter, hearts do." Gammy pointed a parsnip at her.

"I know Gammy, I know." But Devon thought that it was rarely that simple.

"So you want to tell me what happened last night? Why you had to walk home?" Gammy didn't look at her when she asked, just continued to chop vegetables.

Devon ducked her head. "It's no big deal."

Gammy just waited her out. When Devon looked up, the woman had her lips pursed and her eyes raised, silently telling her that no big deal wasn't nearly good enough. Devon sighed and spread out her hands helplessly. "A girl came dressed in prison orange. Said she was Mom."

"Ah." Gammy put down her knife and came to stand next to Devon. "That must've been hard."

"More like humiliating." Devon really didn't want to talk about it. "That's why I left. Gil had been drinking so he couldn't drive me and I didn't feel like waiting around until he was sober."

"You just wanted to get out of there." Gammy nodded, as if giving Devon her approval for her actions.

"You heard something at church, didn't you?" Devon knew how everyone in this town liked to talk and church was the perfect place to gossip.

Gammy squeezed her shoulder, then went back to her chopping. "A few people may have mentioned something."

Devon doubted it was only a few. But it didn't matter. They'd think what they wanted and say what they wanted and the only thing Devon could do was endure it until she could get away from it. "I'm sorry, Gammy."

"And what exactly do you have to be sorry about? You were nothing but a child when your momma went off the rails. You ain't to blame for a thing your momma did—it was all her choosing." Her voice had a tightness to it that only happened when they were talking about Lorelei.

Devon nodded. "I know, I know. But I still feel bad that you're having to go through this too. It's not fair."

Gammy snorted, an inelegant sound from a woman so proper. "My girl, the sooner you realize life's got nothing to do with fair, the better off you'll be." She dumped the cutting board full of vegetables into a large Dutch oven on the stove. "Venison stew tonight! Mr. Caldecott shot himself a beauty and gave me some of the meat once he got it processed."

Devon smiled. Nothing beat Gammy's venison stew, especially not when paired with her homemade cheddar biscuits she always served with it. Devon inhaled, taking in the scent of browning vegetables and meat in the soup pot. The smell of Gammy's cooking perfumed the air and made Devon feel slightly better. This was comfort. This was safety. Nothing could hurt her when she was behind these walls.

"You know anything about a Daniel Holfsteder?" Devon asked, wanting to see if her grandmother had any recollection of the man buried under the gravestone.

"Don't recall that name," Gammy said casually, making a mound of flour on the counter and hollowing out a well in the center. "Who is he?"

"I don't know, but he's buried at the old church just down the road. I saw a woman standing at his grave last night. It was weird. I didn't think there'd be anybody left to mourn for him, but there she was."

Gammy stopped what she was doing, floured hands and all. Her head came up, her eyes blazing like a house fire. "What woman?"There was the same tone in her voice as when they'd been talking about Devon's mother.

Devon shrugged. "I didn't see her too well. But she was dressed all in black and she was crying at his headstone. She had a long black veil and everything."

Gammy went pale, all the color leached from her face so that she was almost as white as the flour dusting her hands. "Have you talked to her?"

Devon shrugged. "Not really, I guess." She put a hand on Gammy's arm. "Are you—"

"HAVE YOU TALKED TO HER?" Gammy's voice rose into yelling.

Devon flinched away, dropping her hand. Gammy never raised her voice to her. "N-no."

Her grandmother seemed to relax the slightest bit, but she was still staring at Devon strangely. "That's something then." Gammy leaned in close. "If you see her again, you just keep on walking. You pretend she's not even there, you hear? And whatever you do, DO NOT speak with her."

Devon felt something yawning and vast open in the pit of her stomach. "What if she tries to talk to me? What do I do?"

Gammy stared at her, the force of her gaze a palpable warning. "You run."

CHAPTER TWELVE

Gil called in the early afternoon to check on her. Devon was elbows deep in studying for her AP History test. She'd been reviewing her notes, but her mind refused to stay where it should. Instead thoughts of Daniel Holfsteder and the woman in the veil kept popping into her head. In truth, the force of Gammy's words had frightened her a little, and she'd been happy to let the matter drop just then. But now that she'd had a chance to calm down and recover from Gammy's harsh reaction, Devon had to admit she was curious.

Who was Daniel Holfsteder? And who was the woman mourning at his grave? And why did Devon have to run from her?

Devon knew better than to bring it up to her grandmother again. The look on her face and the tone of her voice when she'd said to run was one that demanded the matter be dropped. And Devon wasn't about to push Gammy on this, not now anyway. But that didn't mean she couldn't do a little digging on her own.

So when the phone rang, Devon already knew the penance Gil was going to have to perform for her to make up for the long walk home of the night before. The library was open until five o'clock and they had microfiche. Devon knew Daniel's date of birth and his death. Surely there would be something—even a funeral notice—that would give her an idea of what he'd been like when he was alive. Perhaps she'd be able to find something related to this mysterious woman as well.

She didn't even let him stop the car when he pulled up; she just hopped in before it could roll to a stop. Gammy sternly shouted from the porch, "Be back by five thirty!" Devon waved as Gil turned the car around and drove off back down the mountain.

He was quiet as he navigated his Civic down the bumpy gravel road. As they passed the church, Devon looked out the window, craning her neck to see the cemetery around the bulk of the church. It was empty.

Gil's voice pulled her back to the present. "So the party pretty much blew after you left."

Devon made a face. That wasn't surprising. Without her there to torment, where was the entertainment supposed to come from? "Gee, that's too bad." Her sarcasm could have withered plants.

Gil flinched slightly from the venom in her voice. "Yeah, well you did miss the mother of all screaming fights. Brock and Skylar really went at each other once he realized you had left."

Devon whipped her head around to stare at Gil. "I'm sorry, what now?" She couldn't believe that anyone besides Gil would care that she left, let alone Brock. He'd only invited her to his party to be nice; why should he care if she left early?

He nodded, eyes on the road. "Yeah. He came looking for you a little while after you took off. When he found out you were gone, he was pissed. He found Skylar and threw her out."

"Brock threw her out of the party?" She tried to keep the incredulity out of her voice and failed spectacularly.

"Well, he tried." He gave her a quick look and frowned. "Don't be mean. I can tell what you're thinking." He paused to check for oncoming traffic, then rolled through the stop sign. "He really did try to get rid of her. But Micah came up and said something to him before Brock got her out the door."

"What happened then?" Devon asked, curious in spite of herself.

Gil shrugged. "I didn't see Brock after that, so I guess he went somewhere to cool off. Micah came back and hung out with Skylar and her minions."

Devon leveled a look at him that said she knew he had more to tell. "Spill it, G. I know you were rounding up all the news unfit for print before you left. What else did you hear?"

He treated her to a lopsided smirk as he turned the old car smoothly down Main Street. The library was perhaps another mile ahead on the left. "I did do some investigating," he admitted, his dimple flashing. "Turns out Brock didn't think Skylar's costume was…ah… appropriate. He called it a mean joke."

"It was mean," Devon ground out. *Expected, but mean. And no joke.* She didn't know what she'd ever done to Skylar to piss her off so much, but the girl had taken an instant dislike to her in middle school. A stunt like last night's wasn't surprising. "But that's not enough reason for him to get jacked up."

Gil's eyes twinkled. "But that's not all. My source tells me their argument got pretty loud. Skylar was already half-lit when she showed up and she tried to put the moves on Brock to get him to calm down."

Devon felt sick to her stomach. The visual of Skylar crawling all over Brock in that prison jumpsuit was going to give her nightmares. "And?"

"And, he blew her off." Gil's face grew more serious. "That's when she started saying some pretty raunchy things about you."

Devon stared out the window. They were in front of the library and she gestured for Gil to park in one of the spaces out front. "Just say it, okay? It's going to be all over school tomorrow anyway."

Gil pulled into the space and put the car in park. He turned off the ignition before he answered her. "She said that if he wanted to get his freak on with mountain trash, he'd picked the right girl since she'd been taught by a professional." He glanced over at her. "Or something like that."

Devon made an effort to relax hands that had balled themselves into fists. God, she hated this town. She would always be judged by the things her mother had done—or rumors of those things. Devon didn't know how Gammy stood it. "Is that it?"

"Pretty much." He ducked his head.

"Gil!" She hadn't meant to shout, but she was frustrated and angry and hurt, even though she knew none of it would do any good. "If there's something you're not telling, then you'd better 'fess up. I don't want to be blindsided at school."

He sighed. "She named names of guys who'd been with you."

Devon wanted to punch out the window next to her head. "What guys? There have been *no* guys. Even if I wanted to get with any of the mouthbreathers in town, where would we do it? Pretty sure Gammy's not just going to look the other way while I have sex on her sleeper sofa!"

Gil looked like he wanted to crawl into a hole and pull the earth up over his head. She couldn't blame him. This had to be awkward for him, telling his best friend that she'd been branded the town slut. "Look, I know you haven't! And most of the kids like us know it too. It's just..." he trailed off and Devon glared at him.

"It's just what?" She knew she was snapping at him but she couldn't help herself.

"You may have a new nickname come Monday." The reluctance in his voice made her stomach drop.

Devon rolled her eyes. "Out with it."

83

"Pocahontas." He swallowed. "On account of you having to do it in the woods." He looked down, fiddling with his keys. "Micah Landsdown was the one who started it. He told Brock that he'd experienced it firsthand." He looked at her carefully. "I told Brock that you wouldn't have sex with Micah even using someone else's vagina, but, you know." He shrugged half-heartedly.

Devon unhooked her seatbelt and swung the door open. If she didn't get out of the car, she didn't know what she'd do. The cool air hit her like a slap. She took a deep breath, trying to get her anger under control. It wouldn't matter that none of it was true. It wouldn't matter that she denied it; it wouldn't even matter if she could prove Skylar and Micah were lying. Her mom was in jail for drugs and prostitution, so that meant Devon had to be just like her. Up here the apple didn't fall very far from the tree.

The bite in the air stung her nostrils as she took a few more deep breaths. Devon began to climb the steps that led up to the library's front entrance. She could hear Gil getting out of the car. His feet pattered on the stone as he followed her.

"Are you gonna be okay?" he asked when he caught up with her.

She hitched her messenger bag higher on her shoulder. "Maybe." She shook her head, willing herself to focus on why she was here. "I've got work to do. I'll be in the microfiche room. Come get me at five?" That would get them back in time for stew at Gammy's.

"And hey," she said, stopping at the top step. Gil looked up at her. He cocked an eyebrow. "I'm proud you didn't flinch when you just said the word vagina." She managed a wan smile, hoping the joke would show him that she was okay.

She didn't wait for his response. She wended her way to the back of the large open space where the reference librarian's desk sat. Mrs. Dotson smiled at her as she came closer. Devon had been spending most of her free time here since Gammy first brought her back, so the people who worked here felt like a kind of extended family to her. Mrs. Dotson was the weird maiden aunt that would probably turn into a crazy cat lady of that family.

"Well, hello Devon," Mrs. Dotson greeted her as she came abreast of the large half-moon desk. "What are you looking for today?"

"Hi, Mrs. D." Devon pulled her notebook out of her messenger bag. "I need to research something in 1914. Do you have records going back that far?"

"Some." She stood up slowly, her arthritic bones making her move cautiously. "Do you need local, regional, or national?"

"Local. Obituaries at first, I think." Devon figured the man's date of death was a good place to start.

Mrs. Dotson stood up. "It will be on microfiche then. Come along." She led the way to a large room behind her where the readers were.

Devon followed. She knew where the microfiche records were housed—in the grey metal filing cabinets downstairs. She set her bag down in a chair at the back of the room while Mrs. Dotson turned on the reader for her. Devon didn't need the help; she'd done enough research papers and assignments that required her to use the machines that she was probably as well-versed in their use as the librarian, but she didn't want to seem ungrateful.

"If you need help finding anything, just let me know. I'll go unlock the archives now." Mrs. Dotson disappeared out the door holding a ring of keys.

Devon took out her notebook and pen, arranging them to the side of the microfiche machine. She checked her dates again, making a mental note to pull everything in the two months before and after April. The she followed Mrs. Dotson's path to the archives.

Her insides were still roiling over what Gil had told her. None of this was even remotely funny anymore; not Skylar's costume, not the insults to her family, and especially not her new status as class slut. The fact that anyone, let alone Brock, would believe it made her want to hit someone. Preferably someone whose name rhymed with Hylar.

Not that it would make any difference. Devon could beat up the entire senior class and it wouldn't prove anything except that she belonged in jail. Just like her mother.

Devon could feel her mouth turning down into a hard frown. It always did when she thought of her mother. She had vague memories of her from when she was very little, before the drugs and alcohol and men took hold of her mom. Her dad had still been alive then, and while Devon never really thought her mother was happy, she wasn't self-destructive either. Mostly, Devon just remembered her as being sad. Even when things were good, Lorelei always carried sadness with her.

Devon didn't remember many of the fights her mother and father had. They weren't loud arguments, and they were usually started after she'd gone to bed, but she always knew when one of them had taken place. Her mother was almost a mute following an argument with her father, her silence a weapon, one that hurt all of them. Her father would spend a lot of time outside, doing whatever projects were needed on their small house, letting Devon tag along behind him. She'd only been four when her dad died—killed in a car accident where he crashed through a guardrail and plunged down a mountainside to land in a ravine.

She pulled the microfiche boxes for the year she was looking for, trying to put thoughts of her mother and father from her mind as she returned to the viewer. Thinking about the past wouldn't bring her father back from the dead, nor would it make her mother any less...her mother. It was better to let the past sleep.

So why was she so worked up about the headstone? Devon sifted through the film sheets in the box until she found the ones she wanted. She took the first one—from the month of April—and stuck it in the viewer. She spun the dial until she had the April first paper in focus, then began to skim through the articles. Since the paper was so old, she wasn't sure where the obituaries were in the sections, or even if they had obituaries.

But before she had gone very far, she'd found what she was looking for. Daniel Holfsteder had been hung on April 1 for murder. Devon felt her eyebrows take root somewhere above her hairline. Murder? She read on, eager for the rest of the story. The case had been resolved quickly, though the motive was still unresolved. Holfsteder was accused of shooting a man in front of the town hall one night. Witnesses said that the killer who ran away bore a resemblance to the accused. Holfsteder could not provide an alibi, and so was found guilty of murder. He was hung for the crime.

Devon skimmed the editorial pages. There were a few people who didn't believe Holfsteder had been the killer. They expressed their opinion, some of them vehemently, that he had been a convenient scapegoat and that the killer had managed to frame an innocent man. One such man was Keaton Winchester, a lifelong friend of the accused. She made a note of the trial dates so she could go back and find whatever coverage the newspaper had.

There was a photograph at the bottom of the page. Devon scrolled to it so it was in the middle of the screen and rolled the knob to magnify it. The photo was a picture of the crowd of people gathered to watch the hanging. It didn't show the platform or anything like that, so it must have been shot from right in front of it, with the photographer facing the crowd. Devon scanned the crowd of faces, then caught her lip between her teeth. She leaned forward, squinting at the picture.

There she was. Devon could swear it was the same woman from the gravestone. She was wearing a black dress and had a veil partially covering her face. Devon spun the knob until the picture was as big as it would go. The quality was pretty terrible at the resolution, so she couldn't make out the woman's features, but Devon would swear it was the same woman she saw.

How was that possible? This was a photograph taken in 1914. The woman she had seen at the gravestone seemed young—far younger than if this was actually the same woman. Devon didn't understand. And why was Gammy warning her away from her? Had the laws of time and space been changed and no one told her?

Devon jotted down all the facts of the case: names, dates, locations, presiding judge—everything that she thought she could use to find more information. She wasn't exactly sure why she wanted to know more—maybe it stemmed from Gammy's warning from earlier, or maybe it was something else. There was something familiar about this case, something that she couldn't quite recall, but it niggled at the back of her mind like a termite gnawing at a house. Why did she think she'd heard of this before? She had to know more.

CHAPTER THIRTEEN

School on Monday was as bad as she was expecting. The whispering started on the bus, but that Devon could handle. She just sat in her seat, pretending to read a book. She could turn a deaf ear to the murmurs and muffled laughter; at least those were relatively unobtrusive. But things just got worse when she got to her locker. Black spray paint had been used to scrawl a word across the front of her locker and the ones next to hers.

Gil had come by to see her before her first class, and he found her staring at the offending word. He cocked his head as he read it. "I don't get it. They spelled it wrong."

Devon sighed. "I think that was on purpose. Poc-HO-hontas. See how the HO part is underlined?" She gathered up her things and swung her bag over her shoulder. A few guys made that Indian woo-woo sound with their hands over their mouths as they passed her by.

"That's just stupid," Gil said, falling into step beside her. "And I think you might be giving them too much credit. They probably just misspelled it accidentally and made the best of it."

Devon shrugged. It didn't matter, it was still humiliating. What few students didn't know about the party on Saturday night and the rumor started there would know about it now. "Whatever. It's not like it makes a difference either way."

Gil tried to put his arm around her, but she shrugged him off. She didn't want his comfort or his pity. She knew that the torture would last a couple of days, maybe a few weeks, and then something new would pop up to distract everyone. She just had to get through it until then. And she had to do it without showing a hint of weakness. This was high school. Weakness was like chum to an ocean full of hungry sharks.

She got two proposals to go off into the woods behind the school for a little lunchtime action, a couple of lewd notes describing some truly depraved physical acts which made her wonder about the future of her generation, and more catcalls and wolf whistles than if she was passing a construction site buck naked. It wasn't until the end of the day, though, that things got really bad.

Devon had decided to cut through the student parking lot on her way to the town's Hall of Records. She still had to collect some more information about her family tree, plus she wanted to see if there was anything about Daniel Holfsteder. What she'd found in the library had certainly made her more curious about his death and the strange woman who still mourned for him.

Most of the lot had cleared out, many of the students having fled to other hangouts like the Burger Shake at the other end of town. She had stayed behind to wrap up a layout in yearbook class, so she had missed the mad rush at the final bell. She was crossing the lot when she heard someone shout her name.

Devon turned around, her eyes scanning the lot. From a few spots away, Micah Landsdown lounged in the front seat of his Mustang, his driver's side door swung wide. Terrific. Just what she needed at the end of this day from hell. Micah. "Yeah?"

"Come here for a sec!" He waved her over with a lazy hand.

She rolled her eyes. *Really?* "What do you want?" She took a few steps toward him but still maintained a safe distance.

He pushed himself out of the seat. "I want to talk to you." He leaned against the back panel of the car, his arms folded over his chest.

"Yeah, there's not much I want to hear from you." He'd been the one to back up Skylar's claims.

He tilted his head to the side as he looked at her. "How about an apology?"

Devon stared at him, completely at a loss for what to say next. She took a couple of steps closer, positive she'd misheard him. "What?"

He pushed himself away from his car and walked over to her. "An apology. For what I said about you."

She looked up at him, not sure where this was coming from. Micah never apologized for anything. There had to be something else going on here. Devon's gaze swept the parking lot, trying to see if there was somebody else putting him up to this. She saw nothing out of the ordinary. She took a step back, just to be sure.

He took another step closer, keeping the distance between them even. Her eyes flashed up to meet his as anger filled her. "Sorry doesn't take it back, now does it?"

He grinned. Devon gritted her teeth, remembering what a complete asshat he could be. "You know how Skylar can be when she wants something," he answered, as if that excused it.

"You didn't have to lie to back her up," Devon shot back, knowing that this argument was going to go nowhere.

Micah shrugged and she wanted to hit him. So nonchalant, as if her reputation didn't matter a bit. "You're right, I didn't," he conceded, again knocking her off-balance. He stepped closer to her, so that they were only an arm's length apart. "But if you're nice to me, maybe I can do something about it."

Devon narrowed her eyes, suddenly getting where this was going. Did he think she was that desperate to improve her reputation in this crappy town—a town she hoped to have put well in her rearview by this time next year—that she'd be *nice* to him? Clearly the flow of oxygen to his brain had been diverted to other areas.

She crossed her arms across her chest. "So what you're saying is that if I do with you what you already said I did with you, you'll tell everyone that we never did it in the first place. Am I clear on that?" She made sure she put extra sneer into her voice on that last bit. "Yeah, I'm going to have to pass on *that* generous offer."

Devon turned to go, but Micah grabbed her arm. He was fast, but she should have figured that. Still, his grip on her upper arm was really hurting her. "Hey!" she protested, even as he hauled her closer to his face.

"Look, you little hilljack, you're nothing but trash, just like your mama. You should be thanking me for letting people think I'd even touch you."

"Let go of me!" Devon jerked her arm out of his hand, nearly spinning herself around from the force. She was furious, probably angrier than she'd ever been in her entire life. *Thanking* him? For making her sound like a whore?

"Skylar's on to what you're after!" Micah made to grab her again, but Devon stumbled back.

"Just stay away from me!" she shouted back, already running to the street that bordered the parking lot.

She didn't stop until she was almost to the town hall and the stitch in her side was almost unbearable. She had no idea what that was all about, especially Micah's last words about Skylar. Skylar and Brock had dated, sure, but they weren't together anymore. That left Brock fair game for anyone, even Devon. But Skylar was off her meds if she thought Devon stood a chance with him; all he saw her as was writing help with his college essay.

Devon sat on the steps in front of the town hall, taking a look around while she tried to get her pounding heart to slow down. The iron lamp posts lined either side of the street like evenly spaced sentinels. A few people walked on the sidewalks, scuttling between shops and offices. Clouds were moving in from the west, darkening the late afternoon sky. They'd get rain tonight.

The ache in her arm began to really bother her. Devon pulled off her black sweater and pushed up the sleeve of her t-shirt to get a look. Bruises were already darkening the skin of her upper arm, and there was an angry red mark from where she had jerked away from Micah. She cursed under her breath.

"You okay?"

Devon jerked, surprised. Brock stood on the step behind her, a box full of envelopes in his arms. "Yeah, fine." She shrugged back into her sweater. "Off work?" she asked, checking the time on the large town hall clock behind his shoulder.

He shook his head. A piece of hair fell forward, obscuring one eye. "Gophering for Mrs. Welbourne."

Devon nodded, climbing to her feet. She had work to do. She pulled her messenger bag over her head, settling it across her chest. "Ah, okay. See you around." She walked past him on the way up to the double doors.

"Hold up." Brock had turned and followed her. Devon stopped, waiting for him to continue. He stood there, awkwardly shifting from foot to foot. He looked at his shoes so she couldn't see the expression on his face. The silence stretched out between them like inchworm threads that were everywhere come spring, and Devon tried not to fidget.

Finally he spoke. "About Saturday night…"

"I don't want to talk about it." The words were out of her mouth before she could stop them. She knew they sounded harsh, but she didn't care. After the run-in with Micah, the last thing she wanted to talk or think about was Saturday night. "I've got to get some more research done before the archives close."

She thought she saw a flash of hurt on his face before she turned around to walk inside, but she shrugged it off. Devon had enough to distract her without worrying about whether she hurt Brock's feelings. Since he was friends with Micah and Skylar—he had even dated her!—Devon seriously wondered if he even had feelings. She knew it wasn't a fair thought, considering how nice he'd been to her, but she didn't really care about being nice right now.

Devon signed in at the desk, waving at Mrs. Welbourne who was on the phone. She was grateful for the quiet in the archives; there was no one to disturb her. She still had a few more property records and birth certificates to find, but she had made some solid progress on the requirements for the scholarship application. Pulling out her notes and sheaves of copies, Devon began cross-checking her list. Her mother's family had been easy to track, since her Gammy kept everything. Her father's family was a little harder, which was why she had to slog through the public records. Her father's mother lived in this same town, but Devon hadn't visited her once since Gammy had brought her back.

The last time Devon had seen her grandmother was right after her father's death. Grandmother Charlotte had arrived to fetch his things and arrange for his body's transport back home. She remembered Grandmother standing in the doorway, looking tall and forbidding. When Devon tried to give her a hug, Grandmother Charlotte held her at arm's length, as if Devon might somehow dirty her. She marched in, speaking quiet words to her mother that left the woman sobbing. She completely ignored Devon. She'd come to find out later that Grandmother Charlotte had told her mother not to bother coming to the funeral.

Devon pulled out her birth certificate, followed by copies of her mother's and father's. She studied them carefully, trying to remember her father. Her memories had faded with time, but she had a few that still could make her smile. As she ran her eyes along the pages set out side by side, she noticed the blood types listed. Her father was O, her mother B, and Devon herself was AB. But that couldn't be right.

She felt eyes on her and swept her papers together hastily. Brock stood in the doorway, looking at her with the strangest look on his face. It was almost as if he liked looking at her. She felt herself smiling tentatively at him, her anger from before leaving her in the wake of this new mystery.

"Gophering all done?"

Brock smiled and stepped into the room Devon realized she had kind of taken over the place: her folders and notes were scattered across the desk, her messenger bag slung over a chair, the computer monitor turned to face the way she liked. Brock was the one who actually worked here. She wondered if he was ever bothered by the way she had just sort of made the place work for her.

"Yeah, all finished." He scooted around behind the long counter so they were on the same side. "I'd still like to talk to you about something, if you've got a minute."

Devon felt her feet turn to ice. "Saturday night?" Why couldn't he just leave it alone?

He nodded. "You left before we could decide on a time for you to help me with my essay."

Devon had already opening her mouth to deny whatever he'd been about to say, but now she shut it with a snap. "Your essay?" That's what he wanted to talk about from Saturday? "That's all?"

He shrugged, taking a step in her direction. "Well, sure. I mean, what else…" he trailed off, his eyes snapping up to hers. "Oh."

"Yeah. Oh." She found herself staring up at him. His eyes were a muddle of several colors: grey, green, and brown, all mixed together. Devon realized she liked watching the way they changed when the light hit them.

"About Skylar," he began, then stopped, spreading his hands helplessly. "I got nothing." He shook his head. "She was drunk and stupid and mad at me. I'm sorry you got dragged into the middle of it."

"Mad at you?" Devon still wasn't clear how being mad at Brock equated to public humiliation of her, but she was willing to listen.

"Yeah," he said, leaning one hip against the counter. "She's going through a rough time right now. And with us splitting up over the summer," again the shrug. "It's just hard."

"So you broke up with her?" Devon asked before she can stop herself.

"Kinda. I guess." He caught her eye. "We weren't having fun anymore. All we did was fight over the stupidest stuff. It was like we were staying together because everyone expected us to."

"Prom King and Queen," she said, remembering that Skylar and Brock had been voted to the junior court. "She's told everyone that she dropped you."

Brock nodded. "I know. I said she could if that made it easier." He ran a hand through his hair. "I didn't want us to be miserable our senior year."

Devon straightened and crossed her arms. Her upper arm ached when she moved it, reminding her of why she was mad in the first place. "That still doesn't explain the costume. Or the mountain trash thing."

"She was mad I invited you."

"Wow," Devon said, widening her eyes and blinking. "I *never* would have guessed that!"

Brock laughed. "Okay, okay, that was pretty obvious." He brushed his hands on his jeans. "She felt threatened, I guess, when she found out you were coming. She can be insecure sometimes."

"There's insecure and then there's 'call me Pocahontas'." Devon tried to keep the disgust out of her voice and failed. What on earth could Skylar Preston have to be insecure about? Her money, her good looks, her luck with boyfriends? The only thing that she had that Skylar might want was valedictorian, and somehow Devon doubted Skylar really cared about being remembered for her brains. For her perfect back handspring and ability to make letters out of her arms, maybe.

Amazingly, Brock went red. His eyes skipped away from her face and he cleared his throat. Devon watched him, wondering what was wrong with him. She reached over to pound on his back, thinking he was maybe choking, but he moved out of the way.

"I'm fine," he said quickly, still not meeting her gaze.

Devon realized he was still flushing. It dawned on her what she had said. She frowned, wanting desperately to know what Brock was thinking. He couldn't possibly believe that about her, could he? God, what did that say about her? Or him? "You don't actually believe that stuff Micah said, do you?" Her voice was quiet, much quieter than she'd expected it to be. She wanted to shout at him.

His eyes finally met hers, startled. "God, NO!" he practically yelled. "Micah can be a dick sometimes."

"No arguments there," she answered, absently rubbing her arm. "So what then?"

"I guess I just wasn't expecting to hear you...you know...say it."

Devon plopped down in the tall swivel chair in front of the computer, suddenly worn out from the stress of the day. "Why not? It's not true, so why shouldn't I talk about it? I haven't got anything to be ashamed of." She paused, idly picking up a strand of her hair to examine it for split ends. "I just don't get why he'd make up something like that."

Brock inched closer. "Skylar." At her quirked eyebrow, he continued. "He's always had a thing for her. I guess he thought he could get in with her if he trashed you."

"They sound perfect for each other," Devon muttered darkly. Then she thought of something. "So why aren't you trashing me along with them? Not so long ago, you probably would have."

He opened his mouth to say something in protest, but then he shut it. He rubbed his face, and Devon thought he almost looked tired. "You're right. If it was last year, I probably would have."

A stillness fell over the room, the air charged like it was before a summer thunderstorm at dusk. Devon leaned forward in her chair. "What changed?" she asked in a voice barely above a whisper. She seemed to be asking him that question a lot.

This time he finally gave her a good answer. "I did." Brock shrugged and it was like whatever spell had kept everything quiet was broken. He pushed himself away from the counter. "I just don't see the point in all of it anymore. I mean, we're leaving for college. Why does it matter if someone's from the mountain or the town?"

Devon picked at a rough edge on her cuticle, unable to process why she felt so disappointed. He was right; it was stupid to care about something like that, especially with the end of high school looming. It just hadn't been what she'd hoped to hear.

But Brock wasn't done. "I got to know you. And you seemed pretty cool." He gave her a tentative smile.

Devon could feel her face getting hot and she ducked her head. He didn't need to see her glowing like a stoplight. "So do you." Did that sound as lame as she thought it did? She glanced out of the corner of her eye to gauge his reaction. He was smiling, his dimple flashing in and out like a wink.

He leaned over her chair to look at the computer monitor. "What are you working on anyway? I never asked why you needed five generations worth of paperwork."

Devon swallowed at his nearness. He smelled good. He was wearing some kind of woodsy scent that smelled clean, but there was the smell of him layered underneath it. The scents mixed well together and she had to fight the urge to take a deep breath. *Yeah, that wouldn't be weird AT ALL.* Instead she focused on the computer screen, typing in the last parameter of years she was looking for.

"It's for a scholarship. To be eligible, you've got to be able to prove your family has been born in this county for at least five generations." She tucked a stray hair behind her ear.

"How'd you find out about something like that? I've never even heard of it." Brock's breath tickled her ear as he spoke over her shoulder.

Of course not, Devon couldn't help but think. *You don't need to worry about scholarships—your parents can afford to pay the tuition wherever you end up going.* "It's pretty obscure," was all she said. "The guidance counselor found it for me."

"But you're valedictorian." He sounded confused. "I figured you'd be offered a free ride."

She turned the chair around so they were facing each other. It was much less distracting to talk to him that way instead of feeling the shivery touch of his breath on her neck. "I can't count on that." She *wouldn't* count on that; not and risk being disappointed, or worse, stuck here. "Schools are being pretty picky about who they give money to now. I want to be sure I've got everything covered."

Brock shook his head, something like respect in his expression. "You're not going to let anything stop you."

"Nope. Nothing's going to stop me from getting out of here." The determination in her voice surprised even her.

His gaze shifted back to the monitor. "So what's the number of the box you need? I'll go get it for you."

"You don't have to do that," Devon stuttered, unsure of what to do with his kindness. "I can get it."

Brock shrugged like it was no big deal. "I'm going down there anyway. You stay here and keep on your research. I'll bring it up."

"Okay. Thanks." She watched him shuck off his jacket and walk down the stairs that led to the basement archives. Then she opened her mouth in a silent scream of excitement. Brock thought she was cool! What did this mean?!

Skylar and Micah were forgotten in the happy flush that filled her up. She and Brock were talking. Like friends! He had even remembered what her project had been about. She wanted to call Gil right away and talk it over with him, but now wasn't the right time or place.

And tell him what? her inner voice snarked. Devon took a few deeps breaths and calmed herself. She was getting excited over nothing. So what if they were friends? He was nice to lots of people. It didn't make her special, and it certainly didn't mean he was going to suddenly declare his undying love for her in fifth period. She was getting all worked up over nothing. She'd had a crush on Brock for years; it was no surprise that she was trying to read more into it than there really was.

Her mind slowed its racing. *Breathe in through the nose and out through the mouth.* Slowly, she got herself back under control. She had a task to finish—it was only a few more weeks before she needed to turn in all of her applications and financial aid forms. That was what she needed to focus on here.

She dove back into the puzzle of the strange blood types. Devon didn't know much, but she knew that something wasn't right. There was no way this combo of blood types could add up to hers. Had the hospital got it wrong? That didn't seem right, though. She'd been typed since and they'd gotten her blood type correct. Maybe they had made a mistake with her mom's or dad's blood type. Gammy would know—or have records of—her mother's type, but who could she go to so she could verify her father's?

Brock clomped up the stairs from the basement and deposited the box she needed on the counter beside her. Devon thanked him. When he returned to the basement, she pulled up a browser window and began to search for anything she could find on blood types and genetics. After the first few sites, she started to feel a little overwhelmed, so she put that research aside to pull the papers she'd need for her scholarship.

She had sifted through the files in the archival box, stacking the ones the needed to make copies of. She had just turned on the copier and was letting it warm up, when a loud boom of thunder rattled the glass panes in the windows. Devon walked over to the small window and saw nothing but the sheets of water cascading down the wavy glass.

The copier dinged it was ready. Devon made her copies, filed the originals, and returned the folders to their rightful place in the box. She took it back downstairs as another round of thunder made the siding rattle.

"Brock?" She couldn't hear him down here and she didn't know where he had pulled the box from in the shelves.

"Over here!" he called. Devon saw a hand wave from behind a shelf.

She hoisted the box into a more comfortable position and made her way through the silent metal racks of stacked boxes. When she turned down his aisle, she found him sitting on the floor, replacing an old box that had sustained some water damage with a new one.

"Do you ever get leaks in here?" she asked, indicating the old box with the one she was holding. You could barely hear the thunder down here.

"Nah. This one spent some time upstairs though. Some of the offices leak like crazy, especially around the windows. One of the perks of being an old building." He finished what he was doing and hoisted the box back into its place on the shelving unit. "You all done?"

"Yeah. I didn't want to put this back in the wrong place." She found it hard to look at him in the dim light of the archives. They were too close down here, and it was too easy to get lost in his eyes. She tried not to roll her eyes about how corny she was being; she sounded like a love-struck seventh grader inside her head.

He took the box from her. "Over here."

He led the way to the correct aisle and slid the box back home. The lights flickered as another timpani of thunder burst from the sky. They both looked up, as if they could see through the ceiling and straight into the sky. "I'd better get going before it gets too bad out there," Devon said, beginning to make her way through the warren of shelving and back to the stairs.

"Be right up," Brock called after her.

Another boomer shook the building. Devon shut down the computer in case of a lightning strike, and began to gather up her things. She left the light on for Brock, then took herself out to the front of the building.

She stopped at the doors, trying to peer out through the sheets of water that pelted down. She couldn't see the steps, let alone the street in front of the building. She had an umbrella in her bag—Gammy made sure she always carried one—but it would do her next to no good in this downpour. She'd be soaked before she went half a block. And Gammy couldn't drive in weather like this; she could barely see in clear weather as it was.

Pulling her jacket tighter around herself, Devon lingered at the door, hoping that the rain would lessen before the records hall had to close for the evening. She peered out the door, watching the water sluice down in heavy sheets. She could make out flashes of lightning through the watery murk, but very little else.

"Wow, it's really coming down," Brock observed from behind her.

"Yeah." Devon wasn't entirely sure what else to say.

"See you around," he said, turning to go. Devon turned her head and watched him sign out at the front desk.

"Okay," she answered. Devon checked the storm again. The rain hadn't lessened, but she wasn't any closer to getting home. She was just going to have to deal with getting wet. It wouldn't be the first time. She pulled her messenger bag inside her jacket, holding it close to her chest, then zipped up the jacket. She was going to just have to hope that her notes and papers would stay fairly dry with enough layers between them and the rain.

"Hey," Brock's voice called from the other end of the room, "you're not planning on walking home in this, are you?"

Devon turned, the bundle of her messenger bag making her feel like a pregnant kangaroo. "I don't have a car," she said by way of explanation. She sounded almost apologetic and wanted to kick herself. Not everyone her age had a car. She had nothing to feel bad about.

"Come on. I'll give you a ride." He smiled at her and waved her over.

"That's okay. I'm just going to wait a little for it to lighten up." She really didn't want his pity.

Brock checked the clock on the wall before looking back at her. "I don't think it's going to stop much in the next five minutes, and you'd probably need a rowboat even if it did. Come on."

Devon looked back out the door once more. He was right; the rain didn't look like it was going to let up any time soon. "Okay. Thanks."

He waited while she crossed the room to join him at the back of it. Then he led the way down another hall and out a back door that led to a small lot behind the building. He took his keys out and unlocked the doors with a remote, then sprinted out into the wet. Devon followed him.

She slid into the passenger seat, already feeling bad about getting the interior wet. It wasn't a brand new car, but it wasn't old either, and the inside was still in excellent condition. She wondered if it was his dad's old Volvo; if he'd inherited the old one when his dad got the latest model.

Brock leaned over his seat to reach for a towel resting in the back. He wiped the water from his face and hair, then handed it to Devon. "Here, dry off a little." He started the car up and fiddled with the defroster and the temperature knobs.

Devon ran the towel over her wet hair. Amazing how she'd only been out in it for maybe a minute and she was practically drenched. There was no way she would have been able to walk all the way home. She'd have probably stopped somewhere and given Gil a call to see if he could give her a ride. That is, if Brock hadn't offered her one first. She wiped her face free of the rivulets of water coursing down her scalp, noticing as she did so that the towel smelled like Brock. It had his mix of cologne and fabric softener and Brockness that made her want to curl up with it. Instead, she put it in the backseat where it came from.

Brock turned the wipers on high and slid the car into Drive. He took it slow, since visibility was practically nil. He also turned on his lights and hazards so he could be seen more easily. Devon buckled herself in and tried not to grab the door handle or ohshit bar in nervousness. She didn't have much to worry about. There was hardly anyone on the roads right now.

They rode in silence for a little while, the only conversation coming when Devon had to direct him to turn. They were about halfway to the mountain turn-off for Gammy's when she managed to get out, "Nice car."

Brock nodded. "It was my dad's," as if that explained everything.

"He's a doctor, right?" Of course he was. Everyone in town knew who Dr. Cutler was. Most of them went to him. But the thought of his father gave her an idea about some of the questions she had running around the back of her mind.

"Yep." Brock frowned at the mention of his dad.

"Do you know anything about blood types?" *Wow, that didn't sound crazy AT ALL.* She should really work up to questions like that.

Brock's eyes flicked over to her, then back to the road. "That's a weird question."

"Sorry." Devon turned a little in her seat so she was mostly facing him. "I just came across something strange in the records today and I didn't know if you could help me with my questions."

"Just because my dad's a doctor doesn't mean that I am." Then he smiled at her. "But I'll try."

"Cool." Devon took a moment to collect her thoughts. She pointed him to the right turn that led up the mountain before continuing. "Is it possible for a person with O blood type and a person with B blood type to have a child with AB blood type?"

Brock thought for a moment. "You sound like you already know the answer to that."

Devon thought she did, but if she was right, then nothing made any sense. It meant that someone had lied, or was possibly *still* lying. Her hands clenched together into fists in her lap at the thought. What did this mean for her?

Brock continued when it became apparent that she wasn't going to say anything. "I don't think it's possible, at least if I'm remembering my biology right." He risked a look over at her, taking his eyes off of the road for a moment. "I can ask my dad if it would make you feel better."

Devon nodded, not trusting herself to speak. Nothing would make her feel better. Maybe if she hadn't bothered with the scholarship, if instead she'd just counted on her grades and activities scoring her enough money to go to a state college, she wouldn't have found anything out. She felt mad, which in turn made her feel stupid; who could she be mad at? And was it too early to go getting mad at anything? She felt all knotted up inside.

They drove on in another round of awkward silence. Finally, Devon got up the courage to mention the reason why Brock had presumably invited her to his Halloween party and why he was being so nice to her. "Do you still need help with your college essay?"

Brock slowed the car as they begin the climb up the gravel road that led to Gammy's. "Yes!" He ducked his head as if embarrassed at the enthusiasm in his voice. "I mean, I didn't think you'd still do it after the whole Skylar thing."

Devon blinked. *Really?* He thought that about her—that she wouldn't help him just because his ex-girlfriend happened to be a complete bitch-waffle? She said as much to him. "Of course I'd still do it. What she did doesn't have anything to do with you asking for help with your essay. I am a rational person!" *Most of the time*, she amended silently.

"Okay, okay," he said, briefly lifting his hands from the wheel as he gestured in apology. "Can you get together after school tomorrow?"

Devon was distracted by the church as they slowly drove past it. She couldn't help but crane her neck to see if the veiled woman was standing by the grave in this downpour. Brock slowed the car even further to allow her to look. He even peered out the window to see what was so fascinating.

"What is that?" The rain made it hard to see.

"An old church. Most of it's gone now." Devon subsided back in her seat, satisfied that the small graveyard was empty. "I'm just up ahead."

Brock gave the car more gas to get them up over the last rise. Gammy's trailer came into view. "So tomorrow?"

"Sure," Devon answered. "Meet me at the public library and bring all of your applications."

Brock nodded. "And I'll try to have the answer to your question." He pulled the car to a stop in the front yard.

"Thanks." Devon gathered up her stuff in her lap and opened the door. "And thanks for the ride." She sprinted off through the rain to the front door.

CHAPTER FOURTEEN

Gammy was waiting for her, and had the door open before she had even cleared the porch stairs. She pulled Devon inside and they both watched as Brock waited until she was safely indoors before turning the car around and heading back down the mountain.

"Who was that boy gave you a ride home?" Gammy asked as they closed the door against the weather.

Devon stripped off her jacket and hung up her messenger bag on the back of kitchen chair. She felt chilled to the bone, like nothing would ever warm her, and she hadn't even gotten that wet. She knew the only cure for it was a scalding hot shower and she told Gammy as much. Then she said, "Brock Cutler gave me a ride. He works down at the Hall of Records where I was doing research."

"*The* Cutlers?" Her voice was heavy with suspicion.

"Yes." Devon's reply was muffled as she peeled off her sweater.

Gammy's sharp eyes didn't miss much. She caught Devon's wrist and pulled her into the light, examining her upper arm. "He give you this?"

"No!" Devon was shocked that Gammy could even think that. "It was just some guy at school."

Gammy subsided, but she didn't look happy. "Go get warmed up. I'll fix you some stew."

Devon did as she was bid, grabbing her bathrobe from her room before hitting the shower. She sighed as the hot water leeched the ice from her bones, making her feel liquid and light. She took a better look at the bruises on her arm. The marks of Micah's fingers stood out against her pale skin. They weren't bad, not as bad as some of the scrapes she'd gotten running wild in the hills when she was a kid, but it was unsettling to see the evidence of his strength imprinted on her flesh. She quickly rinsed off and bundled herself up in a towel and robe.

Gammy had a bowl of leftover venison stew set out for her. Devon sat, picking up her spoon, but didn't dig into it right away. She looked across the table at her grandmother, who was staring at her cautiously. She'd never seen Gammy look at her that way before.

"Why are you looking at me like that?" she asked her grandmother.

Gammy folded her hands together, clasping the fingers around each other until they made a tight ball. She didn't answer right away. Devon waited, putting her spoon back on the table. Finally Gammy answered her.

"Is there something going on that you'd like to tell me about?"

Devon blinked. There was something in Gammy's voice, a hardness and a warning both that baffled her. "Huh?" She couldn't think of anything more articulate than that.

"The boy who gave you those," Gammy gestured toward her arm, "and the Cutler boy giving you a ride home." She narrowed her eyes. "Awful lot of attention being paid to you, and not the good kind."

Devon was glad she hadn't taken a bite of stew because she probably would have spit it out in shock. "I don't understand." Why was Gammy making her feel like she'd done something wrong? "All Brock did was give me a ride back from town so I didn't have to walk home in the wet!"

"And the one who gave you that?" Gammy nodded her head in the direction of Devon's arm.

"Just some jerk at school. He got mad when I wouldn't be *nice* to him." Devon tried not to shudder at the memory of Micah grabbing her. "I didn't do anything wrong!"

Gammy seemed to relax a bit, subsiding back into her chair. "I know you didn't." Then her voice took on a tone of concern. "You need to stay away from that Cutler boy."

"But Gammy," Devon protested, "I told you he wasn't the one who grabbed me. And we're just friends."

Were they friends? When had that happened? When did she start thinking of Brock Cutler as her friend? Would Brock say the same thing? She thought that he might. Somewhere along the way, a change had happened. Maybe it was all of the time spent in the records office or maybe it was just that being seniors meant there wasn't as much need to care about what other people thought.

Gammy frowned. "We don't mix with town folk, Devon. Bad things happen when we mix with them."

Devon narrowed her eyes. "My dad was town folk."

"And look how that turned out for your mama."

Devon shrank back as if Gammy had lunged at her with a kitchen knife. "That's ridiculous."

Gammy shook her head. "Bad luck followed bad luck once your mama chose your daddy." She raised her eyes to meet Devon's. "I won't have the same thing happening to you." Gammy cut her off when she tried to speak. "Eat your stew."

Devon set her jaw mulishly, watching in loaded silence as Gammy pushed herself away from the table. When Gammy was like this, she knew she didn't stand a chance of changing her mind. She would just have to wait and try and talk to her when she wasn't in one of her moods. Devon picked at her stew with her spoon.

What was that all about anyway—*we don't mix with townfolk?* What was Gil then? He was a townie and Devon had been friends with him for ages and Gammy had never said a thing against it. She ladled food into her mouth, trying to figure out what this was really all about.

She dipped a leftover biscuit into the stew, using the liquid to soften the hardened bread. Gil was gay. Devon couldn't have chosen him, nor he her, even if she'd wanted to. Is that want Gammy meant? She was afraid Devon would run off after Brock Cutler? Devon wanted to snort; the Earth suddenly orbiting the moon was more likely to happen than that, no matter how cute Brock might be.

She took another bite, watching Gammy knit another afghan for her bed. Gammy's bed would probably collapse under the weight of yet another blanket, but that didn't stop her from knitting. Devon felt herself smiling. It was hard to stay mad at the old woman, when she'd done her best to raise her. Gammy didn't want her turning out like Lorelei, and Devon couldn't exactly blame her for that. Still, it did bother her a little bit that here was someone else determined to tell her what to do or who to be friends with. She was old enough—and smart enough—to make her own decisions.

Devon finished off her dinner, listening to the wind whip around the trailer as it rattled through the trees. The gusts threw fistfuls of raindrops at the windows and the side of the trailer, sounding like machine gun pops in the movies. She washed her bowl in the sink, taking a look at the murk just beyond the light from inside. Nothing but darkness surrounded them, and for a moment, Devon felt the need to pull a blanket tightly around herself and huddle in front of the wood stove to keep whatever badness lay in the darkness outside of the firelight at bay. Instead, she placed her clean bowl on the rack to dry and went into the living room to give Gammy a peck on the cheek.

"I love you," she said simply when Gammy looked up at her with a question written in the wrinkles across her forehead.

"I love you too, my girl." She set down her knitting. "I just worry about you sometimes."

CHAPTER FIFTEEN

The day hadn't been horrible: she'd only been propositioned twice and hooted at four times. And she'd managed to avoid Micah and Skylar for the entire day. Devon felt like she could finally relax a little. All that was left was meeting Brock at the library.

She stopped at her locker to switch out books. The halls were mostly empty as students scurried to catch buses and rides home.

A loud bang next to her head made Devon flinch. She jerked away, slamming her locker closed, ready to run. But it was only Gil, grinning at her twitchiness.

"What's got you so spooked?"

Devon tried to smile, but found it too hard. Besides, he'd see through it anyway. "Just have a lot on my mind."

He arched a brow, but said nothing. Devon appreciated his silence. She wanted to tell him everything she'd found out so far, and everything else she suspected, but she couldn't bring herself to start. It was too much.

Gil put his arm around her. "What is it, Dev?"

She was going to tell him everything, but Micah's booming voice kept her silent. "You trying to get a piece of our little squaw?"

Devon jumped, a huge pit opening in her stomach. Gil tightened his arm around her. He turned and scoffed, "Do you have to work at being a Neanderthal or is it a natural gift?"

Micah stopped smirking at them. His lip lifted in disgust. "You want some lessons in how to be a real man, you fairy?"

Gil's eyes narrowed, his lips tightening in a bloodless smile. "Are you offering to teach me?"

Micah grabbed Gil's jacket, slamming him against the wall of lockers. "I'll wipe that smile off your faggot face."

"Hey!" Devon yelled, launching herself at Micah, pulling at his arms.

"And how do you propose to do that, you walking side of beef?"

"Gil, shut up!" Devon kept yanking at Micah, but it was like trying to move a refrigerator.

"Back off, slut," Micah shouted, shoving her away.

Devon reeled back, trying to catch her footing. Someone steadied her, and she turned her head to see Brock holding her up.

"DUDE!" he yelled, letting go of Devon to go help Gil.

Micah glanced at Brock, and that was all the opportunity Gil needed. Devon watched as he grabbed Micah's arms and twisted his body, moving away from the lockers and putting the larger boy in some kind of hold. It must have been really uncomfortable if the redness of Micah's face was any indication.

"Now apologize." Gil's voice was soft, but Devon could see how serious her friend's face was as he kept Micah in the hold.

"Fuck you!" Micah struggled, but Gil adjusted his hold and Micah turned even redder. "Brock, man, smear this queer."

Brock stepped back, shaking his head. "Just apologize, man."

Gil raised his eyebrows at Devon, clearly surprised at the reasonable tone in Brock's voice as much as at the fact that Brock wasn't going to leap to his friend's rescue. Devon shrugged. Brock was just full of surprises.

"You know what? Forget it." Gil flung his hands free of Micah and walked over to join Devon. Micah took a few moments to recover, then stood up straight. He made another move to start something with Gil, but Brock stepped in front of him, holding him back.

"The hell, man?" Micah's voice sounded confused and hurt, like he couldn't understand what his friend was doing.

Devon watched as Brock ran a hand through his hair. "Just get out of here. Before a teacher comes by and writes you up."

Micah looked from Brock to Devon and Gil, as if he couldn't believe what he was seeing. He struggled for words, but even those seemed to fail him. Devon tried not to take pleasure in his predicament, but she wasn't made of such stern stuff.

"What's gotten into you, bro?" Micah's brow knit in puzzlement. "You used to be one of us. Now you're hanging out with the Geek Squad?"

"Nothing's gotten into me." Brock's voice was hard when he finally answered his friend. "What's gotten into *you*? Or maybe it's a who, not a what?"

Micah looked away, his face flushing, this time with embarrassment. Devon watched curiously, knowing that she and Gil should probably leave while Micah was distracted, but not really wanting to. Gil seemed just as interested as she was.

"Skylar's no good for you, man," Brock continued, his voice low and urgent. "Trust me on that one. She's not one to stick around once she gets what she wants."

Micah's head came up. Devon saw his nostrils flare in anger, and watched as his eyes narrowed. He was pissed. But Devon still wasn't expecting him to shove Brock out of his way. He stumbled backwards, clearly not expecting it either, but caught himself quickly.

"Thanks for the advice, *bro*." Micah's voice was mean and dangerous. He glared at Gil before taking off down the hall.

"Are you okay?" Devon walked up beside Brock, still in a kind of a shock over what had just gone down.

"Yeah. You guys?" He looked over at Gil.

"Fine," he said. "But thanks for the assist."

"You seemed to be doing just fine on your own." Brock had a grudging respect in his voice.

"Nine years of jiu-jitsu. You pick some things up."

Devon stared. This was the first time Gil had ever been modest about anything. She knew he'd been taking martial arts classes for years, at first at his parents' behest, but now because he truly enjoyed it. It wasn't something he bragged about, but Devon had thought he'd be a little showier than he was now. Maybe he was maturing.

"You good, Dev?"

She managed a shaky smile. "So far."

Gil nodded at Brock, then gave Devon a significant look. He would want details later. "Then I'm going to take off. Talk to you later." And the tone in his voice told her that, oh yes, he would be talking to her later indeed, and there was no way around it.

"Later." Brock waited until he was out of sight before turning back to her. He shuffled from foot to foot, as though unsure what to do next.

Devon took a little pity on him. "I thought we were going to meet at the library."

Brock shrugged, beginning to walk towards the main doors. "I had to get something from my locker. Figured I'd come by and see if you were around so we could walk together."

Devon managed to keep her face still, even though she wanted to bust out the biggest, dorkiest grin in the history of EVER. He wanted to walk with her! She allowed her girly side a momentary internal SQUEEE! before dragging her brain back to reality. He hadn't professed his undying love for her; he'd only said he was checking to see if they could walk to the library. As far as admissions of passion went, it left a lot to be desired.

She tried to keep her voice casual. "Cool." They were silent as they passed through the doors and out onto the high school grounds. Devon took the lead, able to find the library with her eyes closed from here. When they reached the sidewalk, she asked, "So any idea what Micah's problem is?"

"What do you mean?" Brock sounded surprised.

Devon bit back a sigh. *Hello, Oblivious, Party of One!* "For the past few years, Micah had no idea that I was occupying the same space as he was. And now he's all—" Devon flapped her hands randomly, as if that explained everything. "—freakshow about me."

Brock looked distracted. "To be honest, I don't think it has anything to do with you."

"Gee, thanks." Devon made a sour face. *Way to butter me up there, Romeo.* Yeah, protestations of mad love were clearly not going to be forthcoming.

Brock shook his head. "That's not what I meant." He stopped, and pulled her to a stop with him. She turned to face him. "I think he's bothering you because he's trying to get in good with Skylar."

Devon stared at him, then reminded herself that mouth breathing was not a good look for her and snapped it shut. "Seriously? He's decided to suddenly make my life hell because he wants a date?"

"Not that it will get him far with her," he muttered darkly.

"*You* used to go out with her. Wait, you don't still like her do you? Is that what it was about between you two?" Devon wanted to throw up.

"No, I don't still like her!" His protest was louder than it really needed to be. He looked around and lowered his voice. "I just don't like what she's doing to *him*."

"So that's why you stopped him in the hall when he was about to bash Gil." Devon thought she understood.

At least until Brock spoke again. "No. I didn't like that he pushed you." He looked down. "Or what he called you."

"Oh." It was more of a sigh than a word. She wanted to hold onto this moment forever, to keep it frozen in her head.

He raised his head, almost shy. "I mean, I don't like to see a girl treated like that."

Devon's spell was broken. "Oh," she said, trying not to sound too deflated. "Sure." So much for a white knight on a silver steed coming to her rescue. She decided not to bother telling him about the parking lot.

She saw his look of frustration. "That didn't come out right…" he began, but Devon didn't want to wallow in the awkward any longer.

"Hey, no, it's fine." She began to walk again, her pace brisk. The sooner they got to the library and got his essay done, the sooner she could go home and crawl underneath her bed until her embarrassment faded or the world ended, whichever came first. Why could she just decide NOT to like him and be done with it?

She decided to change the subject. "Did you get a chance to ask your dad about the blood type thing?"

Brock looked just as grateful as she felt at the new topic of conversation. He nodded. "I did. He says that it isn't possible for two people who have O and B blood types to have a kid with AB blood type." He shrugged. "Not sure if that helps you with your research."

Devon could feel her hands beginning to shake. She took a deep breath to try and stop the sudden churning of her insides. She wasn't surprised exactly;

she'd done the internet research that confirmed what Brock had said. But the implications of it—that her mother and maybe her Gammy had been lying to her all of these years about who her real father was—made her sick. She felt out of her depth, like she was close to drowning in strange waters.

"Are you okay?" Brock's voice seemed to come from a long way away. She felt his hand under her elbow, and then he was guiding her to a nearby bench. "You just went white all of a sudden."

Devon dropped into the seat, wincing as her tailbone hit the hard back of the bench. Brock leaned over her, his fingers finding the inside of her wrist and holding it. Devon felt a flush seep over her skin like ink in water. How could one person's touch do this to her?

She pulled her wrist from his grip, slowly looking up to meet his eyes. There was concern there, and not a hint of mockery. Devon managed a weak smile. "I'm okay. My blood sugar just crashed." She made up the lie on the spot. "Forgot to eat lunch."

She watched as Brock sat down next to her and rummaged around in his backpack. He came up with a foil wrapped bar. "Here," he said, unwrapping it for her. "Can't have you passing out in the library on me." He handed her the granola bar.

Devon had no appetite, but she managed to choke down a bite. "Because that would be embarrassing," she snarked around a mouthful of chewy granola and chocolate chips. "As opposed to everything else that's happened in the past two weeks."

Brock grinned. "It would give the gossips around here something else to talk about."

Devon exhaled loudly, knowing it made her sound like a recalcitrant horse. "That's all I need. Something like that's bound to get back to my grandmother. And then she'd probably never let me out of the house." She polished off the rest of the bar and pitched the wrapper in the trash. "Come on, that essay isn't going to write itself." She offered Brock a hand up.

He surprised her by taking it. "True that." He held onto her hand a moment longer than he needed to, before turning away to continue their walk to the library.

Devon followed, trying to squelch the butterflies that had taken up residence in her stomach.

*****

The essay prep session had gone quickly. Brock had surprised Devon by being remarkably good with words once he didn't have his parents breathing down his neck. She came away from the encounter with the impression that Brock had to fit into a very particular mold for his parents and that they would prod and push him until he did. The essay they had worked on was one he wasn't going to show his parents—and it would be the one he submitted to *his* top choice schools. His choices diverged wildly from theirs.

Devon liked this side of Brock. When he didn't have to live up to the public persona of the Cutler family, he was actually really funny. And considerate. And had interests that extended beyond basketball and keggers. He *read*.

None of which was helping her get over the mammoth crush she had on him.

She knew she should have turned down his offer of a ride home, but she was having such a good time talking to him that she couldn't bear to cut it short for the lonely walk to Gammy's. She'd accepted, and now was safely ensconced in the passenger seat of his car, talking about books.

"To Kill a Mockingbird is the best southern novel, hands down," she argued as they turned up the road that led up the mountain.

Brock shook his head. "Uh uh. No way. You're leaving Faulkner out of the equation entirely."

"Oh, come on," Devon countered, slewing around in her seat so she could face his profile, "Mockingbird stands up even now. I mean, can't you see something like that happening in this town? Okay, maybe not with the racism, but certainly there are other parallels."

He cocked an eyebrow at her, as if he knew what she was getting at. But all he said was, "I stand by Faulkner." His eyes darted over to hers and he smiled. "I'm not discounting Harper Lee, but she only had one book."

"We're only talking about one book—not a whole life's work!" Devon loved arguing, especially when there was no real right answer. It could go on for hours. "If we're talking about the whole enchilada, then I have to go with Welty." Devon could see they were coming up on the old church now and she felt the tightening in her chest as the need to look for the veiled woman became overwhelming. She forced herself to look at Brock's hands on the steering wheel.

"That's a little bet—What the fu—!" Brock jerked the wheel hard to the right, nearly spinning them around.

Devon's seatbelt snapped tight as the car bucked and skidded. Brock's eyes were wide as he tried to muscle the car back under control. She looked out and saw a woman in a dark dress moving across the road, toward the cemetery at the back of the church. She braced her hands on the dash as Brock pumped the brakes to get them to stop.

They slammed to a stop, just a hairsbreadth from the trunk of huge oak. Devon hadn't realized she'd squeezed her eyes shut, but now she pried them open. Brock was breathing hard, his head back against the headrest.

His eyes popped open and he fumbled with the seat belt release. "Crazy woman was just standing in the middle of the road!" He opened the door and got out. "You okay?"

Devon managed to get out of the car, her knees shaking. She nodded. Brock took off, following the path of the woman in the veil. Devon started after him, still rattled by the near miss with the tree. She realized she had her bag clutched in her hands in a death grip and slung it over her shoulder as she tried to catch up with Brock.

He was way in front of her, his rage and fear from the near-accident giving him speed that would have made him the envy of his basketball team. Devon ordered her body to stop being so stupid and put on some speed herself, ignoring the tremors in her legs.

She caught up with him as he was rounding the side of the church. When Brock came to an abrupt stop, Devon crashed into his back. "Sorry," she muttered.

Brock didn't appear to be listening. "Where the hell did she go?" He turned around, sweeping the area with his eyes. "She was just here…" he trailed off, then headed toward the chapel's doors.

Devon noticed that they were both closed now, even though she had left one hanging open the last time she'd been here. Something with a lot of cold feet ran down her spine, and the light of impending dusk didn't seem bright enough to drive away whatever might be in that church.

"Brock, hang on—" she called out, but he had already flung open the doors.

The church was empty.

Brock stalked inside. Devon had no choice but to follow after him, even though her heart was racing. What did this mean, that he had seen the woman too? Her thoughts whirled around in her head and she couldn't make sense of anything.

"She couldn't have just disappeared into thin air," Brock was saying as he stomped around the broken down pews.

"You see her too," Devon whispered, but the words echoed hollowly.

Brock spun. "Of course I saw her! She was standing right in the middle of the road—we almost hit her!" It took him a second to calm down and process what she'd said. "What do you mean, *I see her too*?" His hazel eyes narrowed.

Devon couldn't stay another minute. The fear she had when Gammy had first told her about the woman in the veil was back, this time to stay. It started in her feet and moved up, turning her bones to ice so that she was afraid if she tried to talk her teeth would chatter. Brock was seeing the woman too.

He had to be warned. But how could she tell him without sounding crazy? Whatever this woman was, she wasn't just limited to Devon and her family. Now Brock had gotten pulled into it and all because he had the misfortune of giving her a ride home. It wasn't fair.

Devon turned, flinging a careless goodbye over her shoulder. "I have to go." She practically ran out of the church, intent on walking the rest of the way to Gammy's.

Brock caught up with her easily. "What's going on?" he asked, jogging to keep pace with her.

"Nothing." She tried to go faster, but he kept up. "Just go home, Brock."

"Not until you tell me why that woman has you so spooked."

Devon stopped, angrily facing him. "You need to stay away from me!"

"What?" He raked hands through his golden brown hair. "Why?"

"You know why! Mountain and Town don't mix." She took off running, not caring if she looked stupid. "Leave me alone!"she yelled, not looking back.

She had a stitch in her side and pain that had nothing to do with running in the pit of her stomach when she hit the porch. She slammed open the door and fell inside, feeling like a wild thing someone was hunting.

Gammy rose up from the sofa at Devon's sudden arrival. She hustled over to her granddaughter, hand already on Devon's forehead. "What is it, my girl?"

Devon flung her messenger bag down, still breathing hard. She was angry, but at whom she wasn't sure: certainly the woman in the long black veil, maybe Gammy, definitely her mother. She wanted the truth—about everything. She just doubted that she'd get it, even if she asked.

"Brock saw her." She said it as an accusation.

Gammy's look of confusion just made her rage spike higher. "Saw who?"

Devon practically snarled. "You know! That woman you told me never to talk to. She nearly ran us off the road!"

Gammy sucked in a sharp breath. "You were with him? Devon, I told you t—"

"I know what you told me. What I want to know is why? And why is Brock seeing her now?" Devon lowered her voice to a plead. "Please, Gammy. I need to know."

The old woman sighed. "Come inside and let me get some tea." At Devon's hard look, she said, "You may not need something warm to get through all this but I do."

Devon pulled off her coat and boots, then made her way into the living room. She wrapped herself in one of the many afghans decorating the place and sat on the sofa. She watched as Gammy made herself a pot of tea with honey. She raised her eyebrows when she noticed her grandmother pour a heavy shot from a whiskey bottle that she kept in the cupboard.

Devon waited until Gammy sat down in her recliner before clearing her throat pointedly. Her grandmother was not going to get out of telling her what the hell was going on. Gammy took a sip of her tea, made a mollifying gesture with her free hand, and began.

"How many times have you seen her?"

She shrugged. She knew exactly how many times, but she didn't want to worry Gammy. "A few."

Gammy's gaze speared her; it was like she knew everything that Devon was keeping from her. "Uh huh. A few." She took another sip of her tea. "That woman in the long veil—she's no ordinary woman."

"I never would have guessed that what with the disappearing and all."

"Mind your tongue," Gammy snapped, then subsided. "She's a ghost."

"A ghost?" Devon tried to keep the incredulity out of her voice. Gammy had to be pulling her leg.

Gammy's rheumy blue eyes narrowed. "Do you want to hear what I have to say or not?" she challenged.

"Shutting up, Ma'am." Devon sat straight up, like a model student trying to impress her teacher.

Gammy gave her a sidelong look, then started in again. "Yes, a ghost. Our family has one. We've had her for as long as I can remember and past that. Most people don't see her, but then again, most people mind the rules."

"What rules?" Devon blurted out, then pressed her lips together.

"Mountain and Town don't mix—isn't that what I told you when I said not to befriend that Cutler boy? Bad things happen when you do." She caught Devon's blue eyes with her own. "And she's one of those bad things."

Devon shook her head, not sure she was ready to believe this yet. Maybe Gammy was using this as a scare tactic. But when Devon looked at her, she could tell that her grandmother believed she was telling the truth. "So the ghost is the reason I can't be friends with people in town?" She had a thought. "What about Gil? We've been friends forever and I never saw her before."

Gammy leaned back in the recliner, putting her feet up. "Gil is a friend—and he ain't gonna be anything more, what with him liking boys and all." As Devon boggled at her grandmother, she continued. "It's not friends she has a mind to stop. It's more like…friends in the biblical sense…that she's opposed to."

Devon blushed, not believing what she was hearing. Did Gammy just try to talk about sex? The ghost was no longer the weirdest part of her day. "But I'm not even dating Brock. We're barely even friends!"

Gammy gave her a look that seemed to say, *how big a fool do you take me for?* "You like him—as a girl likes a boy, otherwise you wouldn't be seeing her. And he must like you, if he's able to see her too." She shook her head. "You never could do anything the easy way. Just like your mama."

"What does my mother have to do with this?" When it looked like Gammy wouldn't speak, Devon practically shouted. "What about my mother?"

Gammy took another drink from her teacup, buying herself some time. Finally, when Devon thought she would burst, she said, "It's a tale best left for your mother to tell." She held up a hand to forestall Devon's protests. "But she did see the ghost. Just like you."

Devon went still. Her father. Or at least the man who, until today, she thought was her father. "Dad?"

Gammy nodded grimly. "He was from town, but you know that. Your mama didn't heed the ghost's warnings, she was too wild, too in love. She thought the ghost was just superstitious bunk us old people thought up." She looked up at Devon. "Then there was the shooting."

"What shooting?" Devon didn't recall anything about a shooting.

"It was well before your time, little one. Your daddy's best friend shot a man and went to jail for it. He died there too. Strange thing was, he never said a word to defend himself." She sighed. "That was the beginning of the end for your mama and daddy."

Devon rubbed her eyes. "Why haven't I heard about this before?" None of this made any sense.

"You parents didn't like to talk about it. They had all just graduated high school. Jackson Duvall—that was the shooter—was close to your mama too.

Your parents picked up and left as soon as the trial was over. It was too painful for them to stay around here, I suppose."

"And the ghost?" Devon wasn't sure how this ghost had anything to do with this tragedy.

"It's what comes when our family mixes with town folk. She reminds us to keep to our own. You mama ignored the signs, and she was punished for it." Gammy turned the mug of tea around in her hands.

Devon tightened her hold on the blanket she was wrapped in. "Did my dad ever see the ghost?"

"I don't know. He never mentioned it, and your mama never said anything if he did." Gammy took a deep swig of her tea. "So that's why I want you to stay away from Brock Cutler. No good can come of you two being together."

Devon chewed her lower lip, thinking about everything her Gammy had told her; and everything she hadn't. Finally, she asked the question that was bothering her most. "Why do we have this ghost—this curse—anyway? Why us?"

Gammy settled back in her chair a bit, easing the weight off old bones. "She's one of our line. She loved a town man and it turned out badly." She paused and stared off into the distance. "That's all I know."

"And nobody bothered to figure out why she's haunting us?" Devon was shocked.

The gaze from Gammy was reproachful. "Everyone as lives up here is too busy making a living to bother with the why and where. You follow the rules and nothing bad happens. You don't, and you pay the price."

"Mom's rotting in jail because she happened to love the wrong person! Don't you think that price is kind of high?" Devon stared at her grandmother, angry again. How could she just excuse it like that? "She's your daughter!"

Gammy bowed her head. Devon thought she might have gone too far, when the old woman looked up, her gaze fierce. "You don't know what I feel, Devon. And I hope to God you never do."

Devon subsided against the back of the cushions, her eyes caught in Gammy's gaze like a bird before a snake. There was steel in her stare, and power too. Devon felt abashed at her hard words. Gammy had been living with this longer than she had.

But there was still one question that gnawed at her, begging for an answer. After a few moments of silence, Devon finally got up the courage to ask her grandmother. "Was my dad really my dad?"

She expected a look of shock or surprise, or possibly an immediate denial. What she got was a look of immense exhaustion, as if Gammy was too tired to go on. But what scared Devon the most was that it was also a look of acknowledgement, as though Gammy had been expecting this question from her for a long time.

When her grandmother spoke, it was in a voice that sounded a thousand years old. "For that, my girl, you're going to have to ask your mother."

CHAPTER SIXTEEN

Devon rolled into school still half-asleep. She'd stayed up late rereading her mother's diary and obsessing over the photograph of her mother and Jackson. She had a feeling that Deacon had never seen the ghost, but maybe Jackson had. When she eventually tried to go to sleep, she was kept up most of the night thinking about the family ghost and the mystery of who her real father was. By the time she managed a fitful doze, her alarm went off an hour later. She'd be lucky if she made it through fourth period before passing out from exhaustion.

She'd thought about staying home today, but couldn't stand the idea of being in the trailer with her grandmother. There was a tension between them that hadn't ever been there before. Devon couldn't help thinking about the secrets that Gammy still held onto, ones she may never know about. It made her anxious and angry. She didn't want to sit around clenching her teeth in frustration all day, so school was really the best option, even if she did feel like she had to keep her eyelids open with toothpicks.

Devon rounded the corner to the hall that led to her locker and froze. Kids behind her cursed and jostled against her, but she didn't care. Brock was standing next to her locker, evidently waiting for her to arrive and get her books.

Her eyes darted around for an exit, but it was too late. He'd seen her. He was staring at her, as if willing her down the hall toward him. She was even desperate enough to avoid him that she was wishing for a glimpse of Skylar or Micah to serve as a distraction. But it looked like no help would be forthcoming from that direction, so Devon knew she'd just have to pull on her big girl panties and face the boy that she liked but could no longer talk to.

She wasn't sure when she finally decided to accept the possibility that Gammy's outlandish story about a ghost that followed her family's love affairs like a soap opera was true, but at some point in the night she had. Some of it didn't make sense to her, but Devon had never seen Gammy so serious about something so...weird before. She at least owed her enough to try and figure out what was really going, and that was exactly what she planned to do after school.

But first there was Brock. He moved aside as she came up to her locker, allowing her access to her combination lock. The janitor had tried to scrub away the paint, but the faint outlines of the insults were still visible. Devon didn't care; she had bigger problems to worry about than people calling her Pocahontas.

Brock started first. "How are you doing?" His eyes took her in, sweeping her from head to toe. Devon felt a flush of warmth slide through her.

"I'm good," she answered, fumbling with her lock. She took a deep breath to steady herself, managing to get her locker open without further mishap.

He leaned against the locker next to hers. His hazel eyes peered at her. She did her best to resist the urge to look at him. Finally he said, "We need to talk."

No good could come of that, of that Devon was sure. "I don't think that's a good idea." She dropped a book and reached down to pick it up.

Brock beat her to it. He held the book out to her. "Something happened yesterday that spooked you. I want to know what."

Devon took her book from him with hands that just barely shook from nerves. What could she tell him? That she had a ghost that didn't like her talking to him? That her life would be ruined by what could very well be a figment of her imagination? But he had seen it too—so did that mean it was real? And could that also mean that his future was on the line?

Devon didn't know what to do. She wished this was someone else's problem to solve. "I have class."

Brock put his hand on her arm and Devon had to force herself not to jump. It was like his pull on her increased by ten, like he was a magnet drawing her close. "Please, Devon. Talk to me."

She met his eyes then. In them she saw worry and fear and a dozen other things that all made up Brock. Her heart seemed to change its rhythm, rearranging its steady beat to a staccato pattern. Ghost or no ghost, she liked Brock Cutler. And that wasn't going to go away just by wishing it.

"I have to get a pass from first period," she said, her way of acquiescing.

He nodded. "I'll meet you at my car." He took off in the other direction.

Devon managed to snag a pass to the nurse's office and an excused absence from first period. This was the first time she'd ever skipped a class and she kept expecting to be called on it by any number of people. But as the bell rang and the halls emptied out, there was no one to stop her. In only a few minutes she'd found Brock's Volvo and slid into the passenger seat.

She shivered a little, since the car was only marginally warmer than it was outside. Brock leaned over and snatched a gray and red checked wool blanket from the backseat. "Here," he said, passing it over. "Wrap up in this. Skylar and I used to…"

"Ewwww," Devon said, shoving it back at him.

Brock looked offended. "I was going to say, we used to use it for picnics." He shook his head. "Where your mind goes, I swear."

Devon took the blanket back from him. "Sorry."

He waited until she was all wrapped up in it, and then said, "And then we'd have the wild monkey sex on it." Brock grinned hugely.

"Jerk!" Devon laughed, swatting at his head.

He caught her hand easily and held onto it. The tension in the car ratcheted up by a factor of twelve. Devon swallowed hard, her mouth suddenly dry. After a few moments, Brock released it, but Devon could swear she still felt his fingers wrapped around hers.

"So about yesterday," he began, readjusting his lanky frame in the driver's seat. "What happened out there? Who was that woman?"

Devon took a deep breath. "Okay, what I'm going to tell you may sound a little bit...out there. But you have to promise to listen to what I have to say. Deal?"

Brock stared at her, his face suddenly serious. "Deal."

"She's a ghost."

"Exqueeze me?" He frowned, shaking his head as if he had water in his ears.

Devon stared at him, putting on her most serious expression. "She. Is. A. GHOST."

"A ghost?" Skeptical didn't come close to the way he sounded when he said those words.

"Yes." She waited for him to say something else, but all he did was wave his hand at her to indicate she should go on. "Apparently my family has a ghost who doesn't like it when mountain and town folk get together."

"But we're not together." He looked down at his hands. "I mean, we haven't even gone on a date."

"I take it you're over the whole not believing in ghosts thing?" She crossed her arms over her chest. "Wow, that was easy."

Brock ran a hand through his hair. "Oh no, we'll come back to that one. Who told you about this ghost thing?"

Devon clutched the blanket tighter. "My Gammy. When I first told her about this woman I was seeing, she told me to stay away from her—and that I should never speak to her. But I…"

"Wait, you've seen this chick before?" Brock sounded surprised.

Devon nodded. "Pretty regularly since I started going to the records room." She left the *and hanging out with you* part out. "Halloween night was the clearest she's ever been, but I guess that makes sense."

"Huh?" Brock had a lost look on his face.

"Halloween is supposed to be when the veil between this world and the other world is thinnest. So if anything is going to make an appearance, then Halloween is the night to try for it." She'd done some research on it for a paper in her Culture and Criticism class. But she doubted Brock wanted to hear about ancestor remembrance tokens and the Day of the Dead.

He raised his eyebrows. "So you believe this woman is really a ghost?"

Devon shrugged. Now that she was talking about it rationally, the woman in the veil was less scary. Thinking about her like she was a problem to be solved on the SAT was helping her get over her mind-numbing fear. "It makes sense. You look away from her for just an instant and she's gone. She's mourning over the grave of a guy who's been dead for over a hundred years. And then there was everything that happened yesterday."

"I can see her too," Brock said, his voice soft. He turned back to Devon. "What does that mean?"

Devon ducked her head, already embarrassed by what she had to say. "I asked my grandmother about that when I got home. That's when she told me about the ghost not liking it when members of my family get involved with people from town." She looked back up at him, wanting to see his face for her next admission. "So that's why I've been seeing her ever since we started hanging out. I guess she knows that I kind of like you."

The goofy grin that eclipsed his face was something she would never forget. It was a combination of cockiness, pleasure, and a not insignificant amount of pride. "You *kind* of like me?"

Devon couldn't help but roll her eyes at the needling tone in his voice. "Don't go getting all conceited about it. Sheesh."

He turned to face the front windshield. "You kind of like me," he repeated in a surprised voice. Then his head whipped around suddenly. "But why am I seeing her?"

Now it was Devon's turn to grin, and she gave him one that would have put the Cheshire Cat to shame. "I asked Gammy about that too. She said that it was probably because you liked me too." She tried to keep the smugness out of her voice, with only limited success.

Brock's neck went red, and Devon watched in fascination as the flush crept up his face. He was looking everywhere but at her. She was curious what he would say next: whether he would deny the whole thing, or play it off like it was no big deal. She was betting on denial.

What she wasn't expecting was Brock to lean over in his seat, put his hands gently on either side of her face, and kiss her.

"What are you—" she began, but then his lips were on hers, stopping anything else she might say.

The kiss was soft, like a whisper made flesh. Devon put her hands up on his, feeling the strength of his hands under hers. She slid forward, drawing closer to Brock, wanting to breathe him in, reveling in their mingling breaths. She opened her mouth against his, wondering how she had managed to go eighteen years without this wonderful, heady sensation.

Brock pulled back slightly. His thumb stroked her cheek. "You taste like cherries."

"I had a toaster strudel for breakfast." *Oh dear God, just kill me now, please! Why did I have to say that?*

Brock chuckled low in his throat, a terribly intimate sound. Devon realized she was in his car, with no one knowing where she was, and pulled back nervously. She tucked a strand of dark red hair behind her ear to give her hands something to do. She looked up at him, suddenly shy. "So I guess this means you do like me?"

He ran a hand through his hair. "I guess it does." He gave her a small smile. She returned it.

He took her hand. "So now what do we do?"

Devon thought for a moment. She wasn't sure what they should do, or even where any of this was going, but she didn't think this was the time to hash out their future when they'd only just kissed fifteen seconds earlier. "I'm not sure. Maybe we need to figure out how to get rid of the ghost?"

"How do we know something bad is going to happen to us if we get together? I mean, is there any kind of proof?" His thumb rubbed circles on the back of her hand.

Devon looked away. This was the hardest part to believe. If what Gammy said was true, her mother's failure at life was due to the ghost's curse, not anything that Lorelei did. But how to explain that? "My mother," was all she said.

Brock didn't say anything; he just leaned over and pulled her close to him, wrapping his arm around her shoulders. When she was quiet for a few minutes, he prompted, "What about your mother?"

"You've heard the stories, and you were there for Skylar's costume." She tried not to bury her head in his shirt. "My mom and dad—they didn't have a happy marriage. And then my dad died and my mom kind of went...you know." She couldn't bring herself to say that her mother tricked herself out for drug money. "She's been in jail for years."

"And you think that's because of a ghost?" There wasn't a hint of skepticism in his voice now.

"My grandmother does, and she's the one who knew my mother best." She shrugged. "My dad was from town—my other grandmother—his mom, still lives here. And things kind of did go off the rails once they got together." She remembered something her grandmother had mentioned last night. "There was a shooting or something that involved a friend of theirs too."

"Couldn't that have been all there was to it? Maybe it didn't have anything to do with the ghost at all?" He pulled her closer.

Devon relished being held. She took a moment and listened to the steady beat of his heart beneath his t-shirt. It made her feel warm and safe. But there was something else that she felt she had to tell him, something that made no sense. "Do you remember that question I had about the blood types?"

She felt him nod, his chin resting on top of her head. "Yeah."

"Well, there's something that doesn't add up. I have blood type AB. My mom has B and my dad has O." She waited for a beat to see if he would catch what she was saying.

"But that's not right," Brock said, his voice puzzled. "That would mean…"

"That my father isn't my father." Saying it out loud sounded worse than inside her head.

Brock pulled away so he could look at her. "What does this have to do with the ghost though?"

Devon shook her head. "I don't know, exactly. But I feel like everything is connected and if we figure out one thing, we can figure out the rest." She put a hand on his chest. "Does that make sense?"

He smiled at her. It was soft and close, a gift just for her. She wished she could grab it and put it in a box so she could take it out and bask in the special way it made her feel. "As much as anything else does. So what's our game plan?"

Devon felt like she was glowing and that she would never stop. He said *our!* She felt her stomach muscles clench in an unvoiced SQUEE, then tried to pull her mind back to the important matter of her family curse and unknown parentage. Somehow it didn't seem as overwhelming as it had at midnight when she was lying in her bed alone.

She gave him her answer for everything. "Research," she said. "We need to find out about this friend of my parents, about this ghost of mine, and see if there are any books that tell us how to send a spirit to its rest."

"No wonder you're valedictorian." Brock tilted her chin up and kissed her thoroughly. "Library after school?" he asked when he was done and Devon was breathless.

She nodded, because forming words was suddenly something well beyond her.

CHAPTER SEVENTEEN

She thought the end of the school day would never come. She knew she walked through it with a huge smile on her face, but she couldn't help herself. Brock Cutler liked her. Brock Cutler *kissed* her. She had been kissed by a boy—and not just any boy; the cutest boy in school. Gil tried to corner her in third period, but she just tried to smile like the Mona Lisa, leaving him with only empty threats and a serious case of gossip frustration.

Devon nabbed her books out of her locker and headed down the hall to find Brock. She turned down the corridor and stopped when she saw Skylar talking to him. She kept back, making sure she couldn't be seen and peeked around the corner.

Skylar was talking quickly. Devon couldn't make out half of what she was saying, her words were all garbling together. She looked upset though, making Devon wonder what was going on. She looked at Brock's face and noticed he was wearing a neutral expression as Skylar became more and more upset.

Skylar threw her arms around his neck and Devon felt her back stiffen. If she'd been a dog, she'd be bristling. She saw Brock trying to pull her arms off, but Skylar was determined. Devon decided she'd had enough and stepped out into the corridor. Brock's eyes flicked to her, then his attention shifted back to Skylar.

She flung herself at him, her mouth latching onto his. Devon frowned, ready to snatch the hussy bald. She didn't have to though. Brock jerked his head away from Skylar, pulling out of her embrace. "The hell, Sky?"

"You know how good we were together, B. We could get it back, be that way again." There was a pleading note in her voice. Devon almost felt sorry for her. Almost.

"What about Micah?" Brock was scowling.

"What about him?" Skylar grasped at his shoulders, but Brock moved out of her way.

"You're just playing with him, aren't you? Stringing him along?"

Skylar flipped her hair and Devon wanted to smack her. "So?"

Devon walked up, having heard enough. "You ready, Brock?"

Skylar whirled around with a snarl on her pretty, but heavily made-up face. "What do *you* want?"

"I wasn't talking to you." Devon stood her ground, glaring at Skylar. She wondered briefly if this was some kind of dominance behavior. It kind of felt like it was turning into that, but it was too late. She'd challenged Skylar, and short of peeing on Brock to mark her territory, she was going to have to see this through.

Skylar's breath hissed out. She looked between Devon and Brock, shock clouding her features. "Are you kidding me?" She turned her back on Devon to talk to Brock alone. "Really? You've hooked up with this trash?"

"Hey!" Devon protested, walking around Skylar so she stood next to Brock. "Careful who you call trash."

Skylar ignored her. Devon gritted her teeth, resisting the urge to make Skylar acknowledge her. The girl was on a tear. "I get that you might need some space," she was saying, "but when you're done with your cheap mountain strange, I'll be here."

Brock shook his head, his face angry. "I'm done listening to you talk about Devon this way. And you know what? I'm done with you." He faced Devon. "You ready?"

"You have no idea." She began to walk down the hall. A few students still hanging around had seen the whole thing. Devon held her head up, unafraid to meet their eyes. She heard Brock's footfalls behind hers as he caught up to her.

"That was fun," Brock commented drily as they left the school.

"Yeah, I'm hoping we can do that every day and twice on Sundays." She made a face at him. She was surprised that he had been so comfortable being out in public with her. He was from an entirely different crowd than she was. Her popularity had nowhere to go but up, but his social standing was bound to take a hit. She hadn't expected him to be so open about her.

They walked along the sidewalk, keeping pace with each other. Finally Devon couldn't stand it anymore. "Why?"

"Why what?" Brock furrowed his brow in confusion.

"Why me? Why now?" She glanced at him out of the corner of her eye, afraid she was going to make him mad. You didn't question good fortune like this, but Devon had always been more interested in honesty. "You never knew I was alive before."

Brock thought for a moment, still walking easily beside her. "I wouldn't say that," he eventually said. He stared at her, his hazel eyes intent on her face. "I loved the way you smelled sophomore year. You sat next to me and you always smelled so good. Like strawberries."

"My shampoo." Devon was amazed he remembered. That he'd noticed. She said as much.

He nodded, then took her hand. "I noticed." They walked in silence for a few minutes, then he said, "And why now?" He shrugged. "I guess I got tired of waiting for the right time because there is never going to be a right time. There's just right now. And you."

Devon ducked her head, smiling. "That's nice."

Brock bumped into her, causing her to look up. His smile was one of the nicest things she'd seen all day. "I could ask you the same thing. Why me?"

"It was always you. I was just waiting for you to pay attention." She felt herself blush at her bold words.

"I always was a little slow," he said, pulling her close to him as they walked. "But eventually I catch on."

"Took you long enough." She wrapped her arm around his waist, wondering how it was that she felt so comfortable. She'd never have thought she'd be one to snuggle against a boy in public. But then again, she'd never thought she'd get to snuggle against a boy while still in high school. She had always figured it would be an experience that would have to wait until college.

"Too long."

They turned right and continued down the tree-lined street. In spring, the trees would be in bloom, shading the sidewalks and houses, but right now, in the desolate time between fall and winter, they all stood bare, like ladies waiting to be dressed for the ball. There weren't many people out; most were at work or already home from school, but Devon saw several cars slow down as they passed them. The news of the two of them walking down the street together, wrapped in each other's arms would be all over school tomorrow. Heck, it would be all over town.

"Brock, are you sure you want to do this?" Better to find out now if he was likely to cut and run before the gossip really started.

He looked confused for a second, then his face cleared. "You mean us?" At her tentative nod, he squeezed her tight. "Why wouldn't I?"

"Would you like the list alphabetically or by order of importance?" She stopped walking so she could look at him and not worry about tripping over a bump in the sidewalk.

He tucked a piece of hair behind her ear. "I guess, maybe I should ask you the same thing."

Devon went with honesty, as she always did, whether it hurt or not. "I don't have anything to lose. But you—let's face it, I doubt your parents are going to be thrilled when they find out about me. I only have a ghost to worry about. You've got the whole town."

"Your ghost is still spookier than the whole town put together," he answered, his eyes dark. "I can handle it."

Devon eyed him carefully, not wanting to push, but hoping he was aware of just how hard it would be. She had her mother's diary to go by and it hadn't been easy for either her or Devon's father. Things hadn't changed that much in twenty years. Brock gave her a brilliant smile, and she let the matter drop.

They continued their walk. "People are going to talk no matter what we do," he finally said as they began to climb the steps to the library. "You cool with that?"

"Hey, I'm 'call me Pocahontas'. I'm cool with anything."

CHAPTER EIGHTEEN

"I found it!" Brock said just a hair too loud, earning him a quelling glance from the librarian on desk duty. He had the decency to look abashed. "I found it," he whispered again, moving some of Devon's notebooks out of the way so he could sit next to her.

"It's all here," he began, laying out photocopied pages. He leaned his head close to hers, and Devon could smell the fresh scent of his shampoo. It smelled like pine trees and winter. She inhaled deeply, then shifted her attention back to what he was showing her.

She'd given him the easiest piece of the research. She'd already done some work on the ghost herself after she'd found the picture when she was hunting for information on the grave marker, so it wouldn't take much for her to pick it back up. But she had nothing on the more recent shooting and those archives were much easier to deal with, so she gave them to Brock. And he'd come up with something.

"So the man who was shot was a drifter by the name of Benjamin August. It happened in front of the Town Hall late at night on," here he had to leaf through some pages to check the date, "February 21. Anyway, it looks like they didn't have any suspects until someone came forward and said they saw the shooter."

"Who was the witness?" Devon was jotting down notes as fast as she could.

More shuffling of pages. "Dwight Abernathy." He pushed a photocopied picture at her. Abernathy was an older man, perhaps in his fifties, and he looked like he did a lot of work outside. "Anyway, ol' Dwight over there fingered a local named Jackson Duvall." He handed her another picture from his copies from the newspaper. "Duvall didn't have an alibi so he was convicted, although the evidence seems pretty flimsy. He went to prison. That's where he died." Brock paused when he noticed Devon wasn't scribbling. "What's wrong?"

Devon sat staring at the black and white photo of Jackson Duvall. Gammy had told her that he'd been her father's best friend and that he'd been close to her mother. But this wasn't the first time she'd seen him. Her mother had countless pictures of Jackson Duvall: some with all three of them, some of just him, and a couple with Jackson and her. Devon had found these tucked into her mother's diary pages along with some pressed flowers. She'd never found any of her father's pictures tucked away in her mother's diary though. Seeing him staring at her from the newspaper copies came as a shock. He was drawn and thin, looking nothing like the vibrant man in the photographs that her mother had kept.

"Devon?" Brock waved a hand in front of her face. "You still with me?"

She shook her head, as if that would help to clear the cobwebs. Everything was sounding too familiar. She pulled out her copies of the Daniel Holfsteder case reports. "Did he say anything in his defense?"

Brock shook his head. "Just that he was innocent, but that he didn't have an alibi."

"That's just like what happened to Holfsteder." Devon spread the pages out on the table in front of them.

"Who's Holfsteder? I didn't see him mentioned in this case." Brock leaned over for a closer look.

"Daniel Holfsteder is the name on the tombstone that the ghost visits. I saw her standing in front of it on Halloween night. When I went to research him, this is what I found." She skimmed the first article, then pointed at the line of text she was looking for. "He was accused of killing someone in front of the Town Hall too." Her finger moved down the page. "And he didn't have an alibi either."

"Was he convicted?" Brock asked, his voice hollow.

Devon nodded. "And hung for his crime. And look," she shuffled pages until the one she wanted was front and center. She pointed at the photograph of the crowd, specifically a woman staring stoically at the scaffold. "Remind you of anyone we've seen?"

Brock picked up the page to give it a close look. "Whoa." His hazel eyes met hers. "It's her!"

"I know, right?" She grinned.

"This is getting pretty creepy though." Brock put the picture down. "I mean, the cases are almost exactly the same."

"And both men died." Devon's grin was gone. "But why are they so alike? There's got to be a reason. And why is the ghost replaying out what happened in her life if it was so awful?"

"Do you even know who she is? You figured out who her Daniel guy was, but do you have anything on her?"

Devon shook her head. "No, Gammy just told me that she was someone back in our line of kin. I don't even know her name." She brightened for a second. "But I've got tons of family information from the archives and the records room. Maybe I can track her down through those papers."

"Check your Gammy's Bible," Brock suggested absently, still staring at the three pictures laid out in front of him.

"What? Why?"

He looked up, his eyes catching hers. Devon swallowed hard, thinking of what it would be like to drown in them. He had very nice eyes, hazel with a ring of black around the iris, fringed by heavy lashes. "Lots of people pass their Bibles down through the generations, and the names are listed of everyone who had it. It's sort of like a mini-family tree."

Devon put her chin in her hand and gazed at him. "That's actually brilliant."

Brock grinned. "I know. I surprise myself sometimes." He looked over at what she'd been reading. "Any luck?"

She sighed. "There's really nothing helpful in these books. Mostly seems to be a lot of talk about proving the existence of ghosts. We're already ahead of the game on that one."

Brock picked up one of the volumes stacked around her. "But nothing on how to get rid of it?"

"Not so far. I'll check some of these out, maybe see what else they've got." Devon checked her watch. "I need to get back. Gammy's put limits on when I have to be home from school."

"I'll give you a ride." He began to gather up his copies.

"You probably shouldn't do that. It will make her mad." She didn't mention the ghost; then again, she already suspected they had pissed her off.

"I'll risk it. I don't like you walking alone." His voice was firm. There would be no wiggling around it.

"Fine. But you can drop me off at the church and I'll walk the rest of the way. I don't need Gammy grounding me any more than she already has." She shoved papers and notebooks into her messenger bag, then began to stack up the books she thought would be the most useful for checkout.

Brock took the stack from her. "I've got it."

"I can do it, you know." Devon tried for mock-offended and came out nowhere near it.

"What's the point of having a guy around if he won't lift heavy things for you?" He smiled down at her. "Besides I like doing things for you."

"Oh." Devon could feel herself blushing. "Okay then."

CHAPTER NINETEEN

Brock pulled his car over to the side of the road opposite the church. He put it in park and turned in his seat to look at Devon. For her part, she still felt weird when all of his attention was on her like this. She kept wanting to pull her head into her shoulders, like some kind of a human-turtle hybrid as a way of protecting herself. She wasn't used to this kind of attention.

"So what's our next move?" His voice was soft in the confines of the car.

Devon fidgeted with her seat belt release, needing to keep her hands busy. He'd used 'our' again, and it made her heart beat a little faster. The belt snapped off of her. "You see what you can dig up on Abernathy and Jackson Duvall. I'll handle the ghost and what happened to Daniel. Sound good?"

He moved closer to her, his own seatbelt already off. "Sure. I'll tell you what I find via Chat."

Devon lowered her eyes, feeling that mountain embarrassment clinging to her skin. "I don't have internet access out here."

Brock just nodded, not bothered by her admission in the least. "Bet reception is pretty crappy out here anyway. So check back in at school tomorrow?"

Devon tried to put her embarrassment behind her. "Sure." She looked out the windshield, noting how the sun was sinking behind the mountains. Darkness was gathering in the hollows of trees and at the base of their trunks. It would be night soon. "I should get going."

Brock's hand on her arm stopped her from picking up her bag from the floorboards. Her eyes flashed up to his face, suddenly unsure of what she was doing. Everything seemed so clear back at the school, but up here on the mountain, this seemed strange and dangerous. Then his lips were on hers and she didn't care about mountain or town or school or research. All she cared about was the way his breath fanned along her cheek, the way his mouth tasted, and the way her skin seemed to tingle at his touch.

He pulled her closer, and she let him, wanting to sink into him until they shared the same skin. She wrapped her arms around his neck, pulling herself up higher so that she was tight against his chest. His mouth dropped down to her neck, as his hands pushed aside her heavy hair. Devon felt something tighten in her stomach and she shivered at the pure pleasure she felt when he trailed hot kisses down her throat.

Her hands found their way to his hair and she twined her fingers through it. If her Gammy saw her now, she'd have a conniption fit. She was breaking every rule her grandmother had warned her of and she was relishing it.

Devon cracked her eyes open to sneak a peek at Brock when she noticed a dark form standing at the driver's side window. Her eyes popped all the way open and she pulled away from Brock with a shriek. He turned to see what had spooked her and jumped himself.

"Holy shit!" he shouted, lurching away from the window.

The woman in the black veil stood next to the car, watching them. Even though Devon couldn't see the veiled woman's face, she could feel the weight of her stare, glaring at them from beneath the fabric.

Anger surged through Devon. She'd had enough. "That's it!" she cried, pushing her door open. "I. HAVE. HAD. IT!" She stepped out of the car and came around the front of it, but the woman in the black veil was already drifting towards the ruined chapel.

She heard Brock open his door as she ran after the ghost. "Dev, wait a sec!"

But she was furious and wanting to vent it. How dare this *apparition* try and dictate her life! She was just as bad as the townspeople who didn't want to mix with folk who lived on the mountain. Devon was tired of living by everyone else's rules, and being put in certain boxes because of whose daughter she was, or where she lived. It was why she couldn't wait to get away from this place. And now, this spectral pain in the ass was trying to take away the one good thing that had happened to her this entire year. She was over it.

"Hey, you giant perv!" Devon shouted, running to the church doors. "Yeah, you with the boundaries problem!" That probably wouldn't endear her to whoever this woman was, but Devon didn't particularly care. "What the hell is your deal?"

She cleared the doors and stopped, surprised to see that the veiled woman had stopped at the front of what used to be the altar. Devon heard the doors slam shut behind her. She could barely make out Brock's frantic pounding as he tried to get them to open. *Oh boy.* She watched as the woman slowly turned around to face her.

Devon still felt the anger coursing through her, but now it was tempered with a slice of fear. But she was here now—and apparently trapped—and she wanted some answers. She took a step closer to the ghost. "What do you want from me?" she asked, her voice echoing strangely.

The woman reached up, her thin hands pulling the veil back over her head. Devon winced and muttered, "Oh God, please don't have an eyeball hanging out or face rot."

But the face that was revealed was young—maybe twentyish—and would have been quite lovely, if grief hadn't left its mark on her features. Tear tracks gleamed against pale skin, streaking down cheeks sunken with despair. Her eyes glowed dimly, showing no whites. There was only dark desolation in her gaze. Devon felt herself caught in that whirlwind of pain, the ghost's eyes drawing her deeper into the past.

The ghost stepped forward, and Devon took a step of her own to meet her. She felt the pull toward this creature, and she was no longer afraid of her. Somehow Devon knew that the ghost wanted answers too. Devon took another step, mirrored by the ghost, and another, until they faced each other with only an arm's length between them. Brock's door pounding sounded very far away.

Devon watched as the ghost reached forward and carefully, almost gently, took her hand. Devon felt the cold of the ghost's touch leach into her skin, going deep to the bone, and she gasped in pain and wonder. The hand in hers felt real, as solid as her own. She could feel the delicate bones of the fingers beneath hers, almost like bird bones so slight were they.

She looked up at the ghost's face and gasped. Her eyes weren't just glowing, they were burning with a white fire that seemed to steal all of the remaining light in the room. Devon saw clouds of white forming around them: her breath as the temperature dropped quickly. The cold seeped into her, moving up from the stones and through the soles of her shoes and into her legs, but Devon couldn't move, even if she'd wanted to. She felt herself falling into darkness, lit only by two brilliant stars.

CHAPTER TWENTY

She was in the chapel, but it wasn't a burned out relic. The roof was whole, the pews upright and polished to a high shine. Strong sunlight streamed in from the stained glass windows, painting the stone floor in kaleidoscope colors. Devon felt her body, as if ascertaining that she still had one. The woman in the long black veil was nowhere to be found.

The door opened on silent, well-oiled hinges. Two young people came in: a woman and a man, although calling them that was generous. The girl couldn't have been older than sixteen, the boy maybe a year older. They were deep in conversation, almost like an argument.

Devon gasped when the girl turned. It was the woman in the veil except younger. And when she got a better look at the man, she realized that he looked very much like the picture of Daniel Holfsteder that she'd found in the old archives. Where had the ghost brought her? Or when?

The girl and boy took no notice of her, ignoring even her gasp. It was like they couldn't even see her at all. She waved her hands in the air, but they didn't even glance her way.

"Jessamy, please!" Daniel begged, grabbing at the girl's hand. She snatched it away from him, anger plain on her face. "You can't marry him."

"Why not? He asked papa for my hand." Her voice was scathing. "My father approves of the pairing, and Keaton is a decent man."

"I'm not denying that," Daniel said. He scrubbed his face with his hands. "He's my oldest friend. But you don't love him, Jess!"

Jessamy whirled, her blue eyes glaring at him. "Don't you say such things to me!"

Daniel moved closer to her. Devon could see the high spots of color on Jessamy's cheekbones, saw her nostrils flare in anger as Daniel closed in. But she didn't step back out of his path. Devon watched as Daniel took her in his arms.

"I'll say such things to you because they are the truth. You don't love him because you love me."

Jessamy pushed against his chest, throwing herself out of his arms. She straightened her skirts with a finely boned hand. "Be that as it may," she said, her voice low and rough, "HE asked."

Daniel flinched as if she'd struck him with a weapon instead of words. "Jess, you know I would have—if you'd just waited..."

"For what? Your family to change their minds about me?" She barked a sharp laugh, bitter like day old coffee. "For me to be a dried up old spinster woman?" She shook her head. "Keaton's family doesn't mind that I come from the mountain."

"Keaton's family needs the money your dowry can bring," Daniel growled.

"And yours doesn't." Jessamy waved his insult away. "Keaton loves me. And I can build a life with him." She swept past him, and this time he let her go.

She turned back to him once she got to the door. "I may love you, Daniel Holfsteder, but I'll not wait forever." And then she was gone.

The air shimmered around Devon and she was suddenly somewhere else.

*****

It was night now. Devon looked around, letting her eyes adjust to the darkness. There was light, a candle from the way it was flickering, coming from another room. She took a tentative step, unsure of exactly where she was. It looked like some kind of empty animal stall. It had a low door so she could see over it and into what looked like a stable of some sort.

There were candles stuck in various alcoves. Daniel Holfsteder stood in the center, anxiously watching the closed barn door. Devon had an idea of who he was waiting for, and her suspicions were confirmed when the door opened only wide enough to admit a woman in a long coat with a veil covering her head.

"Jess," Daniel breathed, taking quick strides to come to her side.

"I can't stay long," she said, unwrapping the veil from around her face and hair. Droplets of melting snow gleamed and shattered the candlelight.

Daniel caught her up in a fierce embrace, his mouth swooping down on Jessamy's. Devon felt like she was intruding, even though the two of them had no idea she was there. She was a ghost herself, only able to observe the past.

"I love you," he whispered, his fingers lovingly tracing the lines of her face.

Jessamy leaned her forehead against Daniel's chest. "I can't stay. I'm a married woman now."

"But you still came." Daniel smiled down at the top of her head. "I'm glad."

"I am too." She lifted her mouth to his.

Devon didn't know how much time had passed between this vision and the first one in the church, but it had been enough for Jessamy to marry Keaton. She turned away, not wanting to intrude any more than she already was. She only turned back when they began to speak again.

"Leave him." Daniel whispered.

Jess shook her head. "This is impossible. Keaton is our friend, my husband."

Then she looked up, directly at where Devon stood. Her eyes narrowed, as if she could see Devon. The air began to shimmer once more and again Devon was someplace else.

*****

Devon stumbled, landing on her knees in a snowdrift. She didn't feel the cold at all, even as the wind whipped stray flakes into a frenzy around her. She knew where she was; it hadn't changed that much in all of these years. The town hall stood before her, the clock reading ten o'clock. A man stood in front of the building, illuminated against the snow by the full moon above.

She didn't recognize the man from any of the pictures she'd found. Devon took a few steps closer, trying to get a better look at him. He continued to stand, looking up and down the street, but he clearly didn't see her.

A crack broke the quiet of the night air. Devon knew what a gunshot sounded like, and she hit the ground. She doubted a bullet would affect her since she seemed to be invisible in this time, but she wasn't going to risk it. Her eyes scanned the square, but didn't see anything. When she tried to find the man who'd been standing there, she saw a dark shape lying on the ground.

Devon was up before she even thought about it, pelting over to the fallen man. She dropped to her knees next to him, her fingers against his neck for a pulse. His skin was already icy, and blood seeped from the wound on his back. His eyes were open and his mouth worked, but he couldn't see her.

She heard a rustle from farther up the road. Her head came up, eyes searching the darkness. She caught a look at man with an old style rifle slung across his back. He seemed to be confirming his kill, although he didn't come closer. He turned and was gone.

Devon put her hands on the dying man's chest. The air shimmered a third time and she was once again falling through clouds of white air.

*****

Devon pushed herself up from the floor. The woman had replaced her veil, and as Devon watched, she faded into nothingness. Just as she faded away completely, the doors sprang open. Brock stumbled through, caught himself, then rushed to her side.

"Dev!" He dropped down next to her, his hands resting on her shoulders. "What the hell happened in here?"

Devon leaned against him, grateful for his warmth. Her thoughts were all jumbled up in her head, and she was having a hard time making sense of anything. She felt disconnected from herself; unsurprising considering she'd just taken a supernatural trip through time. Her stomach heaved and she swallowed thickly, trying not be sick. Sweat broke out all over her body.

"Are you okay? She didn't hurt you, did she?" Brock's voice was just one level lower than frantic.

She put a hand to her head, as if physical contact would still the roiling thoughts in her head. "I'll be okay."

Brock crushed her to his chest, his lips in her hair. "Don't you dare go after her again by yourself. The doors were locked or something—I couldn't get in to help you!"

"I'm sorry, I didn't know that would happen." She adjusted her position so she could look at his face. Concern and fear stood in his eyes as he looked down at her. Devon put a hand to his cheek, wondering how she had gotten so lucky to find him.

Brock took her hand from his face and placed gentle kisses along her knuckles. "I'm just glad she didn't hurt you."

Devon shook her head carefully, still feeling like it might roll off her neck at any sudden movement. "No, she didn't." Her eyes widened as she realized what she had been witness to. "Oh, Brock, she showed me what happened. I think I understand now."

"What do you mean, she showed you?" His frown was fiercely protective.

"I don't know how she did it, but I saw her past—at least parts of it. Her name was Jessamy and she married a man named Keaton, but she really loved Daniel Holfsteder. And then I saw the shooting and there was no way Daniel could have done it because I saw the man who did do it and Daniel couldn't have done it *anyway* because he was with Jessamy that night." Her words came out in a torrent, like snow melt down the mountain.

"Hang on, hang on. Slow down." Brock held up his hands. "Say that again, at about half speed so I can follow it."

Devon took a deep breath to try and reel herself back in. She felt jittery, keyed up, with a need to do something RIGHT NOW. Even though her body was suddenly bone tired, her mind was alive with the possibilities of what she'd seen. She went over what she saw again in detail, getting Brock up to speed.

When she was finally finished, he ran a hand over his face, rubbing his eye. "It's kind of hard to believe," he said, his voice unsure.

Devon answered him, her words emphatic. "I *saw* it."

"I believe you," he assured her. "But what are we supposed to do with all of this? How does this help us lift the curse?" He paused, thinking. "And what does this have to do with your mom and dad?"

She sagged, the weight of trying to find the right answers crashing back down on her. She rubbed her temples. "I know it's all connected. I can feel it."

"Look, we're not going to do much more today." Brock climbed to his feet, then held out his hand to help Devon up. "You need to go home and get some rest. I can still do the research on Abernathy tonight. We'll meet back up in the morning, okay?"

"But, I—" she began, but Brock cut her off.

"It will keep, Dev. Holfsteder's been dead for a hundred years. What's one more night to him?" He wrapped his arm around her and led her to the door.

Brock's words were imminently reasonable, and Devon could see the logic in them. Still, there was a part of her that wanted to push through her exhaustion and keep working at the problem until it was solved. She hated leaving things half done.

"Devon." Brock's voice was warning, as if he already knew what she was up to.

"For someone who just noticed me, you sure seem to know a lot about me." She bumped into him playfully.

Brock gave her a small, secret smile. "I've been noticing you for years," he said, before he brushed his lips lightly against hers. Then he pulled away. "And I know that look. You're trying to think of way to keep at this." He stopped walking and pulled her around to face him. "So promise me. No haring off on your own. We're doing this together, okay?"

"I promise," she whispered, startled by his seriousness. She hadn't expected him to be this involved in solving the mystery of her family's haunting. It made her stomach do flips.

"Good," he said, mollified. He dropped a kiss on the top of her head, then led her back out to the car.

CHAPTER TWENTY-ONE

Devon looked over at Brock, amazed for the millionth time that he would do this for her. It was the day after Thanksgiving and they were on the road well before sunup. But while most people were up so early to brave the sales and shopping, Devon and Brock were headed to prison.

Devon was going to see her mother.

She hadn't seen her mother in a decade; the last time was when her mother was led away in handcuffs from the dingy motel room they'd been staying in. After Gammy had come to get her and she'd gotten settled, she tried to write a few letters to her mother, but that was always so hard. She'd had no contact with her mother since. And now she was on her way to see her. The lump of lead that was currently sitting in her stomach made her question the intelligence of this enterprise. There was no guarantee her mother would agree to see her; this whole trip could be a waste of time.

Brock took his eyes off of the road for a second to send her an encouraging smile. Devon smiled back, grateful for his help and support. She wasn't sure she could do this if she had to go by herself. She would have preferred not to go at all, but they'd reached the limit of what they could do with archive articles and old photographs. There was remarkably little about the more recent shooting, and none of the major players involved were left alive. Only Abernathy, the witness, but he no longer lived in town.

The only person left to ask was Lorelei. Devon could only hope her mother would tell them what they needed to know. Gammy hadn't been happy when Devon mentioned her plan for a road trip. Gil had covered for her, saying that he'd be driving her so that Gammy would let her go. In the end, Gammy had sent Devon with a box of her mother's favorite homemade cookies.

They stopped for gas and breakfast once the sun started lighting the pavement. For the most part, they drove in silence with only the radio for noise. Devon caught cat naps, her head leaning against the cold window. At least asleep she didn't have to think about what would happen when she saw her mother again.

The prison parking lot was nowhere near full. It wasn't at all like what Devon had been expecting: there were no guard towers, no patrols with guards sporting rifles. There wasn't razor wire or anything terribly prison-like that she could see. It looked a lot like a building you'd find on a college campus, truth be told. The main structure was red brick, the walls set with windows. The land leading up to the main building was nicely landscaped, even in late autumn. The American flag and the state flag flew from two flagpoles that flanked the walk leading up to the doors.

Devon got out of the car slowly, taking it all in while she stretched muscles cramped from sitting so long. The wind cut through her jacket and she pulled it tight around her. She took the box with the cookies from the dashboard. She doubted she'd be allowed in with it, but it gave her something to do with her hands.

Brock came around the front of the car to stand beside her. "You ready for this?"

She took a deep breath and let it out slowly. Then nodded once. "Let's go."

They walked side by side up the front walk and into the brick building. She checked in with the admin behind the main desk and was directed to the visiting waiting area. After the ID check and the review of the rules, Devon was escorted into the visiting room. Brock waited outside, holding the box of cookies and her bag.

She sat at an empty table to wait for her mother. There weren't many people there yet, even though it was a state holiday and visitation was allowed. Her leg bounced constantly as the minutes stretched. Devon was just debating about getting up to get a soda from the machine when she heard a shuffling step nearby. She looked up.

Pale green eyes that matched her own stared back at her. "Devon?" Her mother sounded breathless, as if she'd just run the 100 yard dash.

"Hi Mom." She didn't get up to give her mother a hug. That would have been weird.

"Wha...what are you doing here?" Her mother took the seat across from her, folding her hands demurely on the tabletop.

Devon took a moment to look at her mother, to assess the changes to the woman. The last time she'd seen her, Lorelei had been skinny, underfed, with a junkie look to her. Her auburn hair had been lank and lifeless, her clothes had hung from an almost skeletal frame. Her skin had been a strange ashy color, as if she hadn't been getting enough sun. This woman bore little resemblance to that woman. This woman's skin was clear, and while not what anyone would call a robust color, was at least a more normal shade and not so dead looking. Her hair was cut short, but had some life to it. Her eyes were clear, not clouded with the haze of addiction. And she'd filled out, the sharp angles of her face and body a little more rounded now and softer.

Devon blinked. Prison actually looked better on her mother than regular life had.

"I need to talk to you and I need you to be honest with me. Something's happened."

Lorelei grew pale. "Mom?"

Devon shook her head. "No, Gammy's fine." She looked up, her eyes boring into her mother's. "I've seen the ghost."

She hadn't thought her mother could get any paler, but she'd been wrong. Lorelei moved as though to push her chair back and leave, but Devon grabbed her hand. She spoke quickly. "I've never asked anything of you before now and I'll never ask anything of you again. But I need you to tell me what happened to you so it doesn't happen to me."

Lorelei swallowed nervously, eyes darting around. Devon thought it looked like she wanted to ask for help from the guards. "Please, Mom."

The hand clutched in hers relaxed a bit. Devon kept hold of it, but lightened her grip some. She was afraid Lorelei might evaporate if she let her go, and Devon wasn't willing to risk that until all of her questions were answered. She kept her eyes on her mother's face, watching the subtle play of emotions there. Surprise and fear scudded across it like clouds before the moon, followed quickly by anger and sadness. Then all her face showed was resignation.

"When did you first see the ghost?" Lorelei asked, her voice barely above a whisper.

Devon leaned closer so she could hear her better. "A few months ago. Right before I started hanging out with Brock."

"Brock is from town, I expect." When Devon nodded, Lorelei sighed. "Stop seeing him and the ghost will go away."

Devon's eyes narrowed in irritation. She had not come all this way for the pat, simple answer. She wanted to shake her mother, but knew that would get her nowhere. "That's not going to happen." She thought for a moment, then said, "And I don't think it would help anyway. I think the ghost is waiting for someone to figure out why she's still here."

"I can't help you."

Devon wanted to scream. "No, you *won't* help me. There's a difference."

Lorelei tried to pull her hand away, but Devon latched on, tightening her grip. "You don't know what you're asking."

"I'm asking not to turn out like you." The words were said quietly, but Devon could see they hit her mother like a punch to the stomach. She watched as her mother's eyes filled with tears, though none fell.

The minutes passed as they sat in silence, staring at one another. Finally Devon had enough of waiting. "Okay, fine, you don't want to talk about the ghost? Then how's about we talk about my father." Devon glared at her mother. "Like, say, who is he?"

Her mother's head snapped back. "You know who your father is. Deacon Mackson."

Devon slashed her free arm down, palm flat, like she was slapping the air. "No. I've done some checking and the blood types don't match. There's no biological way my dad is actually my dad." She squeezed her mother's hand. "So I want to know who is."

Lorelei let out a defeated sounding laugh. "I can't win either way." She spread her hands out, as if laying all of her cards out on the table. "The story of your father *is* the story of the ghost. At least in part."

Devon quirked an eyebrow at her. She waited while Lorelei seemed to gather herself and her thoughts. When her mother spoke it was in a voice soft and full of the joy of things past. Her face was transformed into something almost beautiful as she told the story of her life before Devon.

"I was sixteen when I first saw the ghost. I didn't think anything of it, not at first. She just looked like some woman wandering the mountain. I thought maybe there was a commune nearby, or something else that required members to dress in old-fashioned clothes. I was busy with school—and boys—and Gammy made sure I didn't get into too much trouble with either.

"I'd always been a little bit in love with Jackson Duvall since elementary school. He was from the mountains, but his family had moved to town ages ago because they'd done well with some timberland they'd sold." Her eyes were unfocused, describing things that only she could see. "His best friend was Deacon Mackson. They were inseparable since the fifth grade."

"By the time we all were in high school we'd formed our own little group. Not sure how it happened, but because I was friends with Jackson and Deacon, I was accepted by everyone. Those two were on the football team, and they ran track, so they were popular with all of the jocks. Deacon was going for a scholarship—he wanted to be a doctor—but Jackson just planned to kick back and enjoy life after high school. He had no plans for college or leaving. He just wanted to inherit his dad's business and live every day the same as the one before."

She paused for a moment. Her mouth turned down, as if tasting something unpleasant. Then she shook her head, and continued. "During all of those years, I had only seen the ghost a few times. Here and there, off and on, and she never seemed to single me out. I had no idea who she was or what she meant.

"It wasn't until I turned eighteen that my mother told me what the ghost meant to us. She'd seen Jackson and me carrying on at church about something, and she wanted to warn me. Of course, I didn't listen—she was just some superstitious old mountain lady—because there wasn't any such thing as ghosts."

Her hands twisted around each other where they rested in her lap. "Then Jackson got himself a girlfriend. Deacon and I were sort of left on our own." She smiled a private smile, and Devon relaxed, at least knowing that her mother had loved the man she knew as her father at some point. "He was so kind and patient and sweet to me. He didn't mind me missing Jackson; he missed his friend too. It was only a matter of time before we started dating."

Lorelei's eyes darkened, the fear in them palpable. "Then I started seeing the woman in the black veil everywhere. I could swear she followed me to school, standing outside the window of my class and staring in at me. I didn't know what she wanted, but she frightened me. I thought she must be some kind of crazy lady who'd gotten fixated on me—it still didn't occur to me that what my mother had told me was real."

"Gammy didn't try to stop you from seeing Deacon?" That didn't sound like the Gammy she knew.

Her mother shook her head. "Oh, she tried. But I was determined to do what I wanted. I thought I was invincible, that I knew best." She gave Devon a knowing look, but didn't say anything else. "And there was Jackson to consider."

Devon cleared her throat, feeling guilty. "But you married Dad. Wouldn't the ghost have tried to stop that?"

"I'm coming to it." Lorelei's face crumpled a little. Her voice got even lower. "After graduation, Deacon asked me to marry him. His mother was horrified, of course. I didn't say yes right away. You see, I liked Deacon. I knew I could build a life with him. But I'd pinned my heart to Jackson Duvall."

Devon's eyes were wide. Hadn't Jessamy said those very words? "You could build a life with him?" she repeated, feeling an eerie sense of déjà vu.

"I tried, Devon, I did." Tears stood in the corners of her mother's eyes. "Before I said yes to Deacon, I went to Jackson. He knew that Deacon had always loved me and so he'd stepped aside." She shrugged. "He thought I loved Deacon, and he wanted his friend to be happy. That's why he started dating another girl. He didn't want to hurt his friend. Of course, I found all of this out much later, when it was already too late."

"I told him about the proposal. He said I was lucky to have someone like Deacon and he congratulated me. It wasn't what I wanted to hear. I thought he didn't want me, so I stormed back to Deacon and told him yes." A tear spilled down her cheek. "That was a moment I will regret until the very day I die."

"You married Deacon. Knowing you loved another man." Devon couldn't keep the accusation from her voice.

"Yes." Lorelei bowed her head.

"Did he know?"

"Yes, I think he always knew." Lorelei's voice was all sadness. "That was only the beginning of the ghost's curse."

"The murder?" Devon kept her voice to a whisper.

"I'm coming to that." Lorelei wiped the tear tracks from her cheeks with the back of her hand. "Jackson went away after the wedding. I was heartsick, but glad in a way. I thought without him around, Deacon and I stood a chance at happiness. And we were happy as newlyweds. Deacon was applying to colleges so he could go to medical school and I was keeping up the house." She smiled fondly. "It was like we were kids, playing at being adults.

"Until Jackson came back." Lorelei's eyes met Devon's, holding her in place with the intensity of her gaze. "And I was lost."

Devon leaned forward, completely captivated by her mother's story. Lorelei wouldn't look at her as she continued. "It was early autumn. I had gone to visit Gammy and I was coming back down when my car got a flat. It was near the old chapel—is that still there?"

Devon nodded, not trusting herself to speak. Her mother continued. "Jackson was also visiting his relatives. I was walking back up to call Deacon from Gammy's house, when he pulled up. I was surprised to see him—I hadn't heard he was back in town.

"We were very formal with each other, the awkwardness was almost painful. Then the sky opened up in one of those flash rains we got in the fall in the mountains and we ran to the chapel to try and stay dry." Her mother's eyes had that faraway look again. "I don't know if it was the sudden privacy, but we couldn't stop ourselves. I don't know who kissed who first, but once we started, we couldn't stop. The affair went on all through the fall and winter. We both felt horrible about it for what we were doing to Deacon, but we couldn't stop ourselves. I snuck away every chance I got to be with Jackson.

"I don't think Deacon ever knew. We tried to be cautious, but it's a small town and people will talk. It made Jackson and me more careful. We only met at the church, that was our secret place. It would have stayed that way forever, except for…"

"The shooting," Devon finished when her mother just trailed off.

Lorelei nodded, looking at her daughter earnestly. "It wasn't Jackson—it *couldn't* have been him. He was with me that night."

Devon stared in shock at her mother—she had let an innocent man go to jail! "Then why didn't you say anything?"

"He wouldn't let me. He swore me to never saying a word about where we were, he said it would hurt Deacon far too much and he couldn't bear it. He said this was his punishment for betraying his dearest friend."

Devon thought he sounded like a bit of a drama queen, but clearly her mother still loved Jackson, even if he made questionable life choices. "You didn't have to listen to him!"

Lorelei seemed to shrink into herself, her body growing smaller. "I know. But I did because I was afraid. Afraid of what people would say, of what Deacon would do. I didn't want to see the look on his face when he realized his friend and his wife both betrayed him." Her voice was almost nonexistent when she said, "I was a coward."

Devon said nothing. What was there to say, really? She gave her mother a few moments to collect herself, then prompted her. "Then what happened?"

"Deacon tried to find a way to get Jackson out of it—he didn't believe he could ever kill anyone. And in the middle of this mess, I found out I was pregnant. Deacon was over the moon, he was so happy. I didn't have the heart to tell Jackson about it. What good would it have done?" She wouldn't look at Devon.

"What about the ghost?"

Lorelei raised her head, as if surprised Devon was still there. "I would see her sometimes, especially if I was visiting Mom. She didn't appear nearly as much as she had when I was meeting Jackson." She sighed. "I finally told Mom about what had happened and how I was still seeing the ghost. I've never seen her look so disappointed in me before." She shuddered. "She said if I had just listened to her, none of this would have happened."

"I talked Deacon into leaving town. He was all for it after everything that happened with Jackson. I figured the ghost had done her worst. So we packed up—you were only a baby—and headed out. He'd gotten into college so we got an apartment there." Her eyes were wistful. "We were happy there. For a little while.

"Then we got the news that Jackson had been killed while he was in prison. I couldn't bear the guilt of it. I started drinking. Deacon wouldn't look at me. We fought, but what was worse was when we'd go days without talking. We moved again, thinking a change might help. It didn't, it just made things worse. I think I was punishing myself, and by doing so, I punished Deacon. None of it was fair to him."

"I remember the night he died," Devon said softly, her own thoughts turning to the man who'd had a hand in raising her. "You guys had had a fight. He left. It was snowing."

Tears spilled down Lorelei's cheeks. She didn't try to stop them. "The weather was bad. He shouldn't have been out driving in it." She took a shaky breath. "He went down an embankment. It was a few days before they found him." Lorelei looked at Devon, an almost fond smile on her face. "You are so much like him, you know? So smart, so driven. He would have been proud of you."

"But he's not my father. Jackson is." Devon's voice could have frozen skin off the bone.

Lorelei nodded. "I never knew for certain. I didn't want to know."

Devon had a thought. "You said Dad was in pre-med, right?" The unfairness of it all struck her and she wanted to hurt someone. Her mother was the only one available. "He knew."

Lorelei bowed her head. She didn't say a word. Devon sucked in her breath. "You knew that he knew." She waited for her mother to deny it. When she didn't, Devon continued. "He figured it out the same way I did: the blood types."

Devon just stared at her mother. She had no idea what expression she wore on her face; maybe shock, or disgust, or anger, but she knew she felt all three of them and many more. She looked hard at her mother, trying to understand the choices she made, and found that she couldn't. She didn't understand why she'd done what she'd done. She wondered if she ever would.

But there was one thing she understood now: why her mother was in here. "It's punishment," Devon whispered. "You were punishing yourself with the drugs and the men. And now you're punishing yourself by being in here."

Her mother shook her head. "Not punishment. Well, not anymore anyway. And the drugs were about escaping my guilt too. But now, I'd say it's more about atonement."

When Devon spoke, her voice sounded higher and more strained than she expected. "What about me?"

Lorelei looked at her, regret in her eyes. "I'm sorry, Devon. I tried."

Devon gritted her teeth. She didn't believe her mother had tried, not enough to really matter anyway. She'd thought the hurt over her mother's abandonment was long past, but now it burned in her chest. She struggled not to cave in to tears of anger; she didn't want her mother to misconstrue them and think she was sad or that she felt pity for Lorelei.

It came to her that her mother was incredibly selfish. Lorelei only thought about what she wanted. Her desires came first. Even when Devon had been a small child, it had been about Lorelei escaping her guilt and grief, never about what was best for her daughter. Even now, with this atonement rot she was trying to sell, Lorelei only thought of her own feelings. She had a daughter that she could be a mother to, and all she wanted to do was sit in jail and obsess over her lost loves.

Devon felt like she was going to throw up. She swallowed hard. Her mother spoke again, taking Devon's hand "Believe me when I say, you need to heed the ghost. She ruined my life—she ruined all our lives. She'll ruin yours too."

Devon pulled her hand back. She'd gotten all of the information she'd come for. More, in fact, than she ever thought possible. But she was done now; with this place, with her mother, and with the excuses. There was nothing tying her to the town or to her past. It was as exhilarating as it was frightening.

She spoke softly, but her words carried the weight of a judge's decree. "No, the ghost had nothing to do with this. Your bad choices ruined your life. " *Many lives*, Devon thought. "You had a choice! You ALWAYS had a choice. But you just chose wrong. You can't blame your bad decision making on a ghost!"

Devon stood up. She looked at her mother again, as if she was trying to memorize her in this moment. Lorelei was in good shape, probably the best that Devon remembered seeing her. She was clean, sober, and well-cared for. Devon was reminded of Guinevere in the Arthurian legends who became a nun after Camelot went down in flames. That's who her mother was: a penitent praying for forgiveness for the choices she made.

"Thanks for the talk." At her words, her mother stood up, uncertainty in her eyes. Devon made no move to hug her. "Bye, Mom." She turned around and walked away from the table without ever looking back.

Devon had discovered something important, something fundamental to who she was as a person: she wasn't defined or bound by her mother's choices. She still had her own choices to make. She only hoped they would be better ones.

CHAPTER TWENTY-TWO

There was a soft knock on Devon's door. She rolled over to check her clock. It was only 8:16 in the morning. It was a Saturday—the first since she'd seen her mother in jail; she could sleep as late as she wanted to. She pulled the covers over her head, trying to go back to sleep, but the knocking came again. Devon called, "Come in," her irritation only slightly masked by the comforter currently covering her face.

The door creaked open and Gammy stepped inside. She'd been giving Devon a lot of space and time to herself recently, ever since she'd come back from seeing her mother in prison. Devon hadn't spoken to her about it yet, and she wasn't even sure that she wanted to. Right now, it was too raw.

Gammy crossed the room to perch on Devon's bed. She pulled down the covers so she could see her granddaughter's face. Devon groaned and flung and arm over her eyes. "There can't be anything worth doing before nine in the morning," she muttered.

"I'm going up to the Larkin's place in a bit. They've got a sick goat they say I should take a look at."

"Happy goating," Devon said, rolling onto her stomach. "I'll be fine." When her grandmother didn't leave after a few minutes, she rolled back over. "Gammy?"

The old woman sighed. "I don't know what you got into with your mama, and I ain't one to pry. I just want you to know that I love you."

Devon pushed herself up onto her elbows, blinking owlishly. What was this all about? "I know you do, Gammy. I love you too." She frowned in confusion. "Is everything okay?"

Gammy brushed the stray wild hairs out of Devon's face. "I'm fine, my girl. Just fine." She paused. "I know your mama may be a disappointment to you, but she loves you too."

Just not more than herself. But she didn't say the words aloud; it would hurt Gammy. Instead she said, "Did you know about Jackson?"

Gammy looked away, which was answer enough. "Did you know he was my father?" Devon pressed.

"I suspected." She sighed. "But that was your mother's business, not mine. I said my piece about it a long time ago."

Devon came bolt upright. "Grandmother Mackson!" She had loathed Lorelei, and made no secret that she felt the same about her granddaughter. "Did she know?" *Is that why she can't stand to be in the same room with me?*

Gammy's mouth hardened into a thin line. "That woman thought the worst of Lorelei since the day Deacon befriended her. It wouldn't have mattered if your mama came from Heaven itself with wings and a harp. That woman would have still thought she was the devil." She shook her head. "Charlotte Mackson was always too proud for her own good."

Devon flopped back on the bed. She thought she'd gotten answers, but more questions kept popping up. It wasn't just about the scholarship or the ghost anymore. It was about her finding out who her family really was and where she came from. So much had been obfuscation or downright lies that she wasn't sure who she could trust besides herself. And Brock.

They'd agreed to meet up at the library again later. Now that they knew Jackson Duvall—her father—had been innocent, they were focusing their efforts on determining who the key witnesses were and what they'd really seen. Even though it was twenty years in the past, it was still easier than hunting down the mystery man who'd killed the man in Jessamy's time.

She didn't believe there was a curse, not anymore. But there were things that were similar in both instances, and eerily so. Maybe her family was doomed to repeat history until they solved the puzzle. Or until they learned their lesson. It didn't matter; Devon intended to put this mystery to rest once and for all.

"I'll be back before dinner," Gammy was saying, and she leaned over to stroke Devon's hair.

"Okay. I'll try and be back from the library by then." Devon conveniently left out that she was meeting Brock. Gammy still believed in the curse and Devon had no intention of telling her that she'd been talking or time-walking or whatever it was she was doing with Jessamy.

"You work too hard," her grandmother said, getting up from the bed slowly. She straightened and Devon heard the dull cracks of old bones.

"So do you," Devon sassed, a smile on her face.

Gammy smiled back, then ambled to the door. At the door, she stopped, a strange, disquieting look on her face. "You be careful, my girl. Some secrets were meant to stay that way."

Before Devon could ask Gammy what she meant, she had closed the door behind her.

*****

Devon was showered and dressed for the weather. Dark clouds were boiling over the mountains, driven by a steady wind. They promised snow, not necessarily in great amounts, but at least enough to coat the trees. She'd dressed in layers and had her warmest coat on for the long walk into town.

But before she headed down the mountain, she wanted to stop at the church. She hadn't seen Jessamy since she and Brock had gotten back from seeing her mother. In a way, that was a good thing; she didn't think she could take another peeping Jess scene like the last one. But it concerned her that she hadn't seen the ghost—she wondered what it could mean.

She pulled her hat down low over her ears as she came close to the abandoned church. She circled around the back side of the stone building in order to pass Daniel's marker. He'd been innocent, just like her father had been, but he'd refused to use the only alibi he had that would clear him. Again, just like her father. She couldn't think of Jackson Duvall as her dad— that name belonged to Deacon Mackson, the only father she'd ever known.

She knelt down in front of the weathered stone grave marker. She pulled the glove from her right hand and ran her fingers over the cold face of the stone. They were chilled almost immediately, but she traced the letters carved there, ignoring the biting wind. She closed her eyes, calling up the image of Jessamy in Daniel's arms. They had been so in love.

She felt the hairs on the back of her neck stand at sudden attention beneath her hat. Her eyes popped open and she slewed around on her knees to find Jessamy's ghost standing behind her. Devon felt her heart jump in her chest, despite knowing that the ghost didn't actually mean any real harm. The ghost was veiled once more, but Devon could feel the power of her stare through it.

Devon stood, trying to figure out what Jessamy wanted. The ghost reached for her, and Devon held out her hand. Jessamy clasped it and once again Devon felt herself falling through the white air of her breath.

*****

She was in the town jail, in a cell. There was a little light that filtered in from the high window. Devon could see that the small space was rustic and barren, nothing like the modern building in town today. A man was in the cell with her. He had his head down, resting it on his knees, but Devon recognized him. It was Daniel Holfsteder. Jessamy had sent her back in time again.

The door to the cells opened, admitting some kind of official, although Devon wasn't exactly sure of his job. Behind him came a woman; Devon recognized Jessamy. She looked pale and drawn, making Devon wonder how long Daniel had been in jail. Daniel raised his head, following her progress with his eyes.

"You have five minutes," the jailer said.

Jessamy waited until he had closed the door behind him before rushing to the cell holding Daniel. She dropped down to her knees next to the cell bars, wrapping her hands around the metal bars. Daniel put his hands over hers and rested his forehead against them for a brief moment.

"I told you not to come," he whispered.

Jessamy grimaced. "As though I've ever listened to a thing you've said." Devon could tell she was trying to keep her voice light, but there was a tremor to it.

Daniel raised his head, his eyes drinking in her face. "You'll listen to me this time. Please, Jess."

"But I can tell them where you were. We both know you didn't kill that man!" She grasped at his hands.

"No!" He pulled his hands free. "You know why you can't do that."

Jessamy tossed her head. "Do you think I care what people think? They'll be nothing left for me if you're not here."

"There's Keaton." Daniel's eyes were hard. "You're his wife. I'm his closest friend." His voice did not waver. "I will NOT do this to him." He stood up and walked to the back of the cell. He was so close Devon could reach out and touch him.

Jessamy stood when he did. She clasped her hands in front of her skirt, her knuckles going white. "Daniel," she began, her voice as close to a plead as Devon had heard yet. But she didn't continue because the door to the cells swung open again.

Daniel and Jessamy both turned to see the newcomer. The man who entered behind the jailer was tall and handsome, and he moved with the easy grace of someone used to wealth and power. He had lines around his mouth, as though he frowned more than he smiled.

Devon flinched away, feeling like she'd been punched in the chest. She recognized the man. Put a rifle on his back and he was the man she saw the night the drifter was killed in front of the town hall; he was the shooter. She took a few steps closer to the bars so she could be sure.

"Keaton!" Daniel walked back to the front of his cell. "It's good of you to come. You can take your wife home. She's been kind enough to keep me company, but this is no place for a lady, as I keep telling her."

Devon felt like she was in freefall. Keaton? Her mind connected the dots furiously. He must have known about the relationship between Daniel and Jessamy! She bit her lip, trying to make sense of things.

"I had just come by to see if the witness had seen anything else." He shook his head. "Duncan is certain he saw someone running away that looked like you."

"Daniel would never kill anyone!" Jessamy sounded offended.

He held out his hands, trying to placate her. "You and I both know that, but people will find it hard to dismiss an eye witness. What are you doing here, my dear?"

Jessamy squared her shoulders. "I was relaying a greeting from his mother. I saw her this afternoon and she wanted me to give him a message."

Keaton put his arm around her shoulders, drawing her close. "And did you?"

Jessamy swallowed nervously. "Yes."

"Daniel, I should be getting her home." Keaton turned to his friend behind bars.

"I agree." He tried to give Jessamy a significant look, but she lowered her eyes demurely. "Take care, the both of you, and don't worry a thing about me. This will all be dismissed and I'll be back home within the month."

Keaton pulled Jessamy with him. Before he knocked on the outer door to get the jailer's attention, he turned back to face Daniel. "We both know you are innocent. The truth will out." He hustled Jessamy out the door, pulling it closed behind him.

Daniel sat in the dark and waited.

Devon fell through the white mist once more.

*****

She came back to herself to find she was lying on the frozen ground in front of Daniel's grave marker. Jessamy was nowhere to be seen. Devon pushed herself to a sitting position and waited for her equilibrium to return. It wasn't as jarring coming back this time, although she had only been gone what felt like mere moments. But the shock of seeing Keaton more than made up for the short time. She was glad she didn't have to see Jessamy immediately after.

Keaton had been the shooter. He'd set Daniel up, probably knowing he would do anything to protect Jessamy from scandal. This was vastly different than the description of Keaton she'd heard earlier. Devon wasn't sure what to do with what she'd found out. She still wasn't even sure what Jessamy wanted from her.

When her head felt more normal, she climbed to her feet. She needed another opinion on this, maybe even two. She was going to meet up with

Brock, but she wondered if they were spinning their wheels. As she walked down the mountain path and turned onto the main road into town, she knew who she was going to bring in. But first she had to okay it with Brock. They were a team, and he had a say in the decision.

Brock was waiting for her at the library. He took her coat from her as soon as she arrived at the table. "What happened?"

Devon jumped, not expecting that question to be the first out of his mouth. "How did you know?"

Brock smiled, the edges of his eyes crinkling. "You looked like you've seen a ghost." Devon grinned at him. "You looked a little shaky and unfocused when you came in. You saw her again, didn't you?"

Devon nodded. "And this time I saw Keaton Winchester." She looked around to make sure no one was listening. "I recognized him."

Brock's face clouded. "How?"

"I'd seen him the first time Jessamy sent me back." She leaned in closer. "He was the man I saw after the shooting. He had a rifle."

Brock flopped back in his chair. "That doesn't make sense. Not according to everything you heard anyway."

"I know." She shook her head. "Did you find anything?"

He nodded. "Sure did." He pulled a sheaf of papers haphazardly stuck in a folder out of his backpack. "I found a bunch of stuff on the internet on Abernathy and the trial of Jackson Duvall. There's a whole bunch of conspiracy websites that I checked and found some good stuff."

"I don't know if that's exactly reliable material," Devon said doubtfully. "I mean, we're not talking the West Memphis Three here."

Brock pushed the folder toward her. "I know, but have a look. Some of it is pretty interesting."

Devon took the folder from him, flipping to the first sheet of printed pages. She quickly scanned them, her eyebrows rising slightly with each page turn. When she was finished, she closed the file slowly. Her eyes were round when she looked up at Brock. "Wow."

"I know, right?"

"If even half of that is remotely true, that is seriously messed up." She felt a burning sense of rage deep in her chest. "I can't believe that."

"Which part?" Brock's slight smile was sardonic.

Devon shook her head slowly. "All of it?" She scooted closer to him. "Abernathy being employed by Grandmother Charlotte is probably the most surprising part."

"How did that not come out as a huge deal during the trial?"Brock asked.

"Nobody knew about the affair, not really," Devon answered. "But I think this gives us a motive for him lying."

"Do you think your grandmother knew about your mom and Jackson?"

Devon shrugged. "I haven't exactly talked to her about it." She paused. "Actually, I haven't spoken to her in years. I'm pretty sure she hates me. I guess I know why now. So maybe she did know—or suspected that Deacon wasn't my dad."

"Maybe you should go talk to her." Brock took her hand, rubbing the back of it.

"That sounds like as much fun as having my stomach pumped." She grimaced. "But there is something I want to talk to you about. How do you feel about bringing someone else into our little investigation?"

"Who?"

"Gil."

Brock grinned. "Sure. But why him?"

Devon raised an eyebrow. "We need to dig dirt on people. Who do you know that's better at finding out stuff other people don't want found?"

"Think he'll believe us? About Jessamy?"

"I'll drag his butt up to that mountain and camp out with him until she appears if he doesn't." She thought for a minute. "I don't know if we have to even tell him about our ghost anyway. We've got a legitimate mystery going on here. We can leave the Jessamy stuff out of it and just focus on the Jackson Duvall case."

Brock nodded. "I think it could work. Are you going to sic him on your grandma?"

"It would serve her right," she said sharply, her anger spiking. "But I'll deal with her myself. Gil doesn't deserve that if he's helping us out. Could you give him a call?"

"Sure thing." He left the library to make the call.

*****

Gil showed up at the library, looking like he'd just rolled out of bed after Brock had called him. Devon checked her watch. It was 10:30. Gil's brown hair was stuck up in all different directions and his clothes looked like they just happened to be the ones closest on the floor when he needed to get dressed. Devon couldn't remember the last time he'd left his house looking so completely…natural. It made him look much younger.

He clomped over to their table and flung himself into a seat. "This had better be good," he said, sulkily.

"They're going to take away your membership if they find out you went out without proper hair gel deployment," Devon commented, unable to resist digging at him as he sat there all pouty.

"Bite me," he practically snarled.

"I woke him up," Brock explained.

"And you can go straight to hell," Gil added.

"Charming," Brock said.

"I'm here, alright," Gil said, sounding none too happy about it. "What do you want?"

Devon and Brock took turns filling Gil in on everything they'd found so far. They left out everything to do with the ghost and what they'd discovered about Daniel Holfsteder's trial, focusing on all that they knew about Devon's mother and father and Jackson Duvall. Gil remained quiet through most of it, although he did make a shocked noise when Devon revealed that Deacon Mackson could not have been her father. When they finally finished, Gil had his hands tucked under his chin and looked a good deal more awake than he had at the beginning of their tale.

"Well, I must say this is better than any soap opera network TV could dream up," he finally said when they had finished.

"You realize it's my life you're talking about?" Devon said drily.

"It would make imminently watchable Must See TV," Gil replied, grinning at her. "So what do you need from me?"

"Your mother was the same year as my mom. She might remember something. And your parents know everyone—some of their friends might have heard things about my mother and Jackson."

"This town loves gossip, especially about mountain folk. It's hard to believe we haven't heard anything about it, even now." Gil sounded skeptical. "What else?"

"That's it for now," Brock said.

"You okay?" Gil asked, turning to Devon. "I know this can't be easy to take in."

Devon shrugged. "It explains a lot. But I need to talk to my Grandmother Mackson."

Gil made a face. "Good luck with that. You've said the woman actively loathes you."

She nodded. "And now it makes a certain kind of sense." Devon sighed. "And the only witness was a man she employed. There are too many coincidences about all of this."

"When are you going to goad the old dragon?"

"No time like the present."

CHAPTER TWENTY-THREE

Devon stood at the door to Charlotte Mackson's house. She didn't feel up to calling her Grandmother, not anymore. She'd never been close to the woman, and now the space between them might as well have been the distance between the Earth and Sun. She had to admit that she was scared. The woman had always scared her, even when she had her mother and Deacon with her. She'd almost taken Brock up on his offer of company, but knew that there was a good chance Charlotte would say more if it was just her.

It didn't mean she liked it though.

She pressed the button next to the knob, listening to the deep tones of the bell as it sounded inside the house. Devon stepped back so she could be seen easily through the sidelights. She waited patiently, trying not to shift her balance from one foot to another out of nervousness. Fidgeting could be seen as a sign of weakness, and she did not want to appear weak.

After a few minutes, the door opened slowly. Charlotte's face appeared in the space between door and frame. The old woman's face was unhappy, falling into frown lines etched deeply into her skin. "Yes?"

"I would like to talk to you, if you have a moment." Devon tried to sound calm and pleasant.

Charlotte looked at her for a very long time. Devon met her gaze, steady and silent. Finally the older woman nodded, and held the door open. Devon stepped inside.

Her former grandmother didn't offer to take her coat and Devon wouldn't have let her take it if she had. She had a feeling this conversation wouldn't last long and if she had to leave in a hurry, Devon didn't want to risk leaving her winter jacket behind. She followed Charlotte through the house and into the back parlor. She sat on the edge of the pristine white couch, watching while the woman settled into a buff-colored wingback chair.

"What is it you want?" Charlotte asked in her faintly musical voice.

"I went to see my mother," Devon began, eyeing the woman carefully.

Charlotte's lip lifted in derision. "I do not wish to speak of that woman."

Devon's eyes grew hard. In that instant, she matched her former grandmother look for look. "I need some answers."

"I have none to give."

"I think you do." They stared at each other.

Charlotte finally looked away. "Very well. If I answer your questions will you leave and stop bothering me?"

"If you answer my questions, I'll never darken your door again," Devon promised.

Charlotte's mouth tightened. "See that you don't. Now, what do you want to know?"

Devon ordered her thoughts. She wanted to ask the right questions, but she needed to ask them in the right order or risk being thrown out before she actually got her answers. "You hated my mother, didn't you?"

"I think I've made no mystery of my feelings for your mother."

Devon clasped her hands in her lap. "Did you always dislike her or was it only after she married your son?"

"I never liked her, even when she and Deacon and Jackson were just friends. She wasn't the type of girl I wanted my son around, nor was she the kind of girl I thought it suitable for him to date." Charlotte's voice was as cold as a glacier.

"Did you object to their marriage?" So far these were all questions she knew the answers to.

"Of course I did," the woman snapped, clearly irritated by having to answer what she thought was obvious. "But my son was besotted with her. There was no reasoning with him. I threatened to disown him, to cut him out of the will, but he didn't care. He was going to marry her no matter what I said or did." Her glare slammed into Devon. "And we can see how well that turned out."

"Did you know Jackson Duvall or his family?"

If possible, Charlotte's expression turned even sourer. "I did know his family. We went to the same church and our boys were inseparable. Why do you ask?"

"How did you feel about him?"

She shrugged. "I didn't feel about him one way or another. I tolerated him and my son enjoyed his company. I didn't think about him at all."

"But you didn't think he was a good influence on Deacon either." It was a statement, not a question.

Charlotte waved it away, as if it were smoke. "Is there a question in all of this?"

Devon regrouped, feeling out of her depth. "You've never wanted any contact with me, even though I'm your granddaughter, even when Dad was alive. Why do you hate me?"

The older woman looked at her from eyes as distant as the stars. "Hate you? I never even considered you. You were merely the mongrel offspring of your slut of a mother. I don't concern myself with mutts. It made my son happy to pretend I cared for you, but once he was dead—once your mother killed him—I no longer had to keep up the charade. It was extremely liberating." She climbed to her feet. "And now I think it is time you left."

"Long past," Devon said, struggling to keep most of the anger from her voice. She stood and stalked after Charlotte.

Before the older woman opened the front door, Devon turned and asked, "I was wondering who you hired to replace Mr. Abernathy when he retired."

Charlotte Mackson gave her a strange look. "If you must know, his name is William Larch." She opened the door. "You made a promise. I hope you'll remember it." It was equally parts reminder and warning.

"Don't worry. I always keep my promises." Devon stepped out onto the front porch.

The door immediately closed behind her.

Devon walked quickly to the end of yard and opened the gate that led to the sidewalk. She didn't feel comfortable until she was on public property and was at least a block away. For some reason she couldn't get the image of Charlotte as an evil witch, determined to snatch her up and take her back to her hidden cottage and eat her, out of her head.

*****

"What did you find?" Brock asked at the other end of the line.

Devon twisted around to make sure no one was nearby. She'd borrowed the library phone from Mrs. Dotson, but she didn't want to abuse the privilege. "I think there's more than just a false accusation linking the ghost with my mother. Can you meet me?"

"Later, sure. I've got a family thing I have to do now."

"The church at 6:00? Will that give you enough time?"

"Sure thing. See you there."

Devon hung up, heading back to her table. She dropped into her chair with a heavy sigh. Jackson Duvall's setup was slowly coming together in her notes, each piece of the puzzle showing more and more of the conspired whole. She shuffled her notes and made a few more on the related pages.

She had a bad taste in her mouth after the meeting with her ex-grandmother. Devon hadn't expected it to be easy or pleasant, but it had been worse than she expected. She truly believed that woman was just about capable of anything after that conversation. And if she'd suspected that her daughter-in-law wasn't exactly faithful, she wouldn't put it past the woman to have remedied the problem.

Still, condemning an innocent man to prison seemed a little excessive.

Charlotte Mackson had more than the normal share of pride though. So perhaps it wasn't that excessive when Devon really thought about it. She had read that most of the evidence against Jackson had been circumstantial. It wasn't until Abernathy had come forward as a witness that the case had really been built.

But what if Abernathy had lied? Or been paid to by someone with enough money and a deep grudge to make it worth his while to do so? Devon rubbed her forehead. She had to be paranoid. Maybe she was going crazy. She was seeing ghosts, having visions of the past, thinking her grandmother capable of fixing a trial to convict an innocent man all to protect her family's name. She had to be delusional.

Devon gathered up her things, putting everything back in her messenger bag. She slung it back over her shoulder and began her long walk home. The wind was whipping the bare branches of the trees, making the bark of the limbs rub together with a scraping sound. The dark sky threatened rain, but it seemed to be holding out. The clouds scudded like ships across the sea of grey horizon.

She pulled her jacket closed and hoofed it. She took all of the shortcuts she knew, through neighborhoods and cutting across parking lots. Devon reached the main road in good time, and picked up her pace. It was a slow afternoon, especially for a Sunday, with no one on the road. Since she saw no one coming, she strayed into the road where the footing was better.

Devon traveled this way for perhaps half a mile. Then she heard a car coming up at high speed behind her. She walked over to the verge, not really paying much attention. The sound of the engine grew close behind her, and it made her turn. She saw the car's grille coming up quickly, almost as if it was aiming for her.

She threw herself off to the side as the car sped up. Devon tripped over the lip of the verge, rolling into the field. The car swerved off the road, and Devon kept rolling. She saw the barbed wire fencing that blocked off a field, so she threw herself toward that.

Devon felt her jacket catch as she rolled beneath the fencing. For a moment she was caught, tangled up like a tuna in a net. She yanked hard, fear giving her a surge of strength. She heard her jacket rip, but she didn't care. Devon staggered to her feet once she was through and took off running across the empty field.

She risked a look back. The car had swerved back onto the road. Devon didn't stop; she just kept running until the stitch in her side burned her like a brand. She ran on until she was back out the other side of the barbed wire fence. Her breath came in pants as she staggered to the trees. She put her back against one and collapsed against it.

Devon's breath whistled out her lungs, her throat clotted with tears. She wrapped her arms around herself, feeling the tremors that tore through her body. With a choked sob, Devon bowed her head and cried.

After a few minutes, she pulled herself up. Her knees were still trembly. She leaned against the tree, waiting for the weakness to pass. Devon wiped her hands across her face, trying to clear away the dirt and tears. Her mind was still a vast blank, barely registering that she couldn't feel her hands any longer or that the noise was her teeth chattering. She just knew she had to move.

She staggered away from her tree and began to move farther up the mountain.

*****

She didn't remember how or when she got to the church. All Devon remembered was cold. She fell inside the doors, stumbling over the threshold. Her eyes didn't register the form of the veiled woman at the front of the room. The woman appeared to float over to her, and took Devon's hand in hers. This time Devon didn't notice the white air she was falling through.

*****

There was a crowd gathered already. Jessamy watched as they milled around like cattle, each of them trying to jockey for a better position. She had promised Daniel that she wouldn't come, but she couldn't stay away. She'd told Keaton that she was going up the mountain to visit kinfolk in order to be away from the commotion in town. She gone all the way to the chapel where she'd used to meet Daniel, changed her clothes, donned the veil, and then snuck back into town.

She focused on remaining as invisible as possible. Most people weren't inclined to notice her, as keyed up as they were about the impending hanging. But she didn't want word to get back to her husband that she had been in the audience, that she had lied to him. Jessamy wanted a few things to be kept between her and Daniel, especially now that they were going to be parted forever.

She pulled away from the crowd. Jessamy still had time and she didn't want to get caught up with the rest of the mob. Some had brought picnics and were spreading out blankets while they waited for the main event to start. She'd be sickened, if she wasn't already full of grief.

It was hours later when Daniel was led from the jail in chains. Jessamy bit her lip to keep from crying out. He had dropped a stone of weight, his face thin and haggard. He blinked as he walked, as though unused to the sunlight on his face. He didn't look around, he just kept his eyes on the sky.

Jessamy wanted to run to him, to throw herself at his feet, to confess that she'd been with him on the night that man was shot. But it was all too late. She'd made her bed, out of love and cowardice, and now she had to lie in it until she died. It did not make for pleasant dreams.

Daniel stumbled as he climbed the steps to the scaffold. Jessamy kept from crying out through a force of will she didn't know she had. She moved through the mass of people carefully, finding the small spaces between bodies and pressing through. She was a tiny thing, and most folk moved away without knowing it, allowing her passage. She was almost in the front row as Daniel was prayed over by the local pastor.

The hangman slipped the noose over his head. Jessamy wanted to scream, but she just stood there, bearing silent witness to the abomination about to be enacted. She owed it to Daniel, and to herself. She would remember for the both of them.

And Jessamy remembered everything. The soft caress of Daniel's hand against her cheek. The way his breath winged across her neck as he lifted her hair. The sweet taste of his mouth as it closed over hers. The sound of his voice as it breathed her name. Each instance was branded on her flesh.

She pulled her veil up as Daniel's eyes scanned the crowd one last time. His eyes widened as he saw her face in the crowd. She let the veil slip back down, but she could see that Daniel's eyes never left her. He was not alone. She would always be with him. It took her marrying the wrong man to realize that she and Daniel were linked, and they always would be.

There was a sharp crack as the trapdoor fell open, taking Jessamy's heart with it.

CHAPTER TWENTY-FOUR

Devon woke up to an insistent and annoying shaking. She opened her eyes to see Brock's worried face staring down at hers, his eyes dark with fear. She blinked, feeling groggy and strange. She tried to push him away but found she could barely lift her arms.

"Dev, what happened? Can you hear me? Say something!" His hands on her arms tightened convulsively.

She made a pathetic mewing sound since words seemed well beyond her. All she wanted to do was go back to sleep.

"You're freezing!" Before she could do more than flinch, Brock scooped her up in his arms and carried her out of the church. He staggered beneath her weight a little, but then he shifted her into a more balanced hold and continued to his car. He dumped her in the passenger seat, then came around to the driver's side and got in. He turned the car on and cranked the heat to its highest setting.

Devon sank against the seat, feeling vaguely alarmed. Should she feel this way? Why was she so out of it? She didn't remember much of anything after seeing Jessamy's past. That wasn't good. She tried to muster up some good ol' fashioned freak out, but just couldn't seem to reach it. All she felt was cold.

Brock's hands were like brands against her icy cheeks as he forced her to look into his eyes. "Devon." His voice was low and firm. "I need you to talk to me. What happened to you?"

"'M fine," she mumbled. That didn't come out right; why was she sounding all marble-mouthed? Had she had a stroke?

"I think you're in shock." He took his hands away from her face, only to place two fingers against her neck. He was silent for a minute, then he took his fingers away.

The heat was beginning to seep into her chilled body. It wasn't making her head much clearer, but she was feeling a little bit better. But it was making her sleepy too. She knew she had to talk to Brock, to tell him something important, so she fought against the drowsy feeling.

"What happened to your coat?" His gaze swept over her. "You're covered in dirt and there's a huge rip in it."

"Can you turn the heat down just a little? It's making it hard to stay awake." At least her words made sense and were no longer garbled.

Brock did as she asked, then returned all his attention to her. "Dev?"

She started shaking suddenly, and couldn't stop. It was as if thinking of the car sent her back to her initial reaction. Her teeth chattered as she tried to tell him what had happened on the way to the church. "A c-c-car. It t-t-t-tried to run me ov-v-ver," she stuttered out, all the time wondering if she sustained some kind of massive head trauma. She sounded like an idiot.

"What!" He immediately started feeling her extremities for broken bones. "Are you sure?"

Devon gave him what she hoped was a stellar *are you **kidding** me?* look. "I think I know when a car is trying to RUN. ME. OVER."

"Okay, okay." He moved away, clearly wanting to examine her more closely, but needing her to move to do so. "Tell me what happened."

Devon detailed the encounter as best she could. She had no idea of the make or model of the car; she wasn't even sure of the color at this point. The only thing she was sure of was that it wasn't an accident; that car had been aiming for her. She wrapped her arms around her body to try to reclaim the warmth that had fled when she began her story.

Brock pulled the blanket from the back seat forward and wrapped it around her shoulders. "We have to go to the police, Dev."

"And tell them what? That a ghost is leading me to dig up all kinds of unfortunate information that points to the execution of an innocent man over a hundred years ago that may or may not have something to do with a more current miscarriage of justice?" She shook her head. "Why don't we just have them check me into the loony bin right now?"

"I'm serious, Devon. Someone tried to kill you." His brows were pulled low over his eyes, his expression worried and unhappy.

Devon shivered. She wished she could have caught a glimpse of the driver. She had her suspicions of who might be behind it, but nothing that even resembled proof. And she was just a kid—and one from the mountain at that. No one would believe her.

They were on their own.

She leaned forward, her own eyes intense. "I'm serious too, Brock. I didn't see the driver, I don't have a license plate number, I can't even say what kind of car it was. They can't put an APB out on thin air." She slumped back against the seat. "And there's more I haven't told you yet. Jessamy showed me the day Daniel died."

"No wonder you were out of it." Brock pulled her over to him so he could wrap his arms around her. "Tell me about it."

Again Devon talked over what she had witnessed. It didn't really give them any more to go on, although it did explain how Jessamy's picture had wound up in the paper—she was there that day. Devon cuddled against

Brock's chest, needing something firm and steady beneath her. She felt again Jessamy's heartbreak as Daniel's body plummeted through the trap door.

She felt Brock's lips brush against her temple. "You had me worried sick. When I saw you just lying there…," he trailed off and Devon felt the shudder move through him and into her. "That wasn't at all what I was expecting when you told me to meet you up here after your meeting with your grandmother."

"Charlotte!" Devon sat upright, like she'd just been goosed with a cattle prod. "Oh my God!"

"Care to elaborate on that?" Brock said, pulling her back against him.

Devon turned in his arms so she could at least see part of his face. "Gil found out that Abernathy used to work for her—and she confirmed it right before I left!"

"So there was a connection between the two of them." Brock nodded thoughtfully.

"Yes! And she's made no secret about how much she hated my mother." Devon chewed on her bottom lip. "I think she might have known about my mom and Jackson."

"Yeah?" Brock paused, but Devon could tell he was just readying himself to say more. "Devon, you don't think it was her in the car, do you?"

Devon didn't want to say what she really thought. Thinking of Charlotte just made her want to throw up. The woman was worse than unpleasant; she was almost malignant, spreading like a cancer until she destroyed all she touched. Gil had told her the gossip, so Devon knew how Charlotte had been obsessed with Deacon and the idea of him marrying beneath himself. And after their conversation today, she harbored little doubt that Charlotte would do everything in her considerable power to sustain the proud family name.

She shrugged. "Is she capable of it? Sure." She thought for a moment. "Would she actually do it? Probably not."

"That doesn't means she couldn't hire someone to do it. Like she hired Abernathy." Brock lifted her chin up. "I think we've taken this as far as it can go. I don't want you getting hurt."

Devon pushed away from him, not liking where this was going. "I'm not going to get hurt."

Brock gestured to the church, then back to her. "Excepting the last half hour, of course."

"I'm fine now." She set her jaw mulishly.

Brock leaned in and kissed her on the tip of her nose. "*Now*," he emphasized. "But we're getting into dangerous territory here. I'm not sure it's a good idea to push it any further." He paused, ordering his thoughts, then continued. "You found out the truth about your father and your mother, you know who your real dad was, you've figured out who was behind Daniel's conviction. I think you've got plenty of answers."

"You want me to give it up?" Devon tried to keep her voice neutral. No use in accusing him of anything.

He shook his head. "I want you to be careful. More careful than you were today, that's for sure." He pushed back her hair, stroking his fingers down the side of her face as he did so. "What do you really want to get out of all of this?"

Devon slumped back, unsure. That was a good question. What did she want? The answers she found wouldn't bring back either her biological father or Daniel. It wouldn't make Jessamy suddenly happy. It wouldn't get her mom sprung from prison, and it wouldn't keep Lorelei sober when she wanted to get high.

But Devon wasn't content to just solve this mystery. Having the answers didn't matter if you couldn't *do* anything with them. There had to be some way to make them—and the hard work they'd done getting them—count.

"Justice."

Brock raised his eyebrows, looking as if he hadn't expected an answer. "Justice or vengeance?"

"Would it matter?" But she didn't meet his gaze when she asked.

"To some people it would," he said, a sad smile on his face.

"Will you be mad at me if I say I don't know?" Devon really didn't know which was more important anymore.

"Not if it's the truth."

"It's the truth." She touched his face softly with her fingertips, running them across the planes of his cheeks, over the ridge of his nose and down to trace his lips. "I at least owe something to Jessamy," she said, mesmerized by the shape of his face beneath the pat of her hands.

He took her hands in his. "She's not all there is to this," he reminded her. He brought her hands to his lips and kissed the knuckles lightly on each hand.

"I know." She involuntarily shivered at the feel of his lips on her hand. "I have to help her though, before anything else." She met his eyes. "Will you still help me?

"So long as you're careful, yes." He lowered her hands to her lap, but still kept hold of them. "I think we should help Jessamy find whatever it is she's looking for: peace, rest, an adjoining plot with Daniel—whatever. But I need you to stay safe."

"Yes sir." She was going to say more, but a bone-cracking yawn took her by surprise.

"Time to get you home," Brock said, putting the car in gear.

"I can walk," Devon protested, knowing that nothing good awaited either of them if Gammy saw his car dropping her off.

"You can, but you won't because I'm not letting you." He gave Devon a very forbidding glance, one that made her clam up. When she opened her mouth to protest, Brock cut her off. "Look, you were nearly flattened by a stray car, then zipped through time by a ghost. You're tired, you're a mess,

197

and I don't want you walking back in the cold without me. So just buckle your seatbelt and shut up about it."

Devon looked at him in mock surprise. She'd really had no idea he could be this demanding. Or logical, although that shouldn't really have surprised her. "Alright," she managed, trying not to sound too pleased.

Brock began the short drive to Gammy's. When he pulled to a stop in front of the trailer, he warned her in no uncertain terms that she was not to get out of the car without his express approval. Then he got out and climbed the porch stairs to the door. He knocked several times, waiting for her grandmother to open the door. When she did, he gestured to her sitting in the front seat of his car. She saw Gammy's mouth draw down slightly, but her manners were too good to say what she wished to the young man who had done right by her granddaughter.

Brock came back around the car. He flung open the door and scooped her up. She made a surprised little squawk. Then he was carrying her into Gammy's house while the old woman held the door open.

"What did you tell her?" she whispered as Brock set her down on the sofa.

"That you were a complete klutz and tripped down the stairs in front of the library. I was driving past and saw you fall. My heart was then filled with such pity that I had no choice but to take you home." He grinned down at her, a wicked glint in his eye.

"Well, aren't you just the Good Samaritan," she hissed at him, unobtrusively elbowing him in the stomach when he set her down.

"Be nice or I'll tell your Gammy what really happened." He winked at her.

"Blackmailer." But she smiled at him when she said it.

"Now exactly how did you manage to fall down the steps, my girl?" Gammy closed and latched the door, then joined them in the living room.

Devon looked down at her lap, in an effort to hide her smile. "You know me. My mind was somewhere else and I took a header down the steps."

"You're just lucky this young man bothered to stop and give you a ride home." Gammy's voice sounded harsh to Devon's ears, almost as if her grandmother begrudged Brock the compliment. "Thank you, Mr. Cutler."

"Brock, Ma'am. And it was no trouble. I'm just glad she wasn't hurt." He ducked his head shyly. Gammy could have that affect on people.

"Yes, I bet you were." Gammy gave him a slight smile. Then she gestured to the door. "But I think Devon needs her rest. You can see her at school."

"You're being dismissed," Devon whispered from the side of her mouth.

"Looks that way," he whispered back, his lips barely moving. "I'll see you tomorrow." He stopped, watching as Gammy went to the door. Then he leaned in and gave her a quick kiss.

"Thank you," Devon whispered against his mouth. "For everything."

Devon watched him go, shaking Gammy's hand as he left. Her grandmother watched as he climbed into his car, staying at the door until his taillights disappeared around the bend in the road. Then she turned and gave Devon her best parental glare.

"Alright, my girl. What really happened?"

CHAPTER TWENTY-FIVE

The envelope came in the mail on a Tuesday. Devon hadn't been expecting it, even though she had applied for early decision. She stared at the envelope in her hand for several long moments before she slipped it into her bag. She kept the rest of the mail in her hand as she proceeded up the path.

Devon had been looking so forward to finding out where she had been accepted; but now that the first one was here, she suddenly was in no hurry to see what it said. This envelope could change everything. And she wasn't sure if she was ready for it. So many things had changed already—her own father had even changed—this might be overwhelming.

She paced the floor, her eyes drawn inevitably to her messenger bag. She'd have to open it eventually...just not right now.

Devon picked up the phone. She'd never called Brock before for something like this and she felt a little nervous doing so now. She told herself it was just a phone call, swallowing nervously as she waited for him to pick up.

"Hey." Brock's voice on the phone was warm, like melted chocolate.

"Hi." She took a deep breath. "Um, I was wondering if you were busy?"

"No, just studying. What'd you have in mind?" She could practically hear the leer in his voice.

Devon laughed. "Down boy. We'll get to that later." She turned serious. "I have something that I really don't want to do alone."

"Dev?" Brock sounded worried.

"I'm fine," she assured him, a rush of heat flushing her cheeks. "It's college stuff."

"Ah, okay." She could hear him rustling around for something. "Want me to come pick you up?"

"Yes. I can meet you at the bottom of the road."

"See you in twenty."

Devon gathered up her things and left the trailer. She needed movement, a physical way to burn off her anxiety. She walked quickly down the road, passing the church. She didn't want to go in there today. The future was what was on her mind, not the past. As she walked by, there was no sign of Jessamy, for which she was grateful. She had enough on her mind without the ghost complicating things today.

She made good time and reached the bottom a few minutes before Brock was due. She paced back and forth, both to keep her legs warm and to pass the time and keep her mind off of the envelope in her bag.

He arrived perhaps five minutes later. Devon heard his car well before she saw it. Remembering her last encounter with a car on this road, she stepped well back from the highway, just in case it wasn't Brock. But it was Brock, and he pulled to a stop on the side of the road right next to her. She hopped in, grateful for the warm blast of heat and for his smile. Devon leaned over, giving him a hug. Brock pulled her even closer and upped the ante with a kiss. Before it could progress much further, Devon pulled away.

Brock squeezed her hand. "So where are we headed?"

"Someplace quiet and out of the way." She looked up at from underneath her lashes. "Any ideas?"

He thought for a moment, then nodded. "I think I know a good spot." Without another word, he turned around and drove back towards town.

They hadn't gone very far when he turned left, following a winding two lane road up another hill. Devon recognized the gates of the town's cemetery. She raised her eyebrows in surprise. "You sure this is a good idea? I think we've had our fill of ghosts and graveyards."

"There's a small garden just before you hit the older section. We won't be overheard or bothered there. We've only ever seen Jessamy at the old church; I don't think we'll run into her here." He pulled the car into a parking space and killed the engine.

They got out of the car, Brock taking her hand and leading the way. The paths were well tended, the lawn between the headstones neatly mowed. The place felt peaceful, the quiet of the cemetery soothing Devon's frazzled nerves. She had no idea she was so wound up.

The garden was before them. Since it was winter—or nearly so—all of the flowers were gone. There was still some ground cover over the tilled mounds of recently removed plantings. The bushes that dotted the perimeter were still lush. The garden was decorated with large rocks in various places as a way to provide visual interest when the color was gone. It was grey stone and dark earth and wiry grasses, but it was pleasing in a stark way.

A stone bench sat directly in the center of the garden. Brock sat and pulled her down next to him. "Let's see it."

Devon pulled the large envelope out of her bag. She handed it to him.

"It's a big one. That's promising." He looked at the return crest. "Nice. Duke." He handed it over to her. "Are you going to open it?"

She didn't take it. "That's the thing. Every time I think about opening it, I want to throw up a little." She grinned sheepishly.

"Dev, you're super smart. You're like a dream student. They'd be lucky to have you." He pushed it at her. "So just open it already."

Devon sat next to him, her mouth suddenly dry. "Okay." She slid her finger underneath the envelope's seal, dragging it across the paper. "I'm really nervous."

Brock just smiled at her encouragingly. "Stop stalling."

She stuck her tongue out at him. "Fine." She broke through the rest of the seal with a loud rip of paper. Then she pulled out a sheaf of pages, all terribly official looking. She scanned the top sheet, her brow furrowed in concentration.

"What does it say? Besides that you're awesome."

Devon flipped through the rest of the packet quickly. Then she handed it over to Brock. "I'm in." She looked around, not really focusing on anything. "They accepted me."

"You sound like you're surprised." Brock scooted over and handed her the papers. When she looked at them with no sign of taking them, he slid them back into the envelope they came in. Then he put his hand on her shoulder. "You're brilliant, Dev. And you work hard. You deserve it."

Devon frowned, upset now by what the packet hadn't included. "No mention of financial aid though." She scuffed her foot on the ground, moving around bits of rock dust.

Brock put his hand under her chin, forcing her to look up at him. "Stop it, okay? Just stop it. You should take a moment and be proud of what you did. It's what you wanted, right?" When she nodded, he released her chin. "You need to enjoy your accomplishment, Dev. Worry about the money later. For now, just be happy. This is great news!"

Devon sighed. Brock was right, and he was wrong at the same time. She knew she should be happy at the acceptance letter to Duke. And she was, but that happiness was tempered with fear. What was the point in getting excited about being accepted if she didn't know whether she would be able to attend? The tuition was outrageous normally, and she was from out of state. That meant even more money. She wanted nothing more than to be like Brock—he didn't have to worry about how much school cost, because his parents could afford to send him anywhere. If he didn't get a scholarship or financial aid of some kind, he could still attend the college of his dreams.

Devon couldn't. As much as she might wish she could, she was bound by the circumstances she found herself in. Still the letter had mentioned that they were still in the process of determining which of their scholars would qualify for financial aid. Hope wasn't lost just yet.

She tried to take Brock's advice to heart, cutting herself a bit of slack. "It *is* pretty huge," she admitted, her mouth drawing up at the corners.

"You said it!"

"Have you heard back from any of your schools?" Devon tried to make it a little less all about her.

Brock shook his head. "Nah. But I didn't apply for early decision either. All of mine should come in January, February the latest."

"You worried?"

He grimaced, and Devon put a hand on his knee. He said, "It'll just be an argument between my parents—one more in like a marathon session, I guess. Dad will insist on one, Mom will go all passive-aggressive, my grandmother will get called in and she'll have her opinion too. It will be decided for me, like I'm not even there."

"You should talk to them. Tell them what you want to do." She squeezed his leg.

Brock looked at her, moving his knee out from under her hand. "My parents don't work like that. They wouldn't listen, even if I did feel like starting something."

Something in Brock's voice made Devon swallow what she wanted to say. She got the feeling this type of argument had been going on for years, with Brock always in the middle of it. Instead, she said, "Let's take a walk."

She stood up, offering Brock her hand. He took it and they began to stroll through the garden. They followed the path out of the garden and into the older section of the cemetery. After a few moments, Brock spoke. "I bet you think I'm pretty stupid, huh?"

"Why on earth would I think that?" Devon glanced over at him, confused.

"Because I let my parents make all my decisions for me." He tried to pull his hand away, but she wouldn't let him.

"Considering I don't have a father and my mother is in prison, I really don't have a right to say anything about anyone's relationship with their parents."

They continued walking. Devon looked at the headstones, giving Brock time and space to gather his thoughts. She noted that the dates on the markers were getting older as they went farther along the path. Soon they would be in the early nineteen hundreds.

"I wish I could be more like my brother. He's happy going along with my parent's plans for him. He's done everything they've ever asked of him—and done it way better than I ever could." He wound his fingers through hers.

"Why do you have to be like him at all? Why can't you just be you?" *That's surely good enough.*

"That's a nice thought." His voice told her that she was being naïve.

"But not a very realistic one, right?" She squeezed his hand again. "But if your brother is doing such a great job with it, why not let him? You can do what you want to do." Her eyes scanned the statuary and the stones, feeling like there was something here she should see, but unsure what exactly.

"It's not that simple, Dev." He shook his head.

She stopped, turning to face Brock. "With everything we've found out so far, don't you think we've seen enough to realize that it *is* just that simple? Look at the people who tried to do fight against what they really wanted—we've seen what happened."

Devon was planning on saying more, but her eyes fell upon a large obelisk. That wasn't unusual, but what drew her attention was the name on the monument. Keaton Winchester was carved into the stone. "Brock," she whispered, pointing at the obelisk.

He turned to see where she was pointing. "You don't think…" he began, but Devon was already moving, walking quickly towards it.

She stopped a few feet away. "Oh my God," she breathed. Brock came to a sharp stop directly behind her.

There, carved into the stone next to Keaton's name, was another: Jessamy Winchester.

CHAPTER TWENTY-SIX

They were back from winter break. The halls were subdued as kids slowly got back into the swing of things. Devon and Brock hadn't seen each other at all over the holiday break; his family went to the beach for the week. She'd kept herself busy, getting caught up on her reading and hanging out with Gil.

The three of them had agreed to meet in the school library after classes let out to go over the latest information they'd found. As Devon walked down the hall toward the library, she took a good look around the near-empty hallways, the beat up lockers, and the sagging bulletin board notices. Soon this would be a memory. She was shocked to discover she might actually miss the school. Not necessarily the people, but the place itself.

She got a move on once she hit the double doors leading outside. The wind was frigid, whipping her hair into her eyes. Devon tucked her gloved hands into the pockets of her heavy jacket and put on some speed to make it to the library before her extremities fell off. As it was, she already couldn't feel her nose or ears. She should have at least packed a hat.

Gil was waiting for her at what he had dubbed the Nancy Drew table. He enjoyed teasing her about the whole girl detective angle, to the point that she thought she might never stop slapping him if he said one more word about it.

She flung her bag on the table, then began to unwrap herself from her layers of outerwear.

"I've got some good stuff for you," he said, rubbing his hands together like a B-movie villain.

"Take it down a notch, Montgomery Burns," she replied, unspooling her scarf from around her neck. Gammy certainly didn't do things by halves; the scarf could be used to hog-tie livestock. "We need to wait for Brock."

Gil sulked for a moment; he had a near pathological need to share all of the best gossip immediately, which made him perfect for the task she'd given him. He was excellent at ferreting out the secrets people wanted to keep. Gil's problem was keeping any secrets told to him.

Brock showed up a few minutes later, looking tired and drawn. He didn't look like someone who had just come back from a restful vacation. Devon went to him, guiding him away from the table. "Are you okay?"

"Yeah, sure." He put his arm around her, pulling her close. "Why?"

"You look tired. Vacation not good?" Devon put a hand to his cheek.

Brock captured his hand with his. "Trapped in a condo with my perfect brother, his perfect girlfriend, and my parents and grandmother. It was a delight."

"I'm sorry."

He shrugged. "Eh. As long as I never hear the word college again, I'll be fine." He kissed her fingers.

She led him over to their table. When he had shucked off his coat and they were all seated, Devon gestured for Gil to start. "Dazzle us, you silver-tongued devil."

He grinned, leaning forward. "My entire family was in town for the holidays, including my maiden aunt who has more to say about the people of this town than anyone else I know. She was more than willing to talk about the scandal of Jackson Duvall."

"She was a young woman when he went to trial. The Duvalls were new money—only a generation or two off of the mountain. Jackson had been spoiled and allowed to run wild, but Aunt Bitty never believed he was capable of murder. Especially considering how close he was to your dad, Devon."

"What do you mean?" Brock asked, but Devon already had an idea of what Gil was going to say.

"Deacon Mackson was from the best family in town. His father could trace his lineage to the town founders. Deacon's mother had been a debutant from Richmond, and came from massive amounts of old southern money. Aunt Bitty said that Deacon was expected to behave in a certain way, especially once his daddy died. She said Charlotte Mackson was a hard, proud woman, who brooked no disrespect.

"Bitty said that it was obvious Charlotte didn't approve of Deacon's friendship with Jackson, but there wasn't a whole lot she could do about it. She said that it was only after your mom entered the picture," here he looked at Devon, "that she really took a hard line. Rumor has it that she completely lost her mind when your father told her that he was marrying your mother. Screaming, crying, threats—she tried everything she could do to break them up."

"It obviously didn't work," Brock said, looking at Devon as if gauging her reaction.

"Nope. Lucky for us," Gil answered, winking at Devon. "Anyway, they got married—it was a much smaller ceremony than anyone would have expected for a Mackson, but Charlotte was a sore loser—and everything seemed to be okay. Oh, there was some talk that Lorelei wasn't happy with Deacon, but no one thought much of it.

"Aunt Bitty remembered one whispered rumor that Lorelei might even been unfaithful, but everyone assumed that Charlotte had started it herself. You see, my aunt said that Charlotte wanted nothing to do with the newlyweds—she didn't invite them to holidays, she refused to even let Lorelei into her house. Nobody paid any attention to any of the talk."

"That's why it was so shocking when Jackson Duvall was arrested for the murder of that drifter. He and Deacon were best friends and Deacon stood by him throughout the trial. The evidence was primarily circumstantial, Aunt Bitty said, until Abernathy came forward as a witness."

"Didn't anybody find it odd that the one witness to the crime worked for Charlotte?" Devon asked.

Gil nodded. "A few did—Bitty remembered talk of it. But no one could figure out what she had against Jackson. He was Deacon's oldest friend. And when Jackson had no alibi, well, there wasn't anything that could be done for him. The talk died down once he was sentenced. And then Lorelei and Deacon left town and nobody thought anything more about it." He spread his hands. "So that's it."

They sat quietly, staring at each other, unsure of what to say after Gil's monologue. Finally, Devon asked, "Did you find out anything from your mother about mine?"

He nodded. "A little. My mom only had a few classes with yours. But she did say that everyone thought that she'd wind up with Jackson Duvall—it was pretty obvious that they both had a thing for each other. But then he started dating some other girl. She said your mother seemed pretty happy when she and Deacon got together and the three were still close friends. Mom said she doesn't remember much about the trial, except that your mother was pretty upset during the whole thing."

"Did she say anything about Charlotte?"

Gil shook his head. "Nothing new. Charlotte didn't like that Deacon married your mom, but that was about it. She and your mother were always nice to each other in public." He shrugged. "In private, well, that's something else entirely."

Devon looked down at her hands. She wasn't sure what to think now. Gil's information was good, but it didn't tell her anything really new. Everything seemed to hinge on Abernathy's testimony. She knew Jackson had been innocent, so what reason did Mr. Abernathy have to lie? She chewed on her lower lip, unsure if she wanted to continue to look into this mystery.

"Dev?" Brock's voice interrupted her thoughts. "What's on your mind?"

She met his eyes. "I don't know what I want to do next."

He nodded like he knew the thoughts that were flying through her head. Gil sat watching them, a thoughtful look on his face. Finally he said, "We need to find Abernathy."

Brock turned to him. "How do we even know he's still alive?"

"We don't. But let me see if what I can find out." Gil grinned. He apparently wasn't done with the mystery yet.

CHAPTER TWENTY-SEVEN

The flyers papered the school. Posters appeared in the cafeteria, the hallways, and the stairwells. Banners hung above the doors to the gym. The winter dance was coming.

Every time Devon walked by one of them, a lump formed in the pit of her stomach. The winter dance traditionally had the girl asking the guy. Devon had never been to any of the school dances. She'd never wanted to go before. She never really had a reason before.

Gil caught her staring at one. "You asked Brock yet?" When she shook her head, he asked, "Why not? He's probably waiting for you to."

Devon dragged a hand through her thick hair, gathering it in her fist and pulling it over her shoulder. She didn't know why she hadn't asked Brock yet. "I know, but I just haven't been able to yet."

Gil gave her a long-suffering look. "What's the problem? It's not like he's going to say no."

She twisted her hair around in her hands. "It's a dance, Gil. Like, in public."

"So?" He stopped her, his hand on her arm. "Dev, you're dating. Everyone in school pretty much knows it."

"I guess." She wouldn't look at him. She wasn't sure she was ready to make a statement like that, and a mountain girl going to the dance with Brock Cutler was a statement of the highest order.

"Oh, you are just pathetic." He looked away from her, eyes searching the hallway. "Hey Brock!" he called, spotting the basketball player at the other end of the hall. "Devon wants to ask you something!"

Devon glared at her best friend. "You're an ass, you know that?"

He kissed her cheek. "Yep. Bye." He hightailed it out of there.

"What's up?" Brock asked as he came closer. He gave her a smile that made her toes curl.

Devon stared up at him, memorizing the lines and angles of his face. She took a deep breath, steadying herself. Finally she said the words that she had been trying to work up the courage to say over the past few weeks. "Brock, would you go to the dance with me?"

He pulled her close to him, a huge smile on his face. "I thought you'd never ask me."

*****

Devon spun around in front of the mirror on the back of her door. The dress was a deep green, almost black, satin and it swirled around her ankles when she turned. The fact that she was going to the dance was mind-blowing; that she was going with Brock Cutler was even stranger. She was a little nervous about doing this, about going out in public with Brock, about making it official.

There had been lots of rumors surrounding her and Brock over the past few months, but the two of them made sure that nothing could really be confirmed. But now, going to the dance would mean everyone would know. She still wasn't sure this would be worth it. Brock may not know the Pandora's box they were about to open, but Devon certainly did.

"Come on out, Devon," her grandmother called from the other side of the door.

Devon wrapped the black lace shawl around her shoulders and opened her bedroom door. Gammy stood in the hall, holding an ancient camera. Devon was amazed it still worked or that it hadn't been put in a museum somewhere. She followed her grandmother down the hall and into the living room.

"Let me get a good look at you," Gammy said. She walked around her granddaughter, smoothing out the satin as she went. She adjusted the lace shawl that had once been hers around Devon's shoulders. "You look lovely, my girl."

Devon smiled so wide she thought her head might split in half. She'd never been to a school dance, never had a dress this nice. Gammy hadn't been thrilled when she'd mentioned the dance, and that she was going with Brock. But then one day a few weeks ago, a large box appeared on her bed. Inside was the dress she wore now. It was more than she ever expected from her grandmother.

"Thank you, Gammy," she said, so grateful to her grandmother for this opportunity to be a normal girl that she wanted to cry.

There was a knock at the door. Gammy only frowned briefly; she still wasn't sure about Brock. But then she smiled at Devon and went to answer the door. Brock stood there in a long winter coat over his suit, a beautiful wrist corsage in his hand.

"Good evening, Ma'am." He waited on the porch.

"Hello Brock. You come on inside now so I can get a picture." She moved out of the way to allow him space to come in.

He stepped in, his megawatt smile brightening even further when Devon turned around in a swirl of crinoline. "You look beautiful," he breathed, stopping where he stood.

Devon ducked her head, suddenly shy. His words pleased her. She walked over to him, taking his hand. "So do you."

Gammy clucked at them, the camera in her hand. They posed for pictures: one of Brock putting the corsage on Devon's wrist, the two of them standing in their dance finery, another one of Brock helping Devon with her coat. She even snapped photos of them getting in the car.

"That wasn't so bad," Brock said as they drove down the drive.

"She's coming around," Devon answered, trying to ignore the tiny knot in her stomach that seemed to get a little bit bigger the closer they got to school. "Hang on a second," she said as they passed the church. "Stop the car."

"Devon…" Brock looked worried.

"Just for a minute." Devon waited for the car to stop, then opened the door and stepped out. She wrapped her coat closer around herself. The late January air was bitingly cold. She walked over to the cemetery, hoping to catch a glimpse of Jessamy. For some reason, she wanted to see the ghost tonight, almost like she wanted her blessing as well.

She stepped inside the church. It was empty. "Jessamy?" she called. There was no sign of the ghost. With one last look behind her, she returned to the car.

"All good?" Brock asked when she was back in the passenger seat.

Devon nodded. "Let's go to the dance."

CHAPTER TWENTY-EIGHT

Brock parked in his usual spot in the student lot, then led them to the gymnasium where the dance was being held. He took Devon's hand as they walked. They passed a few couples already on their way in, and she noticed the surprised looks on their faces. Brock squeezed her hand—he had noticed them too.

They pushed through the gym's outer doors, depositing their coats at the coat check. Then they pushed open the inner doors, and Devon caught her breath. It didn't look much like the gym she was used to. Archways had been placed at even intervals throughout the cavernous room. Each one was wrapped in greenery and white lights creating a kind of garden party atmosphere. Greenery swags and more white lights dripped down from the high ceilings. Tall plants and small trees stood in corners. Round tables covered in white tablecloths were placed in pods around the room. In the center of each table were mirrored circles upon which sat candles and snow-dusted small logs and pinecones and berries. The mirrors magnified the light of the candles, making the room feel brighter than it was.

It was beautiful. Far more than Devon had been expecting.

"Shall we?" Brock whispered in her ear. Shivers ran up and down her spine.

Devon looked up at him, a bit of trepidation on her face. But it all melted away when she saw Brock's eyes shining at her. "Yes," she said, a smile on her face. She linked her arm in his and let him lead her into the dance proper.

The entrance wasn't as horrible as she'd let herself expect. It wasn't like everyone froze, the needle scratched across the record as even the DJ stopped playing, and nubile girls fainted into their escorts' arms at the horror of a mountain girl coming to what had traditionally been a town dance. A few people did turn to stare, but nobody said anything. She wasn't doused with anything, no one walked by and deliberately spilled anything on her lovely dress. Brock just led her to one of the empty tables and then pulled out her chair so she could sit down.

"That wasn't so bad," he observed, sounding a bit surprised himself.

Someone dropped down into the chair next to her. Devon turned to find Gil sitting there, a giant grin on his face. "So you actually got her to show up," he commented, looking at Brock. "How'd you manage that?"

Brock shook his head. "That's classified. But it did involve a crowbar, some strategically placed brownies, duct tape, and a cat toy."

"A cat toy?" Gil laughed.

Brock answered with all seriousness. "I could tell you, but then I'd have to kill you."

"I am sitting right here, you know," Devon protested, laughing along with them.

"And you look gorgeous," Gil said, kissing her cheek. "Both of you." He winked at Brock who reddened uncomfortably.

"So what do you do at these things?" Devon looked around the room. All she saw were a lot of people milling around in groups, pretty much the same thing they did every day in school. A few couples had lined up to get their pictures taken.

"You're looking at it," Gil replied.

"Don't people dance? I mean, it is called a dance after all."

"Nobody wants to be the first to get out there," Brock told her. "Especially the guys."

"Speak for yourself," Gil said, pushing his chair back. He stood and offered Devon his hand. "Milady?"

She looked at Brock to see if he was okay with it. He got up. "We'll all go."

The three of them trooped out to the dance floor. Gil grabbed a few more people from their class, dragging them up with them. They soon had a decent sized group that hit the floor. The DJ was playing generic top 40 pop, but nobody seemed to care. With Gil as the ringleader, they all laughed and danced and cut up, uncaring about who might be watching. More students joined them, until they were their own mob.

Devon was having a great time, far better than she could have guessed she'd have when Brock had picked her up. She danced with Brock and the others, no longer feeling like an outsider. He swung her around with abandon and their laughter mingled with everyone else's.

The DJ changed the tempo and played a slow song. Gil had found himself a dance partner in Whitney who had come with a bunch of other girls in their class. Devon shuffled uncomfortably until Brock took her in his arms. They swayed to the beat of the song, turning in slow circles. Devon found she was unable to look away from Brock's face as they danced.

He brushed a lock of hair out of her face. Gammy had helped her pull the sides up and curl it, so her dark red hair cascaded down her back in loose ringlets. Brock spun her out easily then pulled her back against him. "Are you having a good time?"

She swayed against him, winding her arms around his neck. "Better than I thought."

"Me too." He lightly brushed his lips against hers. "I'm glad you came into the Records room that day."

"Even with the ghosts and family drama?" she teased, feeling like they were the only two people on the floor.

"Those are just perks. You're the real prize."

A teacher walked past and gave them the signal to separate. They did so with sheepish grins at each other. As soon as the teacher was gone, Devon leaned in once again. "I still can't believe this is real. That I'm here, with you."

"Come on," he said, taking her hand and leading her off the dance floor. "I'll give you some proof."

They stepped out of the press of people; the dance floor was nearly full. Brock began weaving them between the tables, toward the front of the gym where the photographer had set up his portable studio. There was a knot of people gathered around a group of tables, and Brock began to wend his way through them.

"Bro!" Micah Landsdown's voice rang out. He sounded well on his way to plastered. "Brock!"

Brock stopped as Micah stumbled toward them. He pushed Devon behind him just a little, as if protecting her. While Devon appreciated it, she wasn't afraid of Micah and didn't want to look like she was. She stepped up beside Brock. He took her hand.

"Hey, Micah. How's it going?" Brock kept his voice neutral.

"Not bad, not bad." He leaned over to get a good look at Devon. "So you're here with Pocahontas, huh?" Micah seemed to be the only one still calling her that. The nickname had died out after only few weeks.

"Man, just let it go." Brock's hand tightened on hers.

"Good to see you too, Micah," Devon said, refusing to be offended. He was the drunken idiot embarrassing himself here, not her.

"Looking good, Devon," he leered. "When Brock here gets tired of you, remember that I'm more than happy to keep you warm."

"I'll bear that in mind if I ever want to get the syph." She could feel Brock trying to hold in his laughter next to her.

Skylar came up behind Micah. She was wearing a gold sequined sheath dress, and her blonde hair was in a complicated updo. It seemed a little much for a high school dance, but Skylar had never been one for subtlety. She linked her arm in Micah's, who jumped a little, as though surprised she was there touching him. He wrapped an arm like a tree trunk around her shoulders.

"Hi Brock." She greeted him sweetly, fluttering her eyelashes at him. Devon had to resist the impulse to roll her eyes at her. Skylar ignored Devon entirely.

"Skylar." He nodded at her. "We were going to get some pictures. Enjoy the dance." He began to move away, his hand still in Devon's.

"See you on the Winter Court," Skylar called after him.

"That's going to be a nightmare," he muttered. "Sorry about that."

"Again, that went surprisingly better than I thought," Devon assured him. "But thanks." She gave him a quick kiss on the cheek.

They waited in the short line to get their picture taken. Once that was finished, they found Gil at a crowded table and sat down with the rest gathered there. It was an amalgam of people from all cliques and none, but Brock was certainly the most popular person there.

The principal tapped on the microphone set up on a riser at the front of the dance floor. "Hello everyone. I hope you are all having a good time here tonight. I'd like to take a moment to thank the Winter Dance committee for all of their hard work!" Smatterings of applause broke out from random spots in the room. Gil made a face.

"And now, I am here to announce this year's Winter Court." He pulled out a sheet of paper that listed the winners. Ms. Princeton came up to stand next to him, holding two crowns. "First we've got the Winter Maids. And they are: Kimberly Bailey and Amanda Watts."

Devon watched the two girls make their way to the stage. They were both cheerleaders and friends of Skylar's. They stepped up and received a white rose from Mr. Nickolas. They waved to the assembled students.

"And now the King of the Winter Court is: Brock Cutler!"

Brock looked like he'd rather gnaw off his own foot than go up to that stage and take that crown. Devon tried to feel sorry for him, but only managed a small twinge. Gil shoved him out of his seat, saying, "Be a man!" Devon squeezed his hand before he left the table to take his place next to the Winter Maids.

Ms. Princeton placed the crown on his head. He said something to her and then stood there while Mr. Nickolas announced the last member of the Winter Court. "Finally, the Winter Queen is: Skylar Preston!"

Micah hooted and hollered as Skylar made her slow way up to the stage. You would have thought she'd just won the Miss Universe pageant with how slow she was moving and how much she was waving. Devon exchanged a look with Gil. They both watched Brock as he stood in front of everyone, waiting for Skylar to get her butt up there so they could be done with this joke. Unfortunately for Brock, Skylar was determined to take her sweet time. Devon could practically feel the frustration vibrating off of him.

Devon got up so she could get a better look. She wedged her way between clots of students until she had a pretty good view. Skylar had finally reached the stage and she lifted her gold dress above her ankles so she didn't trip when she climbed the stairs. She seemed to be glaring at Brock to come and escort her, but he just ignored her, a slight smirk on his face. Devon smiled too.

Skylar was crowned with little fanfare but a whole lot more waving. She swayed a little on her enormous heels, so the principal propped her up. Then he directed Brock to help her down the steps. The crowd up at the front began to disperse as the DJ spun another slow song. Devon waited for Brock near the steps.

"Nice hat," she commented when he walked over to her.

"I think it brings out the sparkle in my eyes." He batted them at her. "You're just jealous that I'm prettier than you."

"Clearly," she answered, laughing at him. "I think we sh—"

Skylar swept up to them, linking her arm with Brock's. She gave Devon the barest of smiles—it was more like a tightening of the lips and a crinkling of the eyes—and began to drag the poor boy away. "Yearbook photos of our dance," she explained. "Micah can keep her company."

Devon felt the hulking presence of her least favorite behemoth off to her right. She would have preferred just going back to sit with Gil, but Micah grabbed her wrist and dragged her out to the floor. She tried to wrench out of his grip, but his hand was like a manacle.

"Hey, CroMag," she said, keeping up with him so the drag on her wrist wasn't so intense, "you aren't dragging me back to your cave, you know. Ease up!"

In response, he pulled her in so that his boozy breath fanned her face. "Just relax. It's one dance."

Devon pushed against his chest, practically leaning over his arms that were tight around her waist to get away from him. "I prefer to be asked," she said, not really caring that she might be making a scene. "Let go of me!" Unfortunately, they were in the middle of the dance floor which was crowded with couples now; the teachers would have a hard time seeing what was going on.

Micah didn't seem to be listening. Devon had had enough. There was drunk and stupid and then there was this, and she didn't relish another round of bruises from his fingers. She raised her right foot and stomped the pointy heel of her shoe down on the top of his foot as hard as she could. The she gave him a hard shove backwards while he was off-balance and cursing.

Immediately the dancers made room around them. Micah's face was flushed and he glared around at everyone watching him. "What are you all looking at?" he shouted. People shuffled farther back but no one went anywhere.

"What the hell is going on?" Brock's voice was nowhere near happy. Skylar followed along behind, dragging in his wake.

He walked over and put his arm around Devon, causing a murmur to wave through everyone watching. "Devon?"

Devon's eyes widened, but before she could call out a warning, Micah reared back and punched him in the face. It caught Brock on the side of his jaw, snapping his head back. Brock took a few steps back, looking more shocked than hurt. Devon put herself in front of him, in case Micah went for another swing.

"Have you gone crazy?!" Brock shouted, feeling his sore jaw. "Has she made you completely lose your mind?"

"Shut the fu—" Micah shouted, only to be cut off by Skylar's scream.

Devon could feel the temperature in the room drop suddenly. Gooseflesh rippled across her arms and down her back as her body registered the presence of the otherworldly, even as her mind took the time to understand it. She could feel Jessamy's presence behind her, could almost feel the soft weight of the ghost's hands on her bare shoulders.

Skylar continued to scream, but the crowd had begun edging away and muttering. None of them looked at the being behind Devon; they all watched Skylar and her freak-out. Devon took a step towards the Winter Queen. Skylar backed away slowly, all thoughts of Brock and Micah forgotten in her fear.

"You're going to stay away from us, do you hear me?" Devon demanded of the girl. Her voice sounded strange to her ears, almost as if there were two voices talking at the same time but hers was primary. It had an echoey quality about it. "And that includes this brainless jackass, understand?"

Skylar nodded frantically, before scuttling away to the bathroom or the parking lot, or wherever she could go to get away. Devon swayed a bit on her feet, suddenly feeling lightheaded. Brock had his hand under her arm and was guiding her out of the gym. He signaled to Gil to get their coats and then led her to his car.

"How's your face?" Devon asked when he had the heat cranked and the doors closed.

Brock rubbed at the sore spot on his jaw. "It'll be okay." He was quiet for a moment. "Jessamy seemed hella pissed."

"You could see her? I didn't think anybody but Skylar could." Devon gathered her shawl around her shoulders and shivered.

"I could, but I think that's it. Everyone else just seemed to look right through her." He took her hands in his. "Dev, that wasn't the first time Micah tried something with you, was it?" His hazel eyes were hooded, their color dark in the dim light of the parking lot lampposts.

Dev ducked her head. She really didn't want to be talking about this. So much for a nice and uneventful dance. Brock squeezed her hands lightly to get her attention. Finally she said, "No, it wasn't the first time. But I can handle him."

Brock just nodded, as if she had just confirmed his fears. He didn't say anything for a few long moments and Devon began to feel bad for keeping it from him. When Gil knocked on her window, it was almost a relief. She took the coats from him, but before she could really thank him, Brock said in a low voice, "I'm taking her home." Gil just nodded and waved, before heading back into the dance.

"We could stay. I'm pretty sure that was the highlight of the evening," Devon joked. When it fell flat and Brock didn't respond, she cleared her throat and looked out the window.

They'd been on the road for a few minutes before Brock finally said anything. "I don't like him touching you."

"It's not a big deal," Devon assured him.

"It is to me." He turned his head to stare at her. "Why didn't you tell me?"

"Eyes on ROAD," Devon answered nervously. She waited until Brock was looking ahead, then said, "Because it happened before you and I were ever an anything. And I could handle it. I had it under control."

"Not tonight, you didn't." He sounded angry again.

"I got away from him didn't I?" She tried not to sound smug.

"And you summoned a ghost to do it," he bit out.

"What?" Devon couldn't believe what she was hearing. "How do you figure *that?*"

"You're linked to Jessamy, Devon. I think when you're in trouble she feels it. And tonight she came to the school because of it."

Devon sat in silent thought. "Do you really believe that?" She chewed on her thumbnail. "That I conjured her up or whatever?" *That I could do something like that?*

Brock shrugged, careful to keep his eyes on the road. "I don't know what to think. But we need to figure out a way to get rid of her before you leave for college. I don't think you want her following you to North Carolina."

225

"I wish I knew how. We still have no idea what she's waiting for."

"Sure we do." He sounded so sure of himself. "Daniel."

Devon stared at him, wondering if his brains had been rattled a little too hard when Micah slugged him. "Daniel's dead. And as far as we know, he's not hanging around haunting the place." She crossed her arms over her chest. "So how are we supposed to get Jessamy to stop going to his grave? Dig him up?"

"Yes, Dev, that's exactly what I think—it's high time we resorted to grave robbing." He shook his head. "We're not ghouls."

"Then what?" she challenged.

"Maybe he had a touchstone or something else that's keeping Jessamy tied here. It's possible." He turned onto the track that led to the trailer.

"Okay, but how do we find it?"

"That, my dear, I leave up to you. You're the brains of this operation." Brock pulled the car into off to the side of the road across from the abandoned church.

"I notice that I become the brains of this outfit when there's research to be done. How is that fair exactly?" She tapped the dashboard with her index finger.

"It's perfectly fair; an equitable distribution of our respective talents. You get with the thinky thoughts, and I lift the heavy boxes." He grinned at her.

Devon watched him as he slid closer to her in the front seat. "Somebody's been studying for his SATs."

"And somebody talks too much."

She was planning on telling him that she did NOT talk too much, thank you very much, but his mouth closed over hers and what she had to say didn't seem so important.

CHAPTER TWENTY-NINE

Devon looked up as the assistant principal came to the door of her classroom, interrupting the teacher's coverage of the War of 1812. She watched curiously as the two adults whispered to each other at the front of the class. The rest of the class descended into whispers once Ms. Wingate's attention was elsewhere.

"Devon, could you follow Mr. Marcom, please?"

She looked up at her teacher and the AP. Mr. Marcom gestured for her to take her things with her, so Devon gathered up her notebooks, pen and messenger bag. A few people laughed behind her back, but Ms. Wingate's quelling look put a stop to the titters.

Feeling shell-shocked, she managed to put one foot in front of the other in order to follow Mr. Marcom out the door. Once in the hall she asked, "What's going on?"

"We'll talk about it in my office."

Devon felt like throwing up. She'd never had to go to the principal's office, and she'd never been pulled out of the middle of a class before. She had no idea what could have happened. Maybe Gammy had gotten sick? The roiling in her stomach got worse.

The AP deposited her in a chair in front of the principal's office with the admonition to wait. A few minutes later Brock joined her. She looked from him to the principal's closed door, her insides churning. What the heck was going on?

"Do you know wh—" Brock began to ask, but was interrupted by the principal's door opening.

Mr. Harper gestured for the two of them to come in. Two chairs sat in front of his large desk and he waved for them to have a seat. Devon looked nervously at Brock, wishing she knew why they had been called in. She supposed they would find out soon enough.

Principal Harper sat down behind his desk. He wasn't smiling, but he wasn't frowning either. His face was carefully neutral. He said, "I know you two are wondering why you've been called out of class today, and I will explain soon enough. But I need to ask you both a few questions first."

Devon kept her eyes firmly on the principal and her hands folded in her lap. She got the feeling something very serious was going on, and as much as she might want to hold Brock's hand for comfort, she somehow didn't think this was the best idea. She waited to hear what the principal had to say.

The principal slid a few pieces of paper across the desk. "Devon, could you take a look at these and tell me if they seem familiar to you?"

Devon took the pages from him. They were copies of what looked like an English paper. The cover sheet was missing. She began to read; it was a paper about Hawthorne's use of imagery in his short stories. She knew because she had written a paper very much like it last year. She quickly scanned the paper, her eyes flicking over passages of text that were very like what she'd written. There was maybe a word changed here or there, but for the most part, it was her paper.

She placed it back down on the desk. "That's my paper—or parts of it anyway—from junior English."

Mr. Harper nodded. He passed the pages to Brock. "Brock, have you ever seen these before?"

Devon watched as Brock took the pages in his hands and read through them. When he was finished, he shook his head. "No, sir, this doesn't look familiar. But Devon and I weren't in the same English class last year."

"You've never seen these pages?" Mr. Harper frowned. "Are you certain?"

"Yes, sir." Brock's eyebrows were drawn down in confusion. "Is something wrong?"

Mr. Harper clasped his hands together on top of the desk. "You know that we take a dim view of cheating at this school." Both Devon and Brock nodded. "And selling your old term papers and essays would be looked on as cheating."

"Excuse me, Mr. Harper?" Devon was certain she had misheard the man. Selling papers? "Who exactly is selling papers?"

"That, Devon, is what we are here to find out." He gave her a hard look.

"Wait," Brock said, his voice shocked. "You can't think that we're the ones selling them."

Mr. Harper cleared his throat. "I find it hard to believe myself. Miss Mackson, your school record speaks for itself, and your teachers have nothing but glowing recommendations of your character. And you, Mr. Cutler, are a pillar of this school's athletic community."

Brock frowned at that last remark, but said nothing. The principal continued. "However, someone has accused you both of selling papers and brought forth this," he pointed to the pages on the desk, "as proof."

Devon felt the room spinning around her. This couldn't be happening. It COULD. NOT. be happening. Not now. "Who's accusing us?" she asked.

"Until a full inquiry is made, I am unable to tell you that."

"So we don't even get to confront the person who's making up lies about us?" Brock asked, his voice furious.

Mr. Harper's mouth set in a frown. "In due time, we'll get everything sorted out. But for now, I have to contact your parents and let them know you are on academic probation."

Devon knew she had to be as white as a sheet. Academic probation *now*? When she was so close to graduating and getting away from here? "What will that mean for college?" Her voice had barely risen above a whisper.

Mr. Harper looked at her, his face a neutral mask. "Most colleges do not tolerate cheating of any kind, Devon. I think you already know that." He turned to Brock. "If there is anything either of you would like to tell me before I speak with your parents, now would be the time."

Brock took Devon's hand in his. She thought she saw Mr. Harper's eyebrows rise slightly, but he said nothing. "You don't have any real proof," he said, angry now. "You're just taking someone's word over ours."

"Believe me when I say that the student accusing you of this scam will also be investigated." He looked pointedly at their hands before asking them to wait outside his office while he called their parents.

Devon plodded to the chair she'd been sitting in before her world had crumbled in the principal's office. She knew she must have looked like a zombie, but she didn't care. Her mind just refused to wrap itself around the words Mr. Harper had said in there; they were just replaying themselves as random noise bouncing around her skull.

Brock sat next to her, his head in his hands. She shook off her fugue state long enough to put her hand on his shoulder. "Are you okay?"

He swung his head up and his hazel eyes were dark with fury. "I don't believe this," he growled.

Devon could feel her eyes filling with tears and she blinked quickly to clear them. Her words caught in her throat for a second and she couldn't speak. Eventually she was able to steady herself. "I know. I'm not sure I understand what it means."

Brock's face softened. He put a hand up to her cheek, brushing away a stray hair. "You're scared, aren't you?"

A tear slid from the corner of her eye. "Terrified." She drew in a deep breath. "I've been working to get away from here for the last four years. And now this?" Devon closed her eyes, as if unwilling to even contemplate it. "I'm trapped." She leaned her forehead against his, suddenly beyond tired.

Brock pulled back from her, placing his hands on her shoulders so she would look at him. "No. You're not trapped." He glanced at the principal's door. "You can still get out of here." He swallowed nervously, as if unsure of what he was about to say. "I'll tell them I did it."

Devon blinked. His words made no sense. "What?"

Again the look toward the principal's door. "I'll tell them that I stole your paper from you and I was the one selling it. I'll tell them that you had nothing to do with it—that you didn't even know about it."

"But you can't...I mean, your college..." Devon didn't even know what she was trying to say.

"Look, my parents will be furious about this anyway. And they're never going to let me go to the school I want to go to anyway unless I wash out of their top picks." He took her face in his hands. "You have a shot, Devon. Let me do this for you."

Devon felt cold all over, like the temperature in the room had just dropped by fifteen degrees. She huddled in Brock's arms, feeling gooseflesh rise along her arms. It almost felt like when Jessamy was communicating with her. She looked around the room, but saw no sign of the family ghost.

Brock was still talking to her. "Please, Dev. Let me do this."

She thought seriously about what he was asking. If he took the fall for this, he might have some problems getting into college, but his parents would probably fund his way in with a sizeable donation. He might not get a basketball scholarship either, but again, his parents wouldn't have a problem coming up with the money for his education. It wasn't a lot he was sacrificing if she let him take the blame.

Devon didn't have those safety nets in place. If she went on academic probation, there went Duke. Her early admission was contingent upon finishing strong with both her grades and her behavior, and this would ruin her out. And she had no idea what this would do to her chances at a scholarship.

But it wasn't right to ask Brock to shoulder this on his own. Not when they were both innocent. The cold grew more intense, until Devon could swear she was going to see her breath. She shivered. But if they couldn't prove their innocence, what then? Was she willing to gamble her future on this, especially when Brock seemed so willing to help? He would have plenty of opportunities—he'd already had far more than she had—but she only had one. Didn't it make sense to let him take the risk?

She put her hands on top of Brock's, meeting his hazel eyes with her green. "No."

"Why not?" He sounded confused, and a little hurt.

"Because I'm not my mother. I don't need you to protect me. It's wonderful that you want to do this for me, but it wouldn't be right." When he still looked confused, she lightly kissed him on the mouth. "Someone is setting us up. And I'm not going to let them get away with it."

Now that she'd made her decision, she felt warmer, positively blazing with heat. She wouldn't let Brock take the blame for the papers; she couldn't. It would be a lie, and she'd seen where all the lies had gotten the women in her family. If she wasn't able to prove her and Brock's innocence and she lost her full ride to Duke, then so be it. It didn't have to be her last chance, and she wasn't going to compromise what she believed.

"Are you sure?" Brock stared into her eyes, searching for something. Suddenly, he smiled. "You're sure."

She nodded. "We're going to figure a way out of this mess. And we're going to do it the right way."

His smile turned into a grin. "Yes Ma'am." He mock-saluted her. "You're the brains of this operation," he said. "So tell me what we're going to do."

"That's easy," she said, pulling his arm around her shoulders. She had a feeling there wouldn't be many chances for them to see each other in the future once her grandmother and his parents found out. "We find out who turned us in for this." She met his eyes. "And we make them talk."

CHAPTER THIRTY

Devon had been right about not being able to see Brock. But surprisingly, it wasn't Gammy who did the forbidding. Brock's parents had rightfully freaked out over the news of his academic probation. This, coupled with the fight with Micah at the dance, just cemented their opinion that Devon was a bad influence on him. They'd put him in lockdown; he was only allowed to go to school for classes and then had to go straight home. The academic probation had benched him from the basketball team, which also didn't thrill his parents. They'd taken his cell phone and monitored his calls at home. Devon could only catch snippets of time with him in between classes during the day.

Gammy hadn't been exactly happy, but she believed Devon when she told her about the setup. She had instituted a curfew, but as long as Gammy knew where Devon was, she seemed content to let her granddaughter proceed as she usually did.

Since Devon had more time on her hands, she focused as much of her attention on finding Dwight Abernathy. Gil had told her that he had left town several years ago, and between the two of them, they were able to find out where he had settled after he left. But that didn't necessarily help them when they couldn't find an address for him. She was beginning to think they'd never locate the man, when a fellow churchgoer of Gammy's mentioned that he had been placed in an assisted living facility.

Devon tried every assisted living and nursing home in the tri-county area. There were a surprising number of them, and many wouldn't give out information to someone who wasn't a family member. She'd had to think on her feet, inventing a sob story up on the spot, and eventually found him in a small nursing home about thirty minutes away.

Gil drove her to the Manor House—the nursing home where Mr. Abernathy was staying—one Saturday in early March. It was lodged at the base of the mountains, a sprawling one-story building with several smaller buildings behind it. They pulled into the parking lot and took a closer look. It was made of pinkish-red brick, and boasted a set of columns on either side of the entryway. There was a long cement porch—more like a patio—that wrapped the front of the building. Devon guessed that when the weather was fine, the residents could sit outside and get some fresh air and sunshine.

They walked up the somewhat overgrown front lawn. Weeds had sprouted up, and it looked like they didn't have anyone on full time to take care of the natural areas. Gil held the door open for her and they went inside. Devon felt depressed as she looked around the reception area. It reminded her of her mother's prison visiting area—bare, neutral, and utterly impersonal. Even the staff had a sort of dead-eyed look about them.

Gil leaned into her and said into her ear, "I will gnaw a vein open if I get stuck somewhere like this place when I'm old."

They approached the desk. The woman behind it looked up at them with a bored expression on her florid face. Devon smiled, going for friendly and approachable. "We're here to see Dwight Abernathy."

"Sign in." The woman pushed a large log book at them. "Reason for your visit."

Devon and Gil had argued about this on the way down. He had wanted to go with the tale that they were his grandkids, finally come to visit the old man. Devon had nixed that idea—what if the old man didn't have any living family? She'd suggested an interview for a history project. Gil had grudgingly admitted that made more sense, but that his idea had more style. Devon had rolled her eyes.

"Class history project," Devon answered smoothly while Gil scrawled his name in the book in the handwriting of a future serial killer.

The reception nurse waved them on, giving them Abernathy's room number. They walked down a hall that smelled of antiseptic and urine, looking at the numbers on the doors. They stopped in front of the half-open door of room 156. Devon knocked quietly on the door and waited until a gruff voice yelled for her to come inside. Gil gestured broadly for her to go on ahead, and for a moment she wanted to punch him. Coward.

"Mr. Abernathy?" Devon asked of the old man sitting sunken in an easy chair that faced the window.

"Yep. Who are you?" His voice was loud, in the way that hard of hearing people were loud: like he had no idea of his volume setting.

"I'm Devon and this is Gil." She came closer to the man in the chair. He had commas of white fluffy hair above his ears, and a set of glasses sat perched on a beaky nose. He was thin and frail looking, his skin almost transparent. He had to be in his eighties. "We have a history project due in school and we were hoping we could interview you for it."

Dwight Abernathy sat up a little straighter in his chair, almost preening at the perceived attention. Devon waited while he adjusted himself in his chair. "Are you willing to talk to us?"

"Depends on what you want to know," he said slowly, still a little too loud for her comfort. He waved for the two of them to have a seat.

Devon perched at the edge of his bed, unwilling to get to comfortable. There really wasn't a place to sit and talk; the only chair was the one Abernathy sat in. "We were wondering if we could ask you a few questions about the Jackson Duvall trial."

A shadow seemed to pass over his face, but then it cleared. When he spoke, it was in a steady voice. "What you got?"

Devon nodded to Gil. He was going to be asking the majority of the scripted questions. Devon would pipe in if he forgot something or she needed clarification on one Dwight's answers. Gil cleared his throat nervously. Devon had her pencil in hand, ready to begin taking note of Abernathy's answers.

"What do you remember about the night of the shooting?"

Dwight blanched, going whiter if that was even possible, but he swallowed and began to speak. "It was late February. It had been snowing like a sonuvabitch all day long. Nobody wanted to be out in it much, but I had to drop everything and run all of the errands for folks as couldn't do for themselves." He paused, watching his audience for signs of boredom.

"I was out that night, late. I couldn't sleep so I thought walking would clear my head. I lived just off of Oak, just one block over from the Town Hall. I took a shortcut through the public lot and came out in the alley between the Town Hall and the library."

"Pretty dangerous. You never know what might have been out there," Devon commented. The old man ignored her, his eyes fixed inward on the memories that unspooled behind his eyes.

"Turns out I came out right as the shot rang out. I saw this man crumple to the ground, and when I looked up, I saw someone who looked an awful lot like Duvall."

"Did you recognize Mr. Duvall then or did you pick him out of a lineup?" Devon broke in with her question before Gil had a chance to ask his. He gave her a dirty look. She mouthed the word: Sorry.

"No, I recognized him. He was a friend of Deacon's—over at the Mackson house all the time."

Devon stiffened, but managed to hold her tongue and let Gil handle the next question. "So you were also at the Mackson house? That wasn't mentioned in the newspaper articles we read."

The man's eyes clouded over for a moment, as if he were confused. "I used to work for the Macksons. I handled their landscaping and yard work, like I did for almost everyone in town."

"How long did you work for the Mackson family?" Gil asked, glancing over at Devon as she wrote furiously.

"Oh let's see now," Dwight began, closing his eyes for a moment. "Twenty odd years, at least. I still helped out with the yard until I retired."

"Were you ever married?" Devon broke in again, playing a hunch.

Abernathy's face seemed to shrink into itself, the sad, blasted expression swallowed by the folds of his skin as he sank back into his seat. "I was." Tears gathered in the corner of his eyes. "Her name was Rose."

"We're so sorry, Mr. Abernathy," Gil said, shooting Devon a quelling look. "Did she die recently?"

He shook his head, breaking out of his sorrowful reverie. "It was cancer. She's been gone for," he stopped to do the math, "about fourteen years now." He looked over at a framed picture standing on the dresser.

Devon got up and retrieved it, taking a close look at it. It was a wedding photograph, in grainy color, of Dwight and Rose Abernathy standing in front of a church. She was lovely, her hair dark and curling around her face, with pink cheeks and an open smile. Dwight Abernathy looked shell-shocked, as if he couldn't believe his luck. His grin was about eighteen miles wide.

"She's beautiful," Devon said, handing him the photograph.

He nodded, his shaking fingers tracing the contours of his dead wife's face in the picture. Devon gave Gil a look that signaled she was going to take over the interview now. Gil nodded once to show he understood. He pulled out his phone so he could record the conversation.

"Mr. Abernathy," Devon began, her voice low and soft. She didn't want to frighten the man; she just wanted the truth. "I've spoken with someone who insists that Jackson Duvall was with them on the night of that man's death." She looked at him and asked gently, "Is it possible you were mistaken?"

Abernathy closed his eyes. When he opened them, he stared at the photograph of his wife. "She had just gotten sick. We were doing alright, but we weren't what anyone would call well off. I was worried about the money for her treatments, about how I was going to take care of her. I didn't want to put her in a home to suffer." He looked around his room, as if imagining his Rose confined to someplace much worse.

"Jackson Duvall didn't shoot that man, did he?" Devon made sure to keep her voice soothing.

Dwight Abernathy shook his head. "He didn't. I don't know who did."

She risked a glance at Gil, whose eyebrows had decided to lodge near the top of his hairline. *Holy crap*, he mouthed silently at her. She flicked her eyes to his phone to make sure he was recording. He gave her a thumbs up.

"Can you tell us what really happened?"

He sighed. "I guess it doesn't matter now. Everybody's dead, or nearly so, even that poor boy that got sent away for it." He rubbed eyes that suddenly looked sunken and dark. "I never saw who did the shooting. I wasn't even outside that night. But when the offer came to me, it was just too good to pass up, what with Rose's sickness and all."

"What offer, Mr. Abernathy?"

"If I identified Jackson Duvall, I would get two hundred thousand dollars. Half when they arrested him and half when I testified." He looked at Devon with pleading eyes. "I wasn't able to work anymore, what with driving Rose to her appointments and taking care of her. We needed that money."

Devon swallowed, but gestured for him to continue. "I didn't think he'd go to jail, not really. I knew his folks had money. I just thought they'd hire some big shot lawyer and get the case thrown out or something. And when it started to look like he might be convicted, I went back to her and told her I couldn't go through with it. But she threatened me—said if I came clean now, I'd be sent to prison and then who would look after Rose..." He looked down at the framed photo again.

"Who did you talk to? Who paid you?" Devon leaned forward before she could stop herself and had to be reminded to pull back by Gil's hand on her arm. She forced herself to relax, to not be so pushy. The man was talking; if she just let him tell his story in his own time, he'd probably tell them everything. She just had to chill out.

Yeah. Like that would happen.

Still, she tried. She took a deep breath and smiled. "Go ahead, Mr. Abernathy."

He looked up from the photograph for a moment as if ascertaining where he was. Devon put a hand briefly over his, trying to encourage him to speak. Finally, he began to speak once more. "I never could understand why she would want that poor boy to go to jail," he said, his voice confused. "He and her son were thick as thieves."

Devon felt something wind up tight inside her like clockwork springs. She managed to keep herself under control, but she felt like her jaw was going to shatter with the amount of force she was using to keep her mouth shut.

Gil bailed her out. "Jackson Duvall was close with the son of whoever paid you?"

Dwight nodded. "That's right. Deacon and Jackson were joined at the hip in those days. Along with another friend of theirs—a girl. Didn't see her much at the Mackson place though."

She could hear the stutter step of her heart as it pounded in her chest. She felt hot, sweat broke out across her forehead and on her back and stomach. "So Charlotte Mackson was the one who paid you. She's the one who came up with the plan to frame Jackson Duvall?"

Abernathy finally met her eyes. He seemed to look at her and really see her this time, rather than looking through her like he had been. He paled and drew back a little, shielding the photograph with his hands. "You look like him. Like Jackson Duvall." He swallowed. "You his kin? Is that what this is about?"

Devon had always thought she resembled her mother more than anyone, but then again, she hadn't ever gotten to meet, let alone learn the face of her father. She'd only seen newspaper photographs and the photographs her mother had stored in her memory box. This man though, had known Jackson Duvall; he'd sat across a courtroom and lied about him. She imagined the face of her biological father must haunt his dreams every time he closed his eyes. He'd condemned an innocent man to jail. A less charitable part of her hoped that he hadn't slept peacefully since.

She didn't want to tell him that yes, Jackson Duvall had been her father. But she wasn't going to deny her mother either. "My mom is Lorelei Mackson—one of his best friends."

He bowed his head. Devon waited for him to say something else. When he didn't for several minutes, she asked, "Why would Mrs. Mackson want Jackson Duvall framed for a murder he didn't do?"

Abernathy shrugged, surreptitiously wiping his eyes with the back of his hand. "She never said why to me. And I knew better than to ask. It wasn't my business."

Gil spoke. "Why are you telling us this now?"

Dwight sighed, and turned his body so he could face Gil. "Because I'm old, and more than old. I'm dying. And when you know you're dying, a lot of things become less important. And some things matter more." His eyes flicked to Devon. "Truth matters more."

Devon nodded. "Truth matters most," she corrected.

He chuckled. "The surety of youth." He shook his head. "Girl, someday you're going to realize a hard truth of the world when you have to compromise your principles for something you love more."

Devon didn't answer him. But inside, she burned. How could he say that truth wasn't the most important thing? Look at what hiding the truth, denying the truth had done to her family! If being truthful meant she was uncompromising, well, Devon could live with it.

Dwight spoke again, his eyes only on Devon. "And what do you plan to do with what I've told you?" He didn't sound concerned about it. Maybe age took away fear. Or maybe death did.

She chewed on her thumb as she turned that question over in her mind. She had proof now of Jackson Duvall's innocence. But he was long dead, and so was his best friend and rival, Deacon Mackson. Her mother was in jail and content to remain so. She already knew the truth and couldn't live with her part in it. So what did she plan to do with Abernathy's story?

"I'm not sure yet," she answered, because she wasn't. She tucked a stray lock of hair behind her ear absently.

"Sometimes the truth doesn't do anybody any good, at least those that are left alive. You think about that."

"And what about the dead?"

He smiled sadly. "The dead don't care."

Devon thought of Jessamy and knew how wrong he was. The dead cared. Sometimes they cared very, very much.

CHAPTER THIRTY-ONE

She could feel Gil's eyes on her as they walked to the car. They would skip over to her when he was driving. Devon felt like she should say something, anything, to reassure him, but she couldn't bring herself to right now. It was too much to process. She wasn't even sure how to begin to order her thoughts about what she'd learned today.

They drove for a while in silence. Devon knew Gil was giving her some space. It just wasn't helping her. Finally she sighed and said, "So say something."

Gil didn't take his eyes off of the road. "Like what?" His gaze darted sideways eyes off of his road for a second to gauge her mood. "Like your grandmother is a raging sociopath?"

Devon smiled, but it had no joy in it. "It's a start."

"What are you going to do?" His voice was tight, tense.

"We should call Brock," Devon said, wishing he was here with them right now. "But if his mom answers, she won't let me talk to him."

Gil pulled out his cell phone. "Leave it to me." He dialed Brock's number and hit Send. They waited in silence as the phone at the other end began to ring.

"Hi, Mrs. Cutler," Gil said when Brock's mother picked up the phone. "This is Gil Loflin. Brock and I are partners for a project at school and I was wondering if I might speak to him." He paused while she answered him, then he said, "Thank you, Ma'am."

Devon silently clapped. He sketched a bow from behind the steering wheel. Gil's gift for prevarication never ceased to amaze her.

"Hey Brock," Gil said after a few minutes of waiting. "I'm going to put you on speakerphone." He hit a button, then handed Devon the phone. "You still there?"

"Yeah." Brock's voice came through loud and clear. Devon felt a catch in her throat, surprised at how much she was missing him.

"Hi Brock," she said, shocked when the longing she was feeling made its way into her voice.

"Hey Dev." There was something in his voice too. Perhaps he was missing her too? She liked to think so. "What did you guys find out?"

Gil gestured for Devon to handle the recap. She tried to keep it short and simple. "Charlotte paid Mr. Abernathy to lie about Jackson Duvall. He was nowhere near there on the night of the shooting. He made up the whole thing."

There was quiet on the other end. Devon waited, looking at Gil when it seemed the silence had gone on too long. Finally, Brock said, "Okay. So what do we do now? We know she did it, but this happened twenty years ago."

"And who's going to believe us if we say anything?" Gil kept his eyes on the road while he spoke. "Let's face it, we're not the most stellar group of witnesses—I'm gay, and you two are one step away from juvie. We're in high school! Nobody is going to listen to us."

Devon chewed the inside of her cheek. She knew Gil and Brock were right. When she started looking into this, it was all wrapped up with Jessamy, and then it turned into her wanting to know the truth about who her father really was. But now that she had found that out, and now that she knew what had really happened to him, what did she want?

"Hey Dev, Gil? You guys still there?" Brock asked when she didn't answer.

"Hang on, B," Gil said. "Devon's using that enormous brain of hers."

"Somebody has to," she shot back lightly, her mind still running through their options. "I think we should wait before we decide anything. I didn't come at this with the idea of outing my grandmother as a psychopath—that's just been a special bonus. We need to figure out what we should do."

"Cool," Brock said, then lowered his voice. "Hey, my mom's coming back. I got to go."

"Bye. I miss you," Devon said before he got off the line.

Gil wisely said nothing, just kept his eyes on the road. Devon put the phone on the console between them. She looked out the window for a few minutes, lost in thought as the foothills zipped by out her window.

Finally she knew what she had to do, what she wanted to do. Turning to Gil, she said, "Take me to Charlotte's."

*****

Gil offered to wait until she'd talked to her grandmother—to Charlotte, she kept reminding herself—but Devon sent him away. She wasn't sure how long this conversation was going to last. She wanted privacy for it, and she wasn't sure how she was going to feel when it was over with. So he pulled the car to a stop in front of Charlotte's house, admonished her to be careful, then drove away after she'd gotten out.

Devon took a bracing breath, straightening her shoulders. She opened the white gate and walked up the carefully maintained path to the front porch. She remembered the last time she was here, and what she'd promised Charlotte—she'd promised her that they would never speak again. Devon didn't want to go back on her word, but she had to confront her with the truth. Devon had to tell her that she knew what Charlotte had done.

She rang the bell. It was hard for her to stand there, just waiting. She didn't know if Charlotte would slam the door in her face, but she would stand here all day, ringing that damn bell if she had to. Finally she heard footsteps. Charlotte opened the door, a frown of epic proportion on her face.

"I thought we had an agreement," she said in a flat voice.

"We do, and believe me when I say I wish I weren't here." Devon's voice was just as expressionless.

"Then what are you doing back here?"

"There's one last thing I have to talk to you about." Devon took a step into the house. Charlotte didn't move, so Devon was forced to stop or shove her out of the way. "May I come in? I don't think you want me saying what I have to say right here on the porch."

Charlotte raised an eyebrow. "I doubt that."

"Okay." Devon leaned against the doorframe. "I just got back from seeing a Mr. Dwight Abernathy."

Devon waited for a reaction. But she didn't get anything besides the door opening a little further, enough to allow her to come inside. Devon stepped past Charlotte but she didn't go much farther than the parlor. Charlotte didn't offer her to sit and Devon had no intention of staying. This wasn't a social visit.

"Why would you go to speak to Dwight Abernathy?" Charlotte's voice was frosty.

"I know what you did." Devon didn't want to beat around the bush.

"I'm sorry," the older woman said, "I don't understand what you're talking about."

"He told me. *Everything.*"

Charlotte's face showed no emotion. Devon stared at her, trying to read her, but got nothing. They stood in silence for several minutes, staring at each other.

Finally, Charlotte spoke. "How much do you want?"

Devon's mouth dropped open. In all of the scenarios that she played out in her head, this had not even been among the top 100. "What?"

Charlotte frowned, the first sign of emotion she'd given. "I don't believe I was overly complicated in my request. How much do you want?"

"This isn't about money," Devon hissed, anger bubbling inside her.

"Then what is it about?" Charlotte shot back, a hint of heat in her voice.

"You lied! And you paid someone else to lie too!" Devon's voice was getting louder. She couldn't help it; it was either yell or cry. And she wouldn't cry in front of Charlotte Mackson. Not ever again.

A flash of anger crossed Charlotte's face. "I think this conversation is over."

"You can't just buy me off!" Devon shouted. "I know—do you understand that? I know that you framed Jackson Duvall, my *father*, for a murder he didn't commit! I know you paid someone to lie on the stand to convict an innocent man."

"And exactly what proof do you have?" Charlotte drew herself up, a haughty cast to her face. "Do you think anyone will listen to you, the daughter of a junkie whore?"

Devon reeled back, Charlotte's words a slap to her face. She wanted to lash out, to hurt this proud woman who'd always treated her like trash, when really Charlotte was the one who was horrible. Her hands clenched into fists, but she forced herself to stay still, to think.

Like lightning striking a tree, inspiration struck. Devon suddenly knew how to hurt Charlotte. She knew what the woman was most afraid of; she understood why the woman had gone to such lengths. It was all about pride.

Softly, Devon said, "Oh, they'll listen, *Grandmother*. You know how this town loves a good story, even more than they love the truth. In this case, the truth and a good story happen to be the same." Devon began to walk away. She had Charlotte. "How do you think everyone will look at you once they hear about what you've done? Once they hear about what my mother did to your son?"

Devon turned around and gave Charlotte her coldest smile. "It doesn't matter if they believe everything I say. It's enough that they'll wonder if there's any truth to it."

"What do you want?" Charlotte asked again, no longer keeping the hatred from her voice.

"Nothing from you," Devon shot back. "You can't buy your way out of this one."

Charlotte stalked over to her. She wasn't an imposing woman, but the light in her eyes was terrifying. Devon had to stop herself from stepping back. "Say one word, Devon, and you will regret it. I promise you that."

Devon raised her chin. "You'll regret it more. I swear it." She backed away from Charlotte, afraid to take her eyes off of the woman. She stopped when she felt the door at her back and reached back to open the door. Charlotte watched calmly, blinking slowly, as if they had discussed nothing more stressful than what to have for lunch.

Devon slammed the door shut behind her, grateful to be out from under that reptilian gaze. Charlotte had no power over her, but Devon still wanted to get as far from the woman as possible. She rushed through the gate, fumbling in her bag with her phone so she could call Brock. She was only slightly surprised to find her hands were shaking.

CHAPTER THIRTY-TWO

It was freezing cold in early March, the land held in Mother Nature's frosty iron fist. Devon shivered in her jacket and wished for spring. It was one thing to watch the fluffy snow sift down like powdered sugar from the warmth of a sofa; it was quite another to be out in it at nearly eleven o'clock at night. But Brock had asked her to meet him—he'd said he had more information on the term paper setup—so she risked being out past her curfew and possible frostbite to hear what he had to say.

It would be good to see him again. It had only been two weeks since his parents had put the official kibosh on their...whatever it was they were doing, but she really missed the chance to spend time with him. She couldn't call him—and she found that she missed their talks.

It amazed her. Devon hadn't realized how much she'd come to rely on him with all of the family mysteries and ghost sightings, but once he was gone, it became clear to her how much of a partner he'd been. Brock had been a good one to bounce ideas off of, someone who could be trusted to try and see the bigger picture. Now that she was trying to do everything alone, it was so much harder. Brock was the only one who knew everything; even Gil had been kept in the dark about Jessamy.

But he'd found something out that might help them clear their names at school. And, if his call were any indication, he might have found something important. He was risking an even worse punishment than she was, by sneaking out of the house when he was grounded. That made the freezing her butt off worth it.

She curled her hands into fists inside her coat and kept up her pacing. When she looked up to check the time on the old clock, she saw Brock on the other side of the street. He waved at her, his face blossoming into a large smile, despite the cold. Devon began to make her way down the treacherously slick steps to the sidewalk.

Devon was crossing the street when she heard the engine roar as the car it belonged to put on a burst of speed. She froze, unable to move as the dark shape hurtled toward her. She could hear Brock yelling at her, but she couldn't seem to make her body move out of the way. The car's grille was nearly upon her when she felt a hard shove at her back and then she was falling, falling through a mist of white.

*****

Devon pushed herself up, looking at the floor beneath her hands. She was no longer outside; instead, she stood on a wooden floor, one sanded and polished and well taken care of. She looked around, trying to figure out where she was by studying the furnishings. She was in a house, and it was large and neat. She'd fallen in front of the large staircase that led to the second floor. Everything had the feeling of age to it. She wondered where in the past Jessamy had sent her.

She heard voices coming from the upstairs. Devon scrambled to her feet, looking around for a place to hide, then mentally smacked herself. They couldn't see her. She stayed where she was. As the voices grew louder and closer, Devon realized she recognized them. The woman's voice was Jessamy's. Which meant the man's voice had to be Keaton's.

Devon shivered. She remembered Keaton's arrogant gaze from Daniel's jail cell. The urge to hide flared up in her again, but she quelled it. He couldn't hurt her, not when she was out of time like this.

They were arguing, their voices growing louder as they approached the top of the stairs. Devon could see them now; Jessamy wore a dark dress similar to what she wore as a ghost, but Keaton was dressed in lighter colors. She could see the marks of grief on Jessamy in the tired circles under her eyes and the frown lines like commas around her mouth. She was thin, her dress draping over her instead of fitting like it had in previous times.

"I know you've been leaving the house at night!" Keaton shouted.

Jessamy whirled, spots of color blossoming on her cheeks. "Are you following me?" Her voice was low, but it had a dangerous edge to it.

"You're my wife. I expect you to act with some semblance of decorum." Keaton took a step closer to her. They were now almost at the head of the stairs.

"I can't sleep at night, so I walk." Jessamy turned away from him, lifting her skirts so she wouldn't trip on the hem going down the stairs. "There's nothing wrong with that."

Keaton took two quick steps and grabbed her upper arm. "It depends on where you go when you walk." He pulled her close, his face flushed. "You're visiting *him*, aren't you?"

"What does it matter?" Jessamy struggled to pull away from her husband's grip, but she was held firm.

"You're MY wife. It's not proper!"

"HANG PROPER!" she shouted at him.

"He's DEAD, Jess." He tried to put his arms around her, but she resisted. "You have to let him go."

Jessamy paled. Keaton at least had the decency to look contrite for his harsh words. She jerked her arm out of his violently, causing her to lose her balance. Keaton reached for her, but Jessamy twisted away from him. She screamed as she tried to right herself, but it was too late.

Devon watched in horror as Jessamy plummeted down the steep staircase. Her body bounced off of the wooden stairs as if it was made of rags. Keaton cried out, rushing down the stairs after her. When she landed at the bottom of the staircase in a bloody heap, Devon could see that her neck was bent at the wrong angle.

Keaton gently turned Jessamy over. Her head flopped loosely, like a limp chicken's and Devon felt bile rise up in the back of her throat. It was obscene, the way it hung over Keaton's arm. Her face was bloody—Devon figured she must have hit her nose on the way down. Her eyes stared vacantly at the ceiling.

He looked at her for a moment, almost as if he couldn't believe what was happening to him. Slowly, he reached out his free hand and closed her eyes. His mouth worked, but no sound came out. He looked blasted, the lone survivor of a horrible attack. Finally he placed her body back down on the floor and stumbled out of the room.

Devon turned her head away. She jumped back when she realized Jessamy's shade stood behind her, watching the proceedings. "He didn't mean to," she whispered, then seemed to notice Devon for the first time.

She raised her index finger and touched it to Devon's forehead. Then Devon was falling backwards, into the cold, swirling mists.

*****

"Devon!" Cold hands held her cheeks. "Dev!" The voice was frantic, choked with fear and tears.

Her eyes fluttered open at the desperate sound of her name. She was freezing, surrounded by something cold and wet. Snow, she realized as she looked around. She was lying in a drift in the front of the Town Hall. Her eyes focused on Brock, his pale face inches from hers. His hazel eyes looked leeched of color under the streetlights.

"Thank God," he breathed, pulling her up into a bone-crushing hug. "When I saw that car coming at you…" he dug his face into her shoulder so she didn't catch the rest of what he said.

Her eyes followed a blot of shadow just outside of the circle of lamplight. Jessamy stepped forward, looking more at peace and solid than Devon ever remembered seeing her before. She had her veil pulled up, exposing her lovely face. She was no longer drawn and sad; as she watched, Devon saw the ghost smile.

Devon pushed away from Brock. He looked at her quickly and she pointed with her chin at Jessamy. Brock slewed around on his knees, his eyes widening at the sight of the spirit. "She pushed you out of the way," he whispered, awed.

Jessamy walked towards them, her hands outstretched. Brock helped Devon to her feet, checking her over for any broken bones. Devon let him, but her eyes were on her family's ghost. Nothing had been what she thought, she realized. Jess wasn't evil or a curse. Devon took one of the ghost's hands. She gestured for Brock to take the other.

As soon as they touched, Devon could hear Jessamy's light and musical voice in her head. "Thank you, Devon, for freeing me."

"I should be the one thanking you," Devon thought back. "If you hadn't pushed me…" she shuddered as she trailed off. She felt Brock squeeze her hand.

Jessamy's face grew hard for a moment. Her eyes looked beyond them, at the ruin of a car that had plowed into a lamppost. Steam hissed in billowing white clouds from beneath the busted hood. The car resembled nothing so much as an elderly dragon able to spit smoke, but no fire. The ghost studied the wreckage briefly, then turned back to Devon. "You broke the cycle."

Devon was confused, and said so. "I don't understand. What cycle?"

Jessamy's voice fluttered, a breezy sound. "You made the right choice."

Devon remembered the feeling she got when she was sitting in the front office when Brock had offered to say he had been alone in selling the term paper. It had been almost unbearably cold then. "You were there?"

Jessamy nodded. "You did what your mother and I could not. You put someone else before your own wants and desires. I've been trying to atone for my past mistakes, while waiting for some woman with the courage to stand up for the man she loves. That woman was you, Devon."

Brock nodded, sharing a look with Jessamy. He said, "She was never your family's curse. She was a protector of sorts, am I right?" At the spirit's nod, he continued. "She does appear, as a warning, but she doesn't cause the things to happen. That's why your mother saw her. Jessamy was trying to warn your mother about what could happen to her. And trying to get her to make the right choice."

"And Gammy had only heard the legends, so she assumed you were bad," Devon finished for him, her eyes on Jess. "But I still don't get the atone part."

The ghost smiled, a bare upturn at the corners of her mouth. "As penance for what I'd done." She met Devon's eyes. "You, of all people, should know what harm I caused. I should have waited. I should have married the man that I loved instead of marrying the man that loved me."

"The man that loved you framed Daniel," Devon reminded her, not willing to let Keaton off the hook so easily. *Daniel was dead because of Keaton.*

"I know that now." Her smile turned sad. "I wasn't strong enough to follow my heart. But we were all to blame for the decisions we made. I had to make up for my part of it." She paused, holding Devon's gaze with her own. "You are stronger than I ever could be. You are stronger than your mother. Only you could free me."

"So saving me is how you atoned?" Devon shook her head. And all this time, she thought she had to do something to save Jessamy, to put her at rest. But all she had to do was let Jess help *her*. It was going to take some time and serious thought to understand fully the events of the past few months.

Jessamy nodded once. "Yes, that, and something else that I think you will find pleasing."

Before Devon could think too much about that last statement, Brock asked, "But how did you manage to be physical enough to push her?"

"I can gain strength in direct relation to the threat posed to Devon." She smiled again, this time a little wicked. "I was able to manifest at the dance that night because of those two that were threatening you. And I was able to push you out of the way of the car because of the threat to your life."

"The car!" Devon cried, breaking contact to run over to where the car had stopped, its front end crumpled around the light post. She heard matching footfalls muffled in the snow as Brock followed after her.

She skidded to a stop in the dry snow. The steam from the engine had almost stopped as the engine died. Devon slipped her sweater down over her hand and opened up the door.

Charlotte Mackson was pressed against the chair, her face almost covered by the airbag that had deployed upon impact. Devon stumbled a little, but Brock's hand on her waist steadied her. She looked at him, bewildered. "She doesn't drive," she managed to get out before confusion stole her words.

"Does this look like the car that tried to hit you the last time?" he asked, his voice soft in her ear.

She shivered, unable to piece together past events and put them in context with the now. "It was silver. That's all I really remember." She shook her head stubbornly, as if that would make her thoughts arrange themselves properly. "But she doesn't *drive*."

Jessamy stood next to them, looking at the car like it was a sleeping beast about to come alive. Brock glanced at her, then hugged Devon to his side. "Doesn't and can't are not the same thing," he reminded her. He placed his fingers against Charlotte's neck. He waited over a minute. "I don't feel a pulse," he said, his voice hollow.

Devon pushed Charlotte's body back so her head wasn't resting against the air bag. She put her hand in front of the woman's mouth, hoping for even the faintest puff of air against her skin. She felt nothing. After a few moments, Devon lifted her hand away. She pushed the door closed.

"Who is she?" Jessamy asked after placing her hand on Devon's shoulder.

"My grandmother." Then she stopped and thought about what she'd just said. Charlotte was not her grandmother, not by blood or anything else. "I guess she wasn't my grandmother, not really. But I thought she was for a long time."

Jessamy didn't look overly concerned over the accident. Devon guessed she wouldn't be; after all, what could really bother a ghost? But Brock pulled out his phone and dialed the sheriff's department. He stepped away so he could give them the details of the accident while Devon spoke with Jessamy.

"What happens now?" Devon asked. Without her veil hiding her, Jess didn't look scary at all. Devon wondered now how she could have been so frightened of her.

Jessamy shrugged. "I am not sure. But I feel different. I feel..." she broke off suddenly, her head coming up like a hunting dog scenting prey.

Devon followed her gaze and saw a smattering of glowing motes gathering under the town hall light that shone on the steps. The glimmer coalesced into a man in clothing from the same time period as Jessamy. Devon gaped, unable to stop her staring. Daniel Holfsteder stood before them, looking as alive and solid as Jessamy did.

He opened his arms, his handsome face suffused with joy. Jessamy let go of Devon with a happy cry and flung herself at him. Daniel caught her up, swinging her around and off of her feet. Jessamy kept saying his name over and over again until he stopped her with a kiss.

Devon felt an arm around her shoulders and looked up at Brock. He stood watching the reunited ghosts, a proud smile on his face. "You did it," he said quietly, a kind of amazement in his voice.

"We did it," she answered back, snuggling into him. She knew she was going to hurt in the morning from her fall, but right now all she felt was a beautiful energy, like she was tapping into pure happiness.

They watched as Jessamy and Daniel broke off their kiss to stare into each other's eyes. They were radiant in their joy at being together again. Daniel took a moment to look at Devon and Brock wrapped up in each other's arms and gave them a wink and a smile. Jessamy pulled his head back down to hers for another brief kiss, before Daniel placed her hand on his arm and began to lead her away.

Devon watched as the two faded into insubstantiality, their forms fading like mist into the night. She sighed and said, "Wherever you go, you go together."

Brock turned her so she faced him. His arms held her loosely in his embrace and he rested his forehead against hers. Devon breathed in the scent of him mixed with the cold air of winter in the mountains. They had done it. She felt bone tired, but so happy that she was nearly incandescent.

"Think they're happy?" she couldn't help but ask him, although she knew the answer.

"I think it's a good thing they're ghosts and they don't need to come up for air," he responded, looking at her fondly. "Are you happy?"

"Never been happier," she said and meant it with every fiber of her being. Daniel coming for Jessamy was the rightest thing she'd ever had the pleasure to witness. She pulled Brock tight against her. "I think I love you," she murmured in his ear.

He brushed her hair back behind her ears. "I *know* I love you," he answered back.

They stood there holding each other until the sheriff's cruiser came.

CHAPTER THIRTY-THREE

Devon sat on the crumbling wall that bordered the abandoned church's cemetery. Brock sat next to her, holding her hand in his. They both watched the installation of the new headstone in silence. They had decided to go in together and buy Jessamy a new headstone and have it placed where it belonged: next to Daniel. She and Brock had split the cost.

Charlotte had died in the accident. She and Brock had lied about it, telling that they saw her lose control of the car on the slick road and crash into the post. Being as old as she was, the shock of the impact had been too much for her. And Charlotte had never changed her will to remove Deacon, or his heirs, as her beneficiary—Devon assumed it was because she didn't want anyone to suspect the scandal—so Devon had inherited everything.

Brock put his arm around her shoulders, pulling her close to him. They had a blanket wrapped around their legs to keep them warm as they sat in the cold watching the work. Devon snuggled against his side, feeling satisfied. Jessamy deserved some happiness after all this time.

The workman finished installing the headstone. He waved at the two of them, then climbed in his truck and drove away. Brock and Devon sat on the wall for a few minutes, enjoying the quiet and each other. Finally Devon gathered up the blanket and hopped down from the wall. Brock took the blanket from her and draped it over the wall, then took her hand.

They walked to the stone marker. Devon wished that they could have moved Jessamy's remains here, but she thought the ghost would appreciate the gesture of the headstone regardless. Not that she ever expected to see Jessamy again. But it made Devon feel better.

"Think she's happy?" she couldn't help asking Brock.

He stood behind her and wrapped his arms around her waist. His breath ghosted over her cheek as he answered her. "I don't think happy is enough to cover it."

Devon sighed, leaning against Brock's body. "Good."

"Are you?"

She nodded. Everything was so perfect, Devon thought she might be living a dream. Jessamy had taken care of the academic probation situation for them by simply frightening the student who had made up the complaint into telling the truth. Devon remembered with a smile the cryptic message Jessamy had said that Saturday night. When she and Brock had arrived in school that Monday after Charlotte's accident, they were immediately called into the principal's office for an apology. He notified Brock's parents and Devon's grandmother that very morning that they were off academic probation and the incident had been removed from their student records because a junior had come forward to admit that Micah Landsdown had paid him to say that Brock and Devon were running a term paper scam. Devon wasn't surprised to hear through the gossip grapevine—Gil—that both Micah and Skylar were suddenly suffering in-school suspension. As far as she was concerned, it couldn't happen to a nicer couple.

Today she'd received an acceptance letter from the final college she had applied to, along with offers of financial aid. Devon was still waiting to hear about the five-generation scholarship that had started everything, but she felt a huge weight was lifted from her shoulders. Even if she didn't get the money from it, she had gotten a great deal more than she ever expected. Devon had found out who her parents were—all three of them—and had managed to put to rest not one but two skeletons from her family's closet. Knowing that Jessamy and Daniel were at peace was more than any scholarship was worth.

She wondered if Charlotte knew what her secrets had come to. The woman had spent so much time and effort trying to protect the family name that it had wound up killing her. Devon still got her father's money, and she was still thought of as a Mackson. Devon had no intention of changing that either; Deacon Mackson had been her father in every way that counted.

So she, Brock, and Gil had decided it was better to keep Charlotte's secrets. None of them would reveal what they had learned about her grandmother's part in the murder of the drifter and the framing of Jackson Duvall, nor would they ever speak of Devon's true parentage. They vowed they would take it to their graves.

"Penny for your thoughts," Brock said, resting his chin against her shoulder.

"I was thinking about my mother," Devon answered.

"Ah. Come to a decision yet?"

She and Brock had talked a lot about whether Devon should tell her mother everything they'd found out over the past few weeks. He hadn't pressured her, just let her use him as a sounding board. Devon knew she would have to see her mother if she wanted to talk to her and tell her about everything she'd been through. She just wasn't sure if it would make a difference.

"No." She shook her head. "I guess I'm still mad at her."

Brock tightened his arms around her. "It's okay to not know what you want to do."

"I should tell her." Devon knew this. She felt bad that her mother sat in jail in a sort of self-induced exile, a punishment of her own devising. But what she was most afraid of was if her mother would choose to stay there, even after she knew the whole truth. What would that mean for how she felt about Devon?

"There's not a time frame on this," Brock reminded her. "You'll see her when you're ready."

Devon turned in his arms, wrapping hers around his waist. "You're pretty smart, you know that?"

"That's high praise coming from the valedictorian." He ducked his head down to kiss her.

Devon gave herself up to the sensation of his lips on hers, of his hands sliding up her back, of his body pressed against hers. Brock slowly broke off the kiss, running his hands through her thick hair. She opened her eyes and smiled up at him. "That was a pleasant distraction," she whispered, leaning her forehead against his.

"So, my mom wants you to come over for dinner this Sunday." Brock held her loosely in the circle of his arms.

Devon raised her eyebrows. To say that they were less than enthused over Brock's choice of girlfriends—once they'd found out about Devon anyway—would have been a gross exaggeration. But once Brock had proved that he was serious about Devon and their relationship was more than a pre-college fling, his parents had slowly accepted it. They still weren't thrilled with it, but they were trying.

"You sure that's a good idea?" Devon still liked to keep a safe distance from his parents. They were nice people, but she didn't feel comfortable around them yet.

"Oh, come on, Dev. My mom is way less scary than your Gammy—I thought she was going to burn a hole in my chest with her glares the first time I came over." He let her go, taking her hand instead. "I still stuck around."

He led her back to his car. "So you'll come?"

Devon pursed her lips, thinking it over. "Maybe."

Brock frowned. "Maybe?"

Devon grinned slyly. "If you make it worth my while…"

Brock leaned forward, pushing her back against the car door. "And exactly how am I supposed to do that?" His smile was wickedly inviting, and it turned her knees to liquid.

She moved so her lips were against his ear. "You're creative. I'm sure you'll think of something."

They were so busy kissing that they didn't notice the two pale shapes that watched over them from the churchyard. Jessamy and Daniel shared a slight smile, private and full of emotion, then faded slowly into nothingness.

ABOUT THE AUTHOR

Jeanette Battista graduated with an English degree with a concentration in medieval literature which explains her possibly unhealthy fixation on edged weapons and cathedral architecture. She spent a summer in England and Scotland studying the historical King Arthur, which did nothing to curb her obsession. To satisfy her adrenaline cravings--since sword fighting is not widely accepted in these modern times--she rode a motorcycle at ridiculously high speeds, got some tattoos, and took kickboxing and boxing classes. She gave up the bike when her daughter came along, although she still gets pummeled at the gym on a regular basis.

When she's not writing or working, Jeanette spends time with family, hikes, reads, makes decadent brownies, buys killer boots, and plays Pocket Frogs. She wishes there were more hours in the day so she could actually do more of these things. She lives with her daughter and their two psychotic kittens in North Carolina.

You can read more about her and her books at

http://www.jeanettebattista.com